# Love at Sunset Lake

## THE ABUNDANCE SERIES
### BOOK 1

## SALLY BAYLESS

KIMBERLIN BELLE PUBLISHING

Printed in the United States of America
First Printing, 2016
ISBN: 978-1-946034-00-7

Kimberlin Belle Publishing
Contact: admin@kimberlinbelle.com

Extracts from the Authorized Version of the Bible (The King James Bible), the rights in which are vested in the Crown, are reproduced by permission of the Crown's patentee, Cambridge University Press.

Publisher's Note: This is a work of fiction. Names, characters, places, and incidents are a product of the author's imagination. Locales and public names are sometimes used for atmospheric purposes. Any resemblance to actual people, living or dead, or to businesses, companies, events, institutions, or locales is completely coincidental.

Cover Design © Jennifer Zemanek/Seedlings Design Studio

*This I recall to my mind,*
*therefore have I hope.*
*It is of the Lord's mercies that we are not consumed,*
*because his compassions fail not.*
*They are new every morning: great is thy faithfulness.*

Lamentations 3:21-23

# Chapter One

Tess Palmer didn't need to be perfect. She only needed to get every detail right.

Every time.

And as a special events caterer, her to-do list this Friday ran for three entire pages of details.

She stopped at a light in a pricey St. Louis suburb and glanced at the clipboard on the console of her van. For the next event, a simple surprise birthday party, she'd gone over her list so many times that the edges of the paper curled. The future of her catering business was at stake, after all.

She drove two blocks farther, passed a row of dogwoods in full bloom at the entrance to a subdivision, and parked as instructed in the client's three-car garage, where her commercial van could be hidden from the guest of honor.

Up since five, Tess had triple-checked the food, recounted the plates, and examined every tablecloth for spots. She'd even taken more care than normal with her appearance, using a double coating of hairspray to keep her hair in a bun, dousing her white blouse with extra starch, and wearing her newest black pants. This event was going to be a success. She'd make sure of it.

A stack of plates in one arm, she walked to the door that led into the house from the garage and knocked.

Madeleine McCullen pulled the door open wide and, although she was well past sixty-five, fluttered her hands like an excited five year old. "My son just sent a text. His wife doesn't suspect a thing, thinks I'm picking up drive-thru burgers for our lunch." She ushered Tess into a huge kitchen.

"We can definitely do better than drive-thru." Tess set the plates on the island and flashed an encouraging pre-event smile.

A silver-haired Peter Pan, at five-foot-nothing and maybe a hundred pounds, Madeleine made Tess—five seven and more on the sturdy side—feel like a Clydesdale.

But Clydesdales know how to work, and Tess was all about work.

Madeleine tapped Tess's stack of plates with the click of a long, manicured nail. "You've got more of those?"

"Three more loads. Plenty for fifty guests."

Madeleine stepped closer, surrounded by a cloud of magnolia perfume. The hot-pink sequins on her blouse caught the light. "Dear…" Her voice hit the same too-sweet note that it held each time she'd called to change the menu.

Tess gripped the edge of the granite countertop, stomach tightening. A week ago, she'd made it clear that everything had to be final, including the number of guests. "Fifty people, right?"

"Well..." Guilt flashed across Madeleine's eyes. "My other daughter decided to fly in from Dallas. With her husband and teenage son."

Tess released her death hold on the granite. "Three more people? No problem. I always allow ten-percent extra." Paying attention to detail, planning for overages like this, riding herd on indecisive clients like Madeleine—it had taken four years, but Tess was getting good at catering.

"I told her she could bring her in-laws," Madeleine said. "And her best friend."

Tess stopped congratulating herself.

"And their families." Madeleine slipped the words in soft and low, as if that made the news easier to take.

It didn't.

The nerves in Tess's stomach contracted into a knot. "How many people total?" She tried to sound calm but failed.

"I added it up." Madeleine pulled a small piece of paper from her pocket. "Sixty-five. That's why I think you'll need more plates."

With effort, Tess kept her mouth shut. Sixty five? Fifteen extra people? Plates were the least of her problems.

She needed an additional dessert, more appetizers, and more drinks, all ready to serve in less than four hours. And her kitchen was thirty minutes away.

But she had to pull this off. In catering, there were no second chances, and she was counting on referrals from Madeleine to boost her business over the hump, safely into the world where she'd make a solid profit every year.

"Excuse me. I need to make a call." Tess backed toward the garage. "And make sure I have more, um, plates."

"I thought so." Now smiling, Madeleine smoothed her gray pixie cut. "Good thing I asked about them when you first got here."

Tess gave a tight nod.

"Hey, where's my beautiful bride of forty-seven years?" A barrel-chested older man wearing a green golf shirt with a country club logo walked in from the garage and blocked Tess's escape.

Madeleine's brown eyes sparkled. "Right here, Harry."

He wrapped her in a huge hug and then, one arm still around her sequined shoulders, beamed at her as though she was his own personal Miss America.

Tess looked away and braced herself for the all-too-familiar wave of sadness. Now was not the time to dwell on what was missing in her life. She had a food crisis to handle. "I'll be back." In the garage, she climbed into the van and wiped the moisture from her palms on her pants. Then she pulled out her cell phone, dialed Rose, and hurriedly explained about Madeleine's extra guests.

"How are we supposed to feed heavy hors d'oeuvres and birthday cake to another fifteen people?" Rose's voice shot up an octave on the last word.

"I don't know. But remember what the sous-chef at her country club said?"

"'If we get Madeleine's approval, the jobs will roll in,' but—"

"No 'buts.' We have to do this." Sometimes when a job went off course, Tess had to push Rose past panic. "It's a buffet, that helps."

"True," Rose said with less tension, more resignation.

"I'll take stuff inside and then pick up more crackers and some fancy olives. Call you from the store."

The second Tess hung up, her phone rang.

An unfamiliar number with the area code for Sunset Lake, out in north-central Missouri, where Great-Aunt Leticia had lived.

The reality of her death two days ago swept over Tess anew.

But the call wasn't from the funeral home or the minister. She knew those numbers.

With exactly three hours and twenty-seven minutes until the McCullen party, anybody else would have to wait.

She let the call roll to voice mail and unloaded the rest of the food, squeezing what she had to into Madeleine's refrigerator, then backed out of the driveway and headed toward the highway. Ten minutes later she reached her exit and steered up the off-ramp.

On the incline, the van slowed dramatically, even when she punched her foot on the gas. *What was going on?*

The van inched up the ramp, finally reaching the top. Back on level ground, it drove normally again.

Tess blew out an exasperated breath. Once this event was finished, she'd have to get the engine checked. Silver Platter Catering couldn't survive without wheels, even if van repair wasn't in the budget. But how was she going to pay for it? Forget about borrowing from family. Her brother, the boy genius, was doing his residency in pediatrics and struggling with student loans. And asking Mom for money would only lead to a resounding no, followed by a discussion of Tess's failures.

Tess snagged a parking spot, grabbed her phone, and called Rose. "I played with a new ice cream last night, Coconut Lemon Bliss. We can have a server put mini scoops in glass dessert cups at the end of the buffet.

"I saw that in the freezer."

Wait, she hadn't made that much ice cream. "Why don't you crush some graham crackers to line the bottom of the cups?"

"Okay. And I found dough for those yummy cheese straws."

"Perfect. Start those. I'll be there soon."

An hour and a half later, with small culinary miracles complete, Tess turned off the highway and headed back to the McCullens'.

Rose sat in the passenger seat, cheeks still pink from their frantic loading. Although a year younger than Tess, Rose appeared older than her twenty-six years, the toll of late nights as the single mother of a toddler. She balanced the birthday cake on her lap, and the scent of its buttercream frosting filled the front of the van.

The rest of the food—enough for sixty-five—was secured in the back.

"I can't believe we did it." Rose pushed her dark bangs off her forehead. "I'm glad you had that new ice cream made. It's amazing, like nothing I ever tasted."

"Thanks." Tess looked over at Rose. "But Madeleine's daughter-in-law isn't the only one with a birthday today, and don't think I've forgotten. I didn't have time to give it to you, but I got you a present. It's nothing huge, just a season pass to the zoo for you and Charlie. I figure he's old enough—"

"Nothing huge?" Rose's voice grew higher and filled with emotion. "It's way more than you should have done."

"Nonsense. You know I love birthdays. And you're one of my best friends." A bit of an understatement. Tess's old friends had moved to another galaxy, orbiting husbands and babies. If she didn't count clients and wait staff, on most days, Rose was the only person Tess talked to.

Not that Rose knew that. When she wasn't at Silver Platter, Rose spent time with her son and her mommy friends.

When Tess wasn't at Silver Platter, she made checklists.

"I'm so glad we work togeth—" Tess glanced down at the floorboard, then at the huge hill they were climbing—or trying to climb. Only a fourth of the way up. She jammed her foot down.

Instead of an encouraging *vroom*, the engine made a weak moan.

Useless. Her pulse sped and she shot a look at Rose.

"Are we out of gas?" Lines formed around the edges of Rose's mouth.

Tess pointed at the full gas gauge. "And I was fine on the highway where it was flat."

"We're at least two miles away." Rose's tone said she'd given up, like it might as well be two hundred miles.

Tess yanked the steering wheel hard to the right and turned onto a side street. Not. Giving. Up. "We'll cut through by The Ice Cream Station and avoid that big hill. Maybe we can make it that way."

"Leave it to you to know a back way past a place that sells ice cream."

In spite of her worry, Tess grinned. She did sample a lot of ice cream. But she liked to think of it as research.

On the side street, the van eased along, almost as if nothing was wrong. Two minutes later they reached a stop sign. Beyond it, the road dipped, then climbed again.

Rose leaned forward, peering ahead.

Tess tightened her grip on the steering wheel. They only had that hill and about half a mile to go. But with the time they'd lost cooking for fifteen more guests, there was no way to carry all the food in on foot. She studied the road ahead and looked back at Rose. "If I get up enough speed going down this hill, maybe I can coast up the next one."

Rose lowered her head and began to pray under her breath.

Tess kept her focus on the road, not heaven. God probably wouldn't help her, but maybe he would intervene—for Rose.

Jaw tight, Tess floored the gas.

The old van raced down the hill, bottomed out, and began to climb. Three-fourths of the way up, however, gravity took hold.

"C'mon, c'mon." Tess's heart pounded. She sucked in a breath and pressed harder on the gas, straining her thigh muscle to ram her black clog against the floorboard.

Yard by sluggish yard, the van crept up the hill.

With a jolt, as if fueled by its dying breath, it rose the final inches to the crest.

Tess exhaled. "We made it."

Rose slumped against the seat. "Once we unload, I'll call my cousin's friend and see if he can look at the van tomorrow."

"Thanks."

Tess turned into the McCullen driveway and, with one hand, lifted the collar of her blouse off her chest to let in some cool air. Time to act like nothing had happened. Time to wow Madeleine McCullen and ensure the future of Silver Platter Catering.

Six hours later, packing up in the kitchen as the last guest left, Tess leaned against the counter and caught her breath. In spite of fifteen extra guests, her ancient van, and the hills, the party had been a success.

Madeleine walked in, looking less fresh-from-the-salon, more droopy pixie.

Though Tess and her staff did the heavy lifting, being a good hostess was exhausting.

"You were fantastic." Madeleine's eyes met Tess's, her sincerity clear. "Those crab things. And that ice cream… Give me a week or two to talk you up, and your phone will be ringing off the hook."

Excitement filled Tess's chest like a swig of carbonated soda. Exactly what she needed—good reviews that would bring in more catering jobs. Her hard work would pay off in success. "Thank you, Madeleine. Your recommendation will mean a lot."

"You've got it." Madeleine rubbed her lower back. "I'm going upstairs to take something for this. Just show yourself out when you're done." She slid off her pink mules, picked them up, and padded toward the hall, leaving behind a faint scent of magnolias.

Tess bundled up the dirty tablecloths, the last load. Now she only needed to help Rose strap the trays back in the van.

Oh, the call she hadn't taken. Probably some question about the funeral. With Dad long dead and Leticia's brother in the hospital, Tess had ended up in charge.

She pulled up her voice mail and hit Play.

"Hello, this is Jewel, from the law firm of Redmond and Sons. Mr. Al Redmond would like you to come by Monday right after the funeral for Leticia Palmer. You're named as a beneficiary in her estate."

Tess stopped in the doorway to the garage, leaned against the door frame, and listened to the message again.

One more sign that Leticia was really gone. If only Tess had visited her great aunt more often after high school.

She blinked back tears. It was okay. Leticia had lived a long, healthy life.

But that message…

A tingle of hope began to rise in her chest. Years ago, Leticia had hinted that she might leave Tess some money.

Maybe, if her luck held out, it would be enough to fix the van.

❧

Jack Hamlin tugged on his hiking boots, grabbed a jacket, and stepped onto his back deck, ready to check on the wood ducks.

Sunset Lake spread before him, forty acres shimmering in the morning light. The air smelled of last night's rain and rang with the conversations of red-winged blackbirds.

In the shallow cove near his house, several Canada geese and a pair of blue-winged teals were feeding. Beautiful birds, but not his favorite, not the baby wood ducks. Not yet. Their unhatched eggs were still in their nests, high in trees or in manmade boxes on metal poles.

But it was mid-April. One day soon the ducklings would start to hatch. Then each baby wood duck would make a bold leap from its nest and plummet until it bounced on the ground or splashed into the water. But they would never leap from those nests, never reach the lake, if their eggs were eaten by raccoons or snakes.

Jack squinted at one of the nesting boxes, far across the lake on one of three dead trees knee-deep in water. His urge to check the boxes, to make sure the storm hadn't affected them, was probably paranoid.

The weatherman hadn't called the storm that hit mid-Missouri last night a tornado, but one of the three trees looked wrong, like the wind had definitely done a number on it.

Halfway down the deck stairs, Jack spotted a different type of problem on the far side of the lake. In the distance, behind the home of his neighbor, Leticia Palmer, a cedar leaned at a precarious angle and threatened her power line. Further proof the weatherman might have been wrong.

Jack would check on the nesting boxes, then deal with the cedar by the power line.

Leticia wouldn't be needing electricity, seeing as he was attending her funeral today, but he'd taken care of her property for years. It didn't feel right to stop now, even if the church was going to inherit the place.

He took a hatchet and a pruning saw out to the dock and went back to the garage for his canoe—the same canoe he'd used here since he was a kid. Soon he was on the water, paddling toward the first nesting box.

Sunset Lake was his home, his solace, and—when he loaded his backpack with gear and set up his easel by the water—his studio.

Near Kaitlyn's Point, where a long finger of land stretched into the water, he startled a frog, sending it into the lake. Jack drew in a deep breath and watched the ripples fan out from the frog's entry point.

After several minutes, he passed the dam and rounded a bend. There, the first nesting box sat five feet over the water, atop a pole a few feet from shore. A metal cone encircled the pole beneath the box to protect it from predators.

The box looked fine.

Probably, he should assume the rest of the boxes were all right, deal with the cedar, and get to work. He needed to add more detail to his current painting of a pair of American black ducks. The gallery where he showed his work wanted it for an event late next month.

But he'd paddled all this way already. Might as well keep going.

Around the next bend, he had a clear view of Leticia's house. Two stories, but designed to look long and low, with a huge deck facing the lake.

He'd liked Leticia. Ever since she moved in fifteen years ago, the retired Latin teacher had been a good neighbor. When he'd bought his childhood home from his parents and suggested a mutual covenant to protect the habitat at Sunset Lake, she'd readily agreed. And she'd left him alone.

No "come over for dessert," no mention of a friend's daughter she wanted to introduce, no invitations to church.

Perfect.

Because he didn't need to socialize, didn't want to get involved with another woman, and didn't have much use for God.

He paddled closer to the next box, which at Leticia's request was directly out from her house, where she'd been able to view it easily with binoculars.

There it was. Good thing he'd come to check on it.

The three dead trees rose from the water, the bases of their trunks submerged. Two of the trees were little more than stumps. The third was taller and retained a few branches.

Well, sort of retained, after the storm. Now one huge branch dangled, halfway broken off the trunk, and

17

stretched into the water a few inches from shore. Another branch, higher and also partly broken off by wind, now leaned toward the top of the nesting box.

A raccoon could scamper out from shore on the lower branch, scoot up the tree to the second branch, and shimmy down it to the nesting box—a sneaky way to skirt the protective metal cone and access the box from above.

And have duck eggs for dinner.

Jack leaned back and considered his options. The lower branch lay toward the shore in a particularly shallow area. If he cut that branch, it would land in a position that would still allow a raccoon access to the tree.

If he cut the top branch, though, the one that hung down toward the nesting box, it should fall in the water completely. A raccoon would be able to get to the dead tree, but not the nesting box.

That should work. If he could reach the upper branch.

With a bit of maneuvering, he positioned his canoe beside the tallest dead tree and wedged the stern between two branches—broken off long ago—that stuck out of the water. Not perfect stability, not by a long shot, but better than nothing.

He picked up the hatchet from the floor of the canoe, made sure the blade cover was securely in place, and slid the hatchet handle through a belt loop on his jeans.

He swallowed.

Now came the hard part.

On both sides of the canoe, in addition to the two branches that stabilized it, other branches stuck up through the surface of the water. Underneath, hidden by the reflection of blue sky, peril lurked. If he fell...

The back of his throat tightened. This probably was not the time to consider which arm or leg he'd prefer to impale on a submerged stake.

"This is such a great idea," he said under his breath.

The mother wood duck poked her head out of the box and peered at him, giving no indication that she appreciated his sarcasm.

Jack grabbed the trunk of the dead tree, and—ever so slowly—stood.

He wobbled.

He clung to the tree trunk with both arms, sucked in a breath, and forced himself to steady the canoe with his feet.

Thanks in large part to the restraining branches, it worked. He exhaled.

At last, he was in position.

He held the tree trunk with one arm and freed the hatchet from his belt loop. Then he flipped off the blade cover and hacked at the branch.

Three whacks later, it gave a loud *creeee-eeech* and broke apart.

As he'd envisioned, it fell into the water. The pathway to the nesting box was removed. Raccoons around the lake cursed his name.

Jack leaned forward a fraction and gently tossed the hatchet into the bow of the canoe. Then he straightened back up. He'd ease straight down in to his seat and—

"You shouldn't stand up in a canoe!" The warning cut through the air like a tornado siren.

Jack jerked toward the sound.

A blonde woman stood on the shore.

The canoe thrust forward, away from the stabilizing branches.

His throat slammed closed and he lurched for the tree.

If he could grab—

Too late.

The canoe shot toward deeper water.

For a fraction of a second, he remained standing, like a surfer riding a wave. Then the canoe slowed.

Before he could sit, he swayed right.

He leaned left and hunkered over, trying to steady the canoe.

But he overcorrected.

The canoe tipped.

And he splashed into the water.

His elbow rammed into an underwater branch, and his feet hit the bottom and sank into the muck.

He gasped and stood up. The water didn't even come to his waist, but it was so cold that chunks of ice should have been floating on the lake. His elbow throbbed. And he must have hit his shin against the canoe as he fell. All because of some blonde.

"Are you okay?" She ran to the edge of the lake.

He wiped a slimy bit of duckweed from his cheek. "I'm fine." What a ridiculous question. Of course he wasn't okay.

The canoe bobbed a few feet away, upside down, with the paddles close by.

His hatchet and pruning saw had to be at the bottom of the lake. Sunk in the mud and impossible to find.

And he needed to get out of the water before he froze to death.

He bent his elbow and drew in a sharp breath. Probably not broken but plenty painful. Carefully he navigated the underwater branches, righted the canoe, and slid the paddles inside.

Mama Duck gave a series of faint, unsettled squawks.

He didn't know for sure, but judging by the tone, she was glad he was leaving.

Ungrateful bird.

Farther from Leticia's, in a spot where the lake bottom was clear, he dragged the canoe toward shore. He wasn't going to attempt to climb into it in the middle of the lake while wearing stiff jeans and a bulky canvas jacket. Not with his elbow and shin hurting. And not with an audience.

Because the woman was still there, watching and leaning out toward the water like a concerned mom at camp. At thirty-two he didn't need mothering.

He pulled the canoe out of the lake and limped, dripping, onto the grass, boots globbed with mud, clothes strewn with duckweed.

The blonde scurried over.

Jack narrowed his eyes, trying to place her.

Pale hair in a tight bun. A face without makeup, authentic and attractive, despite the obvious lack of a brain behind it.

"Can I help you?" she said, now right beside him, her blue-gray eyes wide.

21

"I think you've helped quite enough." He took a step back. Favoring his left arm, he stripped off his jacket and examined his elbow. The jacket was torn, but the skin was unbroken. And, though it felt like he'd have a massive bruise on his shin, his jeans weren't even ripped.

"What were you doing out there?" Her tone implied he needed mental help.

"Removing a branch brought down by the storm." He wrung out the hem of his T-shirt and put his jacket back on. At least it blocked the wind. "If you'd left me alone…"

Her mouth tightened and her chin shot out. "That branch wasn't hurting anything. It would have simply fallen in the lake one day."

Heat rose in Jack's chest. The woman didn't have a clue what she was talking about. "That branch"—he jabbed a finger toward where it had hung—"was the perfect access for a raccoon to reach that nesting box."

"So?"

"So if no one eats the eggs, in a few days they will hatch. Which is what we want, unless you hate baby ducklings."

Her lips grew even tighter, bunched up into an uneven line. "I do not hate ducklings. But why do you care so much? Are you from the state conservation department?"

"Jack Hamlin. I live over there." He pointed at his house. "And you're here because…?"

"I'm Tess Palmer, Leticia's great-niece. Here for the funeral."

Jack didn't respond. That explained her black skirt, dark blouse, and black high heels, but not why she was at the lake.

"I wanted to come here before the service, to say goodbye." She made a vague gesture toward the water. "It seemed fitting." She trailed off.

All right, she understood Leticia. He'd give her that. He tipped his head a few degrees in acknowledgment.

"I figured Trevor wouldn't mind me walking around." Tess gazed at the lake.

"Trevor?" Jack looked around. He didn't need to be surprised by another stranger.

"Leticia's brother, the one who will inherit the place."

"Really?" She had a surprise coming. Everyone in town knew Leticia was leaving her house to the Abundance Community Church. Jack took a step back. Whatever, he'd had enough chit-chat. He needed to take a hot shower and get dressed for the funeral.

"Trevor lives in Oregon, but he's in the hospital, so he won't be here today. May never be here. I remember when I was in high school, he told my mom that if he owned this place, he'd sell it to someone who'd put in a hotel."

Jack flinched. "A hotel?"

"Can't you see something small and rustic? With kayaks, paddle boards, a few of those personal watercraft?" She sounded ready to write the brochure.

"No, I can't." Jack repositioned the canoe. There was no need to let the mere mention of personal watercraft spike his blood pressure. Trevor's scheme was a non-issue, because the church would not be building a hotel.

"I'll be over on Leticia's land this afternoon." He pointed to the leaning cedar. "To make sure nothing falls on that power line. I had planned to take care of it after the nesting boxes."

"You're really serious about protecting the ducks. From raccoons and all."

"Yep." Jack shoved off and climbed in the canoe.

His kind of serious included very strong opinions about the right and wrong places for noisy, intrusive personal watercraft. And about hotels.

If anybody in Leticia's family tried some stupid development scheme, they'd hear how serious he was—from his lawyer.

# Chapter Two

Shifting straight from mourner to hopeful heir felt greedy.

Greedy and wrong.

Tess drove her brother's Honda down the main drag of Abundance, the town closest to Sunset Lake. Good thing he'd asked her to keep his car and drive it once a week while he did his residency in Boston.

Rose's friend hadn't offered a loaner while he worked on the van.

Along the lazy street, huge baskets of pansies hung from dark-green metal light poles. A banner announced a pancake benefit breakfast for the local fire station. And not one of the street parking spots was metered. Three hours from the St. Louis suburbs by car, but it felt as if she'd gone back in time.

Tess turned off the GPS on her phone, parked two doors down from the office of Leticia's lawyer, and looked at her reflection in the rearview mirror.

She should have rescheduled. But the lawyer had asked her to come by right after the funeral.

And if Leticia left her money, Tess needed it. Any minute, Rose would text with the mechanic's estimate for fixing the van.

Tess dusted some powder on her nose, which was still red from crying, and went inside the office, an older house with a mansard roof. She spoke to the receptionist tucked behind a sliding-glass window and stepped into the lobby, which looked like it had once been the parlor.

Across the room, Jack Hamlin looked up from a magazine.

Tess sank into a brown leather chair facing him and smoothed her straight black skirt. She'd seen him from a distance at the funeral but didn't expect to find him here. Did Leticia leave him something too?

Jack leaned forward. "I didn't mention it earlier," he said in a low voice, "but I'm sorry about Leticia."

"Thank you." She tried not to stare at him. Earlier, when he'd been dripping wet in jeans and a T-shirt, she'd mostly noticed muscles.

And mud.

And the fact that—even though standing up in a canoe had been his idea—he'd been mad at her.

Now she saw short, light-brown hair and hazel eyes, a neat beard, and a well-cut dark suit. When he didn't look ready to throw her in the lake, the man was handsome enough to make her heart falter like a blender hung on a hunk of ice. Cheeks growing warm, she averted her eyes and studied the room.

Huge baseboards and crown moldings, an ornate gold-and-burgundy rug, and tables with ball-and-claw feet. Intellectual magazines neatly arranged in staggered rows on the coffee table. Normal office noises were partitioned behind the glass window with the receptionist, giving the place the feel of a historic home. The only anachronisms were a Keurig machine and a window-unit air conditioner.

The ceramic doorknob to the adjoining room rattled, and the lawyer—it had to be him in the three-piece suit— guided a couple into the lobby.

An apple-shaped woman and a pudgy man, both in Sunday-best polyester, both in their fifties. Maylene Wheeler, Leticia's cleaning woman, and her husband.

Tess gave them a polite smile.

Maylene hitched her cream vinyl purse higher on her shoulder and stomped out. Her husband gave an apologetic look and darted after her.

The lawyer gave a disappointed glance after them, then cleared his throat. "Miss Palmer? I'm Al Redmond." He shook her hand and gestured Jack into the next room. "I need to speak with Jack for a moment and I'll be right with you."

"Thank you," she said.

Jack tossed his magazine on the coffee table and stood up.

Tess reached out and aligned the magazine with the others.

As if it was a physical force, his gaze fell on her. She slowly looked up.

Straight into his eyes, which were laughing at her.

She glared at him and slid back in the soft leather seat. What a jerk. All right, she was tidy. There was nothing wrong with tidy. The world would be a better place if everyone was tidy.

Jack walked toward the lawyer. Next to Jack, who had to be about six feet tall and looked like he spent lots of time outside, the lawyer seemed short and pasty. He led Jack into the next room, and the door closed behind them.

Tess stretched her calves and re-crossed her legs the other way. These black heels were fine for a quick funeral in a St. Louis church but not so good for a visit to the lake or lengthy graveside condolences in Abundance.

Mom had refused flat-out to come to the service, said she and Leticia never had gotten along. But if Tess had known she'd be the only family member present, standing there after the service talking to strangers, she'd have begged her mother to attend.

Okay, maybe not.

Still, someone from the family should have been there besides Tess. She'd barely seen Leticia since high school. Uncle Trevor, eighty-five, with a broken foot, had a good excuse. But what about his kids? One of them lived in Kansas City, two hours away.

With none of them here, she probably should call Trevor and offer to clean out Leticia's fridge before she drove back.

Before the secretary called Friday, Tess had planned to attend the funeral out of gratitude for the summers she spent at Sunset Lake, out of love for Leticia. Here, all she could think about was the guy at the bank who told her she'd reached her credit limit and the fact that Leticia might have left her money. Tess crossed her arms.

What was taking so long? The longer she sat here, the more cold-blooded she felt.

At least she could check her email while she waited. She dug into her purse. In the bottom, under her pack of multicolored fine-point gel pens, her phone lit up, still on silent from the funeral. She grabbed it and found a voice mail from Rose.

She hit Play.

"Tess? He says we need a whole new engine. That the van could die at any time, and..." Rose slowed in the way that meant bad news. "And it will cost like four thousand dollars."

Tess's stomach cramped. She slid down in the chair, arms over her mid-section. The apple Danish she'd eaten for breakfast hardened into a medieval weapon, one of those iron balls with spikes.

There was no way Leticia had left her four thousand dollars. She was a retired Latin teacher. And had other relatives.

But Tess had no other options.

With the van out of commission, she'd use her brother's Honda a lot more than once a week. But his little car couldn't haul all it took to cater an event. And Rose's mother dropped her off each morning.

The doorknob rattled again.

Tess straightened up and tried to hide her worry.

"I could have sworn Leticia said you suggested this contribution." The lawyer led Jack back into the lobby.

"Uh, no, we never discussed a gift to a conservation group." Jack sounded confused. "But it's great that she left money to help preserve wetlands for waterfowl."

The lawyer's chest puffed as though he'd given the money himself. "She wanted you to know about it." He turned to Tess. "Miss Palmer?"

Tess stood. What was it with Jack and ducks? She looked in his direction.

He was focused on her legs.

She reached to smooth her hair, to make sure none had escaped her bun, and stopped, hand near her neck.

Preening? Really? Right after Leticia's funeral? For some guy who had gone overboard—literally—to protect ducks?

Ignoring Jack, she scurried into the conference room and sat at a large cherry table.

"Please accept my condolences on the loss of your great-aunt. She will be missed here in Abundance." Al Redmond's voice was deep and resonant, perfect for a courtroom.

"That's very kind of you."

"Concerning the house..." The lawyer drew out the pronouncement and slid a thick folder across the table.

"If you can loan me a key, I'll be happy to clean out the fridge. Uncle Trevor's in the hospital."

The lawyer leaned forward. "Actually, Leticia had me draw up paperwork three years ago to put the house in trust for you."

Tess's chest hollowed and she melted halfway down into her chair. "I inherit the house?" Her words came out shaky.

"Yes, I believe she hoped you might move your business to this area." The lawyer coughed twice. "You can read through the rest of it, but basically her trust designates two hundred thousand dollars each to your brother and three cousins, makes several smaller charitable bequests, and leaves the remainder to the local church."

Tess raised a hand to cover her mouth.

"You were aware that Leticia invested heavily in the stock market?"

Tess managed the slightest shake of her head. Her brother got $200,000 cash? First thing out of this meeting, she'd call and ask him to loan her enough to get the van fixed.

"Distribution of the money will take a month or so." He looked down and flipped through some pages.

So much for the loan. Silver Platter couldn't survive that long without a van.

"But the house is yours today," the lawyer said. "Also, with the exception of the items listed on page nine of the trust, which you will need to bring to my secretary so we can ship to the beneficiaries, she left you the contents of the house."

"What about Uncle Trevor?"

"If you look at page four, subparagraph H…"

She opened the folder, pulled out the first set of stapled pages, and found the right page.

Al read aloud from his copy, his tone now sour, as if Leticia had ignored his esteemed guidance. "'To my brother Trevor, two thousand dollars. It is my hope he will buy a new television set and subscribe for one year to a cable service that provides access to news programs supporting a number of political views, not just his own.'" The lawyer tapped the page. "Leticia insisted on writing that part herself."

Tess read the paragraph again. It sure sounded like Leticia. "Does Uncle Trevor know?"

"I reached him this morning on his cell phone and went over this document with him. I was concerned that it might be unexpected. Her earlier estate plan did leave him the house."

"Was he upset?"

"No, she'd already told him."

With slow, careful movements, as if the will might shatter, Tess closed the sheaf of papers and straightened it on the table.

No need to call Uncle Trevor.

But she did need to clean out the fridge.

Because the house at Sunset Lake was hers.

ය

Even after a stop at the bank, Jack was still off-kilter.

He'd talked with Leticia about protecting the wetlands around Sunset Lake when they handled the deed restriction for their properties, but he'd never asked her to contribute to a conservation group.

Her donation had been a huge surprise.

Then that woman Tess had stood up. And Jack found that when he wasn't dripping with ice water, her long legs and black high heels shorted out his brain as if he'd inhaled turpentine.

What he needed to get his brain working was takeout lunch from Cassidy's Diner. And, since he'd be there already, a whole pie to go.

The diner wasn't much to look at. Ten immobile stools at a gray counter with a wide silver edge. Eight sagging, duct-taped red booths. Two replacement booths in a burnt umber that in no way matched and, according to Jack's mom, had been put in after a fire when he was in college. All in all, not much seating, but always delicious food. And always full, always loud. A stop at Cassidy's would be worth it, though, in spite of the noise.

He stepped inside and drew in a deep breath. The aroma of fried onion rings filled the air, along with a hint that Grace Cassidy had been baking, a scent as seductive as fine perfume.

The grill sizzled behind the little window that opened to the kitchen, and one of Grace's sons whacked the order-up bell with a ding.

Those noises didn't bother Jack, only the talking.

Back when he was a graphic artist in Chicago, he wouldn't have even noticed the jabbering. Now, after so much time alone, all that chatter made his head throb. With luck, he could keep his own conversations to a minimum. At least he didn't see any of his relatives, like his Aunt Patsy. That woman was quite a talker.

Jack nodded in response to several waves, took a seat at the counter, and carefully kept his focus away from Maylene Wheeler and her husband, Bob, three stools down. Jack had spoken to Leticia's housekeeper twice in his life. That was plenty. Both times she'd cornered him in the grocery store and told him what a grand job she could do cleaning his house, how she could make his life better.

Right. Having her around would improve his life about as much as keeping mosquitoes as house pets.

He studied the chalkboard.

*Monday's Pies: Apple Sour Cream Crumb, Coconut Cream, Strawberry-Rhubarb*

Strawberry-Rhubarb? A stop at the grocery for vanilla ice cream and his meals would be tasty for a week. Well, maybe three days.

Jack scanned the menu and decided what he wanted, but left the pages open. He did not want to look available for conversation. From the corner of his eye, he saw that Maylene and Bob were studying papers, probably the same ones she carried when she stormed out of the lawyer's office.

Maylene's cheeks were red. "All right, let's see what other fool things she did," she said in a peevish tone.

Still looking down at the menu, Jack listened more closely. He wouldn't mind learning if this Trevor person really had inherited Leticia's house.

"To Badersburg University, fifty thousand dollars," Maylene said. "Can you believe it?"

"Isn't that where she worked?" Bob sounded shocked.

"Thirty years, she told me."

"There's no way I'm giving money to the feed store after I retire."

Jack's eyes met those of Grace, the diner owner, who was on the phone behind the counter.

She shot a glance at the couple, as if she was on hold and also listening to the conversation. A minute later

Grace hung up. She tucked a wisp of brown hair behind her ear, walked toward him, and flipped open her order pad. "Sorry about that. The kitchen exhaust cleaners are coming tonight and called to confirm. What are you having?"

Jack nodded. As much fried food as Cassidy's sold, he could only imagine the amount of grease that needed cleaning. Cooking his meal would only add to it.

Ever efficient, Grace took his order in seconds and hurried away.

He pulled out his phone and pretended to check his email.

"Five thousand dollars to the Abundance library, that's nice," Maylene said.

"Makes sense, since she was a teacher," Bob said.

Jack silently agreed. And smiled at the thought of the gift. He'd spent many hours at the Abundance library as a kid, looking at art books and graphic novels.

Grace returned. "Reuben and rings coming right up. And here's your cherry Coke and a whole pie to take home, so nobody will cut into it." She set down a to-go cup and a carry-out box. "That's the last one. The mayor will be real perturbed this afternoon when there's no strawberry-rhubarb left."

Jack patted the pie box. "He'll get over it."

Grace chuckled. "You should come by more often, Jack. This time of year I make strawberry-rhubarb every day."

Jack gave a non-committal shrug. Even for pie, he'd only endure the noise of the diner so often.

"I still can't believe she only left me a lousy twenty thousand," Maylene said in a loud whisper.

Bob flushed.

Grace's eyes grew wide and she walked past Maylene, as if hoping to hear more.

Jack took a drink of his Coke and stirred it to mix the cherry syrup up from the bottom. How much money had Maylene expected? She cleaned Leticia's house one morning a week, as evidenced by her car coming and going on the other side of the lake, but didn't even show up when there was more than an inch of snow.

"It is quite a lot of money, dear," Bob said.

"Not nearly what she promised."

"You know what riled me?" Bob said. "The way Al got so defensive when you asked if Leticia was in her right mind."

Jack slid a glance down the counter.

"'I assure you,'" Bob cleared his throat with a double cough, a perfect imitation of the lawyer. "'I would never execute a document for someone not in full possession of their faculties.'"

Maylene let out a snort.

Bob looked straight at Jack, his eyes hard, a silent warning to quit eavesdropping.

Jack studied his phone.

"I, for one, think the old bird was loony." Bob plunked down his glass.

"Folks at the church must think so."

Jack tapped the screen of his phone but listened intently. That didn't sound good. If the church had inherited Leticia's property, Pastor Corey planned to use the house as a retreat, take small, quiet groups out once a month. A wonderful plan he'd shared with Jack at the post office one day while trying to convince him to come back to services.

"She left the church all the rest of her estate, after the bequests. How much do you think that is?" Maylene asked.

"Not a clue. Hope it's enough for a new roof. What about the house?"

"Her great-niece gets it," Maylene said. "That blonde girl."

Jack took a quick peek at Maylene. Tess had said her uncle would get the house.

"C'mon." Bob grabbed up the papers and left a ten-dollar bill on the counter. "We're supposed to babysit the grandkids."

Grace brought Jack a second Styrofoam box. She stacked the boxes holding the pie and his lunch in a bag and handed him the bill. As soon as Maylene and Bob turned, she angled her head toward them and discreetly rolled her eyes.

The couple walked to the register.

Jack replayed their conversation in his mind, and tightness grew in his shoulders and neck. Leticia's bequests careened like a wobbly bicyclist from one side to the other of the line of promises she'd made.

What if she'd done that with other legal matters?

The tension spread down into his chest, and he grabbed his takeout.

Diners were four deep, waiting to pay. He pulled out his wallet and shoved his ticket and some bills under the salt shaker. He glanced at what Bob had left on the counter. Not much of a tip, and Aunt Patsy had told him that Grace had been struggling. Jack slid another five under the salt with his own ticket. Then he sped outside, dialed Al Redmond, and paced. Would Al be in? And taking calls over lunch?

Five rings and the secretary placed him on hold.

Three minutes later—and twelve passes pacing back and forth in front of the diner—the lawyer came on the line.

"Al, can I have a copy of the covenant for the Sunset Lake landowners after Leticia signed it? The one I dropped off about six months ago?"

"Jack, didn't she tell you? Once she made that donation to the conservation group, she said the deed restriction wasn't necessary."

A lump like a piece of one of the diner's Styrofoam food boxes caught in Jack's throat. He forced his words out. "No. She didn't tell me." And it didn't make sense. "Was the donation given specifically to help Sunset Lake?"

"No, it was an unrestricted gift. That's what she wanted."

Al said something else, but the words buzzed in Jack's ear without meaning.

Leticia had lied.

Lied.

Another woman he shouldn't have trusted. The donation on behalf of waterfowl habitat was great, but it only would help broad conservation efforts. Not Sunset Lake in particular.

Sure, because of the fringe of wetlands, the lake had some legal protection, but with the way Tess's eyes had lit up when she talked about the hotel, not enough.

Not nearly enough.

Because Jack had to protect the lake. And not just for the ducks.

For Kaitlyn.

# Chapter Three

The house was dark, with heavy drapes pulled over the wall of glass that faced the lake.

Dark and silent and empty.

Leticia should be leaning in from the back deck, urging Tess to fix a cup of tea and come join her.

But Leticia was gone.

Tess flipped on a light, set the trash from her drive-thru lunch on the breakfast bar, and slipped off her heels. She walked past the kitchen and through the shadowy living room, both remodeled from what she remembered. At the west wall, she tugged back the massive drapes to reveal French doors flanked with large windows.

The room filled with light.

That was better.

In the living room, the furniture echoed the outdoors in blues and greens. On the other side of the glass, beyond a wide deck, a celebration of spring erupted. White and purple blossoms covered the dogwood and redbud trees in the yard. Beyond Sunset Lake, more flowering trees dotted the woods, breaking up the dark-green cedars and the pale green of the new leaves on the oaks and hickories and maples.

Across the lake sat the house that—though she didn't remember him from when she visited Leticia in high school—must belong to Jack Hamlin. Wide and low like Leticia's place, Jack's house was smaller with what might be cedar siding.

On the water, several groups of his beloved ducks floated and soaked in the sun.

Tess unlatched the French doors and stepped out onto the deck. The boards were cool against her bare feet, but the April afternoon was mild. Somewhere close, maybe on a cove hidden around a bend in the lake, Canada geese honked. She sank into a mesh chair that faced the water.

This had been Leticia's favorite spot, where whenever weather permitted she'd eaten her breakfast and read the Bible.

Tess ran one hand along the smooth arm of the chair and closed her eyes, remembering the smell of her great-aunt's coffee, the peace found here with Leticia.

Tess had thought that she'd accepted the loss. But surrounded by memories, the funeral only hours past, her chest ached with sorrow, a hollow surprise, and questions. Why had Leticia left the house to her? And what should she do with it?

The house was gorgeous, but three hours away from St. Louis, three hours away from Silver Platter. She looked out over the water. If only she could do as the lawyer suggested and move to Sunset Lake, have a catering business in Abundance.

A warm breeze flowed over her, fresh with the hint of spring and growth.

With Leticia, Tess had felt that she could exhale every ounce of worry from her lungs, that she was good enough just as she was. Part of that feeling had come from what Leticia shared from her Bible. That Tess's sins could be forgiven. That God loved her. She had believed it, had prayed with Leticia, had been washed in peace.

But she hadn't felt that peace in a long time. And she didn't expect it again anytime soon.

She lowered her head and hunched over, arms wrapped tightly around each other.

Another breeze swirled past and hair that had escaped her bobby pins tickled her cheek.

Tess looked back up, her gaze drawn to the water. Maybe some of that peace hadn't come from Leticia and hadn't come from God. Maybe it had come from the lake. If so, that alone would be reason to move.

It would be wonderful to wake up each morning, drink her coffee out here, listen to the waterfowl and songbirds, and soak in all that blue and green instead of asphalt and concrete and stress. Not to mention that she wouldn't have to pay rent on an apartment.

Tess gripped the arms of the chair and inched forward in her seat. She needed to go in and make a call. To Mom, the very reason Tess had been so glad to spend her summers here.

Best to get it over with. If Mom learned about the house from one of Trevor's kids, Tess would never hear the end of it.

She walked back inside, grabbed her cell phone, and dialed.

"Tess." Mom picked up quickly and spoke fast, as though she'd been expecting the call. "How was the funeral?"

"Fine. No one else from the family was there, but lots of people from town were." Kind, down-to-earth people.

"Not your cousin from Kansas City?"

"No."

"Humph." Mom paused, letting her disapproval sink in. When it came to communicating criticism without words, Mom was a master. "How was your meeting with the lawyer?"

"Did you know Leticia invested in the stock market?"

"Why do you think I sent you there?" Mom's words held a note of incredulity. "I hoped you'd make a good impression and she'd leave you money. I tried to get your brother to go, but he refused, said he had to play baseball."

Tess's stomach clenched and she sank onto the edge of the couch. Her blessed summer reprieves had been one of Mom's plans?

"So did she leave you any money?"

"No." Tess paused, drawing out the moment, imagining her mother's face. It was true. Leticia hadn't left her any *money*. And there was a perverse pleasure in letting Mom think her manipulation had failed. But Tess couldn't pull it off forever. "She left Patrick two hundred thousand dollars. She left me her place at the lake."

Mom let out a cry of victory. "Excellent. She owned most of that lake. The property and the house have to be worth even more than two hundred thousand. You can sell the place and bail out your little business."

Tess gave a rueful smile. Her little business. "The lawyer said Leticia hoped I would live here."

"Live there? On what? Those people can't afford meals like you fix."

Tess pressed her lips together. Like Mom was better than the people of Abundance. But she was right. Silver Platter Catering was designed for a big-city market. A typical event was lobster salad in puff pastry cups, bouquets from the florist, and a string quartet. Abundance was a potluck with crepe-paper streamers and a playlist on somebody's smart phone.

But the lake was so appealing.

"I could take out a small loan against the property and set up my business in Columbia. It's less than an hour from Abundance and a lot bigger." As she said it out loud, Tess liked the idea more and more. The two larger towns on either side of Abundance, Prattsville and Miller's Junction, weren't quite big enough. But Columbia was. If hard work could show results in St. Louis, it could do the same in Columbia.

"But you've got established clients in St. Louis. In Columbia, you'd be starting over. Don't you realize how many new businesses fail?" Mom's voice rose and grew harder.

Tess's chest became rigid, her breathing rough, and she squeezed the sides of the phone with her fingertips. Mom was consistent, if nothing else. Always ready to expect disaster.

"If you take out a loan, you could lose that business and Leticia's place as well."

Tess clenched her teeth. A good daughter would think her mother was just worried about her. Tess, on the other hand, thought Mom was far more worried about how those failures might reflect on her.

Fine. So Silver Platter had been trying to get over this financial hump for four years, ever since she opened it. And with her track record, she was fully capable of ruining two parts of her life in one fell swoop. She didn't need Mom to remind her. "Forget it," Tess said. "You're probably right." She said goodbye, hung up, and massaged her temples. Moving to Sunset Lake was a bad idea anyway. Rose depended on her job and needed to be in St. Louis, where her mother could watch her son while Rose worked.

And if Tess sold the lake house, she could pay off her debts, stop renting work space, and buy her own kitchen, maybe something with more room so she could hire more staff and compete for bigger jobs. And she could still have a significant stash to get her through hard times. At long last she'd be able to leave behind the shadow that had hung over her for the past four years. She could relax, maybe even find a great guy and start a relationship.

Because her social calendar was pretty sparse. She was working so hard to become a success, to leave the ugly past behind, that she didn't have time to date.

But still the lake called to Tess. And, with Madeleine's upcoming recommendations, Silver Platter might be able to succeed without money from the house. Was there some way she could keep Leticia's place and come out every once in a while?

She couldn't get to Sunset Lake very often, not with her schedule. Her last day off had been three months ago. And even if she wasn't at Leticia's, she'd have to keep the utilities on and pay taxes.

No. As much as she hated to admit it, Mom was right.

Tess looked over at the house across the lake, and one more longing fluttered in her chest. For all his craziness about ducks, Jack Hamlin added to the appeal of the lake. He seemed solid and dependable. Look at how he said he'd take care of Leticia's power line even after she died. And he was definitely handsome.

But Great-Aunt Leticia hadn't left her the house so she could move to the lake on the whim that the neighbor might find her as interesting as the ducks. So no, Jack Hamlin didn't matter.

Tess pulled up a search engine on her phone and typed in *Real Estate, Abundance, MO.*

A newspaper article popped up that featured a new real estate agent in town, a woman with local ties.

Perfect. Someone who'd have the time it took to sell Leticia's house.

Uncle Trevor was right. Sunset Lake would make an ideal setting for a boutique hotel.

ߒ

47

Jack had wolfed down his diner carry-out in his SUV, then sat in his lawyer's parking lot and stared at the glass door of the red brick office until the secretary got back from lunch.

"Is Pete in this afternoon?" Finally inside, Jack stood, tapping the fingers of one hand on the edge of the secretary's desk.

Her mouth pursed. Not attractive on a woman whose crimson lipstick bled down the lines that fanned out below her lips.

He kept tapping.

"Pete should be back any time. But he'll only be here a minute, because he's got a hearing at the courthouse. How about I schedule you for tomorrow?" The secretary turned on her computer, and it hummed to life.

Jack wasn't interested in tomorrow. "I'll wait. I can walk with him when he goes to the courthouse if I have to." He sat in the vinyl guest chair closest to the door, ready to spring up the instant Pete arrived.

"He'll drive. And you'd have to walk back."

Jack didn't budge. The courthouse was only six blocks away.

The secretary spread her hands in an airy your-call gesture, intently studied her monitor, and gave a sigh of disapproval.

Jack settled in to wait.

Leticia had lied. Right to his face. Right after they had that long talk about birding. She'd been a birder for years. And he'd told her about how—after he'd painted a pair of mallards on a whim—he'd learned the secret. He'd thought bird watching would be boring, that it only appealed to ninety-year-old British women who wore tweed. Actually, birding was a treasure hunt. She'd laughed, agreed, and said she didn't even own tweed.

They'd discussed how important it was to his career to protect the wetland habitat at Sunset Lake. Sure, much of the year he worked from photos in his studio. Often he spent several weeks out of state, taking images of birds that were never seen in Missouri. But some of his best work had been done outside his studio, en plein air on Kaitlyn's Point, during long stretches when he stayed at the lake until he reached the end of his stash of frozen burritos, cheese crackers, and Kellogg's Frosted Mini-Wheats.

He'd even told her how much it meant to him to keep the lake the same as before the accident, before Kaitlyn died. Leticia had acted like she cared.

Jack crossed his arms over his chest. He should have known.

He could trust his family. The Hamlins stuck together.

And he could trust the gallery owner who showed his work. Any deal that was good for Jack meant more commission for Mort.

But after that wreck, he could never again trust a woman. And never again trust God. No loving God could have let Kaitlyn die.

Jack glared at the door and willed Pete to hurry up. There had to be a way to fix the mess with Leticia.

Five minutes later he sat across the desk from Pete.

The lawyer dug through the piles on his desk, yanked out a file, and opened it. "I can't talk long, Jack," he said in a rush. "I have to look over my notes before this hearing."

"Remember the deed restriction for the Sunset Lake properties?"

"Of course. I wrote it."

"I talked with Al Redmond. Leticia verbally agreed, but she never signed it."

Pete ran a hand over the back of his neck. "Without her signature, you can't prove anything."

"Her great-niece inherited. What if she's all gung-ho to sell the place to some developers?" Tension grew in Jack's temples. "She thinks Sunset Lake is a great place for a"—he swallowed, as even the thought brought a bitter taste to his mouth—"a hotel."

"You could fight it, file for an injunction—"

"Would it work?" Jack leaned forward.

"Nah. It would only slow the process down. But the legal fees might pay for the bathroom remodel my wife wants."

Jack shoved back in his seat and glared at Pete. "Is there anything else I can do?"

Pete sobered. "Not unless you find a copy that Leticia signed and had notarized but didn't give her lawyer."

Jack perked up, but only for a second. If Leticia did have such a copy, it would be in her house. Fat chance Tess would drag it out for public view. "So Leticia's relative can sell the land to anyone she wants, for any purpose?"

"She owns it."

Blood built and pounded in Jack's temples.

"A buyer would have to abide by federal laws protecting wetlands." Pete sounded sympathetic but not hopeful.

"Federal laws." Jack spat out the words. "You know as well as I do that a developer can follow the letter of the law and still not act in the best interest of the habitat." He rose. "I should have driven Leticia here myself and watched her sign the papers. I believed her when she said she'd taken care of it."

Pete tipped his head a few degrees to one side, his brows raised, as if in silent agreement that the mess was Jack's fault.

Jack spun and strode out, ignoring the secretary's perfunctory wave.

Sunset Lake was not being developed commercially. Somehow, he had to stop it.

He had too many memories tied to the lake the way it was. And too much of his heart.

# Chapter Four

Stacey Gilcroft needed this listing.

She stood on the front porch of Leticia Palmer's house—listed at twenty-eight hundred square feet in the county records—checked her manicure, and smoothed her hair.

Her nails looked good. She'd done them last night in a nice, rosy pink. And her shoulder-length hairstyle was easy, as long as she didn't count the time she spent coloring it over her bathroom sink, making sure those threads of premature gray didn't show through the brown. Or the bite that the overpriced haircut took out of her dwindling cash.

But when a woman came back to her hometown after fifteen years away, she had to look her best. Especially if she was starting a business.

Stacey rang the bell and drew in a cleansing breath. The call yesterday from Tess Palmer had been a godsend.

Stacey could do this. Be calm and professional. Not desperate.

The door opened. A woman with a severe blonde bun and tension around her eyes held a cell phone to her ear and gestured Stacey inside. "Hi, I'm Tess," the woman mouthed.

Stacey gave a small wave and introduced herself in a low voice.

"Take a look around. Everywhere," Tess whispered with her hand over the phone. "I need five minutes." She pointed Stacey to what looked like bedrooms and spoke into the phone. "Certainly. Silver Platter Catering would be happy to handle your party."

Stacey nodded, pulled her portfolio out of her bag, and headed down the hall. So that was Tess Palmer, Leticia's great-niece. Stacey stepped into the first doorway. If she, personally, had inherited a house and lakefront acreage, she wouldn't look so worried. But sometimes, even when a woman was the talk of the town, there were things other people didn't know.

Stacey understood.

Using her brand-new tape measure, she checked the first-floor master suite, baseboard to baseboard, and wrote down the dimensions. She drew a star and added *remodeled bath*, like she'd learned to do in her online real estate class. Then she measured a small study with a daybed that looked like where Tess was sleeping.

Tess rushed in and gave a smile that couldn't quite overcome the stress in her eyes.

Stacey wiped the dust from the baseboards off her fingers and handed Tess one of her new business cards. "I'm so glad you called. This is a great house."

The smile on Tess's face deepened.

"Want to show me the rest of it?" Stacey said.

"Sure," Tess said and she walked toward the living room.

Stacey stopped beside the couch.

Across the lake, over at Jack's, a red truck reflected a glint of sun. Probably a Ford. Probably his cousin Earl Ray's.

Her nerves tightened, and she turned back to her potential client. She had to stay focused. "Such a lovely place. Lakefront property. I don't think I'll have any problem finding you a buyer." Well, she wouldn't if the house were in California. But it might be a challenge here, smack-dab in the middle of Absolute Nowhere.

Lesson 4 of her online course had made it clear to keep her mouth shut on that point.

Tess turned the business card over in her hand. "You just opened your agency?"

"Yes, I recently moved back from L.A., but I was born and raised here."

"Were you in real estate in California?"

"For years." As the office secretary, not a real estate agent, but Stacey wasn't volunteering that. She stepped through the dining room and into the next room. "What a gorgeous kitchen. Definitely a selling point. I'll have to get lots of photos so we can show everyone what a great house this is."

"It's got nice high counters." Tess ran a hand in front of the toaster. "I would have gone with a gas stove, but that's just me."

Stacey looked at her. "Oh, yes. I heard you're a caterer. Normally, I'd agree, but for out here all electric is a good choice. The gas lines don't run this far and most people don't want to mess with propane." There, her frantic homework this morning had paid off. She sounded downright knowledgeable.

"Shall we?" Tess gestured toward the stairs. "The basement's almost empty, but you need to see the second floor." Her tone held a note of dread.

Stacey climbed two steps and her phone rang. "I'm sorry. I have to take this." She gave Tess a forced smile and dashed down the stairs so she could duck into the kitchen for privacy. The second she picked up, yelling filled her ear.

"Stacey Lynn, where's my car?"

"Dad, I'm working," Stacey whispered. "Not so loud."

"Okay, okay, but where's my Chevy?"

She pressed her lips together. She was supposed to be helping Dad, not driving him insane. "Didn't you see my note? I borrowed it."

"Without asking? Didn't you learn anything from your mother and me when you were little?"

"You were in the shower. I was late. I was coming out here to Sunset Lake and didn't think I had enough gas."

"How am I supposed to get to the store? We're out of milk and bread and my best snacks."

"I left my keys on the counter." Like that would appease him. He hated her car. Said it didn't have enough leg room. "And you shouldn't eat so many of those greasy onion things. You have to get better test results if you want to avoid that operation."

"I don't need heart surgery."

"It's a strong possibility, and you know it." Maybe if she reminded him enough, he'd accept it. With Mom dead, somebody had to get through to him. "Got to go, Dad. I'll have your car home in an hour." She hung up and shut off the ringer, then scrambled upstairs and pulled her professional real-estate-agent demeanor back in place. Dad was not ruining her chance at listing this house. She darted into the only room with an open door. "I'm so sorry."

"What? Oh, no problem." Tess sounded distracted, as though she hadn't even noticed that Stacey had been gone.

Stacey looked past her and saw why.

The room was a nightmare. Piles of trash, plain and simple. Faded artificial flowers. A clear plastic bag of mousetraps. Farther back, stacks and stacks of boxes. Those bits of dust on the downstairs baseboards were nothing. Up here, everything wore a thick fur of dust, surrounded by the smell of dead mouse.

Stacey tried to keep the disgust out of her voice. "What other rooms are up here?"

"A bathroom with silver wallpaper and an avocado sink and tub." Tess picked up a straw cowboy hat that had seen better days and set it back down. "And a turquoise toilet." She paused, then led Stacey into the hall. "And there's this room." She opened another door. "More boxes." Her shoulders sagged.

Stacey couldn't even walk all the way into the bedrooms, but she guessed their size as best she could and measured the bathroom. Downstairs, with Tess holding one end of the measuring tape, she got dimensions for the rest of the rooms.

Then Tess sank into the living room couch. "I can't believe the upstairs is such a mess. But somewhere up there, if I remember right from when I was in high school, I think there's Depression glass that belonged to Leticia's older sister."

"Don't get overwhelmed." Stacey took the chair across from Tess. "I saw a place in California that was worse. A man collected moss. Seriously, tray after tray of moss. It sat for at least twenty years before his nephew inherited. Totally gross." She wrinkled her nose. "If you want this place to show well, though, you do need to clean those rooms out, so people can see how big they are." She peeked at her notes. "And I think you need to have that dead oak taken out at the corner of the house. If not, a big storm could mean pricey roof damage."

For a split second, Tess seemed to think logically, and her eyes filled with agreement about the tree. Then she let out a soft moan. "I don't have time. I need to be back in St. Louis tonight. I'm catering a huge wedding, with events starting this weekend. I'll have to wait to put this house on the market."

A rock formed in Stacey's stomach. She pawed through her papers, looking for answers that weren't there. If Tess didn't sign today, she might list with someone else. "Tell you what, why don't we take care of the paperwork today to save you time?" A nervous quaver pinched Stacey's words, but she had to keep going. "You said on the phone that Leticia had the property appraised not too long ago, right?"

"The lawyer gave me the papers."

"That will make it easy to set a price."

At the word *price*, Tess perked up.

"I'll get the listing online and round up some names of people who could handle that tree and sort those two rooms." Surely Dad would have some suggestions. "Then I'll come back for a couple of hours and help you clean the first floor. With two of us working, we can get a lot done fast."

"You'd do that?" Tess's face brightened.

"Happy to." Stacey flashed her most confident smile. She edged forward and rested one finger at the top of her portfolio, ready to pull out the listing agreement.

"It's a deal," Tess said.

Stacey slid out the agreement. Her first listing. Next up, her first sale. The rock in her stomach was gone, replaced by a litter of Chihuahua puppies, bouncing for attention. "You won't regret it. I will find the perfect family to live here."

"Actually…" Tess rested her hand on her chin for a second. "I was hoping you'd also market it to commercial developers. With all the acreage, my uncle once suggested it would be a good place for a small hotel."

An image of a red truck flashed before Stacey's eyes. A hotel? Oh, buddy. That would not go over well with Tess's neighbor, Jack. Or his cousin Earl Ray.

59

While Mom was alive, she'd kept Stacey updated. Because sure, Stacey had spent time in California, and Jack had worked for a while in Chicago, but she and Jack had grown up together in Abundance.

She and Jack and Earl Ray.

Earl Ray Hamlin...with his green eyes and broad shoulders and those cool new glasses and the goatee she'd seen in a photo on social media and—

She needed to focus on real estate.

She was the seller's agent. No matter what her ultimate goal was in coming back to Abundance, her job was to make money for Tess. "Let me check something." She skimmed her research on the property. "Commercial development is possible, but it would have to be done carefully, because of the wetlands."

"Do you think a developer might buy it?"

"Yes, I do." Stacey held out the listing agreement and offered a pen. The idea did make sense. "You and I will make a great team. Sign here." Even if the house sold to a developer, the deal might be quite lucrative. She could come away with a hefty commission.

Although it might not make up for the fact that certain people in town, like Earl Ray, would hate her. More than ever.

&#x43;&#x292;

Three hours later Tess waved goodbye to Lou, the tree trimmer Stacey had recommended, as he headed down the drive after giving an estimate.

Ducks and geese glided on the lake, and spring covered the hills in a profusion of blooms. The setting definitely provided enough beauty and tranquility to appeal to any potential property buyer. And inside, thanks to Stacey's help, the first floor looked great.

Tess walked back through the front door and into the living room, where Stacey had plumped and arranged the sofa's throw pillows with precision. Listing with her had been a good decision. She'd helped clean, suggested the tree trimmer, and supplied the numbers of two women that she said Tess could trust to sort the bedrooms upstairs.

Maybe something in them would be worth four thousand dollars.

Tess had left messages at both numbers and only needed one to respond so she could know everything at the lake was taken care of. Then she could drive home.

With the demands of her job, it was bad enough that she'd had to stay last night.

She certainly hadn't planned on it yesterday morning. She'd found a pair of tennis shoes in her car but had to make a run to Walmart for a toothbrush and something casual to wear.

But soon she'd be back in St. Louis.

Her phone rang. She read the number, grabbed her notes, and moved to the couch to talk to tomorrow's breakfast client. Five minutes later, after promising that, along with coffee, tea, juice, and water, she would have Pepsi products available—and not a drop of Coke, she hung up and called Rose. "How are you doing?"

"All right, but there's no way I can handle the breakfast, all the appetizers we're supposed to drop off for the bachelor party, and prep the food for the shower, especially not your new Triple Truffle Chunk ice cream."

"Don't worry," Tess said. "I'm leaving soon. I'll help prep for the wedding events and take care of the corporate breakfast client." And she would, even if she had to stay all night at Silver Platter.

"Good," Rose said. "It's overwhelming. And not as fun without you here."

"Thanks." Tess hung up and drew in a deep breath. It was nice to be missed. As stressful as Silver Platter was, she was good at running it. Good at taking care of all those details.

And as she'd learned over the past year, good at creating ice cream flavors. She made a note on her clipboard to test her latest idea, fresh strawberry puree and chunks of extra-crisp gingersnap cookies swirled into a crème brûlée ice cream. It was hard to imagine that wouldn't be tasty.

After a moment she punched in the number for the first name on Stacey's note again. Maybe it was a landline and no one had noticed the answering machine blinking.

After ten rings, a man answered. No, his mom couldn't help sort those bedrooms. She and his dad were celebrating their thirtieth wedding anniversary in Hawaii.

Tess fingered the fuzzy fringe of a throw pillow, tugging the pillow out of alignment. That only left one possibility, a woman named Enid.

She called the next number a second time but it rang and rang, never even letting her leave a message.

A tense feeling spread down from her throat and into her chest. She rolled the edge of the pillow back over on itself, pressing it flatter and flatter.

What if there was no one to help?

She hugged the mangled throw pillow, and the tension in her chest grew as twisted as the exit at 40 and the inner belt back in St. Louis.

What was she going to do now? There was no way she could sort all that stuff, no way to show the house as is. And she really needed those bedrooms sorted, needed the house to sell.

Her gaze slid past the throw pillow to Leticia's Bible on the end table near the French doors. That Bible would have been the first place her great-aunt would have turned if she had Tess's troubles.

Tess looked away, then scooted down the couch, and picked up the big leather-bound book.

Leticia had written a list of verses in the front. Maybe one of them would help.

She lifted the front cover, held it a moment, then let it drop.

No. The answers weren't there. Once upon a time she'd believed they were, but now God just felt distant and disapproving. She'd have to find her own answers. Even if she didn't have a clue how.

A car crunched to a stop in the gravel driveway.

Tess gave the pillow a nervous fluff, tried to line it up as perfectly as Stacey had, and glanced out the narrow window beside the front door.

Jack Hamlin was walking toward the porch. Same neat beard and light-brown hair, but the classy suit from the lawyer's office was gone. He'd returned to casual dress with jeans and a green flannel shirt, a streak of paint across one sleeve. His hazel eyes looked hard and his jaw tight.

Great. Exactly what she didn't need—the grumpy neighbor.

He pounded on the door.

She opened it slowly.

"You can't hire that idiot." He waved a hand over his shoulder at the driveway.

"What idiot?"

"Lou of Lou's Lawn and Garden. I saw his truck from across the lake."

She caught her thumbs in her back pockets. Frankly, as long as she could come up with the money, she could hire anyone she wanted to. "He seemed fine," she said in the don't-push-me tone that she usually reserved for a certain pair of immature servers. "Came right over after I called."

Jack gave a loud, disapproving sniff. "Hard up for work. I'm not surprised." He inched closer, seeming more interested in making his point than in respecting her personal space. "I hired him once to take care of my yard when I had to be out of town." Jack's words came out faster and built in volume. "He used fertilizer that ran into the lake and tried to tell me he hadn't." He fisted his hands at his sides. "Like I wouldn't know."

"Whoa." Tess held one palm up like a traffic cop and inched it toward Jack until the heel of her hand brushed his flannel shirt mid-chest.

His shoulders stiffened and he backed up a fraction of an inch.

"Lou won't be fertilizing anything," she said. "I'm only getting an estimate for having the dead oak removed."

"The man can't be trusted. What if he drops a limb on the roof?" Jack's voice wasn't quite as loud, but it still held an imperious note that grated on her nerves. "Talk to C&K Tree Trimming."

"Fine. I'll get another estimate."

He let out a breath as if he'd averted a nuclear spill. "Good. And if you ever need lawn care, don't use Lou." He stomped out and slammed the door.

Tess sat down at the breakfast bar.

At least he was gone.

But her chest was even tighter than before. Stacey hadn't mentioned lawn care. Tess lived in an apartment and hadn't even thought of it. She dropped her head into her hands.

To get this house on the market, someone would have to mow Leticia's yard.

And sort those boxes.

And make sure the tree trimmer didn't drop a limb on the roof.

Details—what she was usually so good at. But how could she handle details here while running a business in St. Louis, three hours away?

# Chapter Five

"Yo, Jack, you home?" Earl Ray walked in the back door of his cousin's house.

"In here," Jack called from his studio.

Earl Ray dumped a bag of barbecue on the kitchen table. If he didn't stop by occasionally, Jack might go three weeks without seeing another soul. Some greasy beef, covered in tomato sauce and sugar and carcinogens, was good for him.

Earl Ray pulled out forks, foil-wrapped packages, and plastic tubs, then yelled toward the studio. "I brought brisket." Maybe Jack's favorite supper would help him deal with the news. And maybe that news would be easier coming from family.

Jack walked in the kitchen. He grabbed plates from the cabinet and a couple of cans of pop from the fridge. He inhaled deeply, eyes closed in appreciation.

Earl Ray shook his head. If his cousin would actually cook for himself, carry-out wouldn't be such a big deal.

But Jack got so obsessed with painting, he forgot about his stomach until he was starving, and even then he thought food prep was unwrapping a pizza.

To Earl Ray, the hickory-smoked meat, crispy curly fries, and fresh coleslaw didn't have the usual appeal. No matter. He moved Jack's backpack off a chair, sat down, and distributed the cups of sauce—spicy for Jack, sweet for himself. He looked at Jack. No reason to put off telling him. "Have you heard that Leticia's house is for sale?"

Jack's shoulders sank. "No."

Earl Ray served himself moderate portions and covered the brisket in sauce. "That's what they said after I finished that estate sale and stopped by to check on my bike."

Driving his Harley off the back of a pickup bed had been, in retrospect, a bad idea. Bad for the bike at least. He'd had a blast, sailed through the air, and come away without a scratch.

Jack flopped down in the chair across from Earl Ray and his jaw grew tight. "I hoped Tess would keep it."

"Can't say as I blame you. Saw her at the funeral. She would make one fine-looking neighbor." He pushed his glasses up his nose and studied Jack, hoping for some sign of interest, some indication his cousin was ready to live again.

Jack glared at him. "I don't care what she looks like. I just don't want her to sell." He piled brisket on his plate and cracked open his pop. "Who's she got for an agent? Maybe Marv?" A note of hope slipped into his words. "I bet he only sells one house a year."

"Not Marv." Earl Ray studied his plate. This was the part he'd rather avoid. "Stacey."

"Your Stacey?"

Earl Ray gave him a dirty look and jabbed at some brisket with his fork. One of the plastic tines snapped off.

Stacey wasn't his. Not anymore.

"As if ruining your life wasn't enough." Jack picked at the edge of a ketchup packet, then got up and grabbed a bottle out of the fridge. "Why's she back here, anyway?"

"I heard it's because of her dad's heart trouble. I think Stacey and her brother and sister were worried about him." Earl Ray fished the broken piece of fork off his plate.

Jack sat back down. "That doesn't mean she needs to sell real estate."

Earl Ray bit into a potato wedge. Jack was right. It didn't. And it didn't make having her here any easier. "Why don't you buy Leticia's place?"

"She owned way more of the lakefront than me. No way I can afford it." Jack paused and squeezed ketchup on his plate. "Unless…" The note of hope was back in his voice. "Unless Tess priced it really low to move it."

Earl Ray took another bite of brisket, wiped the grease from the potato wedges off his fingers, and pulled up the listing on his phone.

There was Stacey in a little photo in the corner. He zoomed in.

He had dropped some extra weight before she moved back, but at thirty-three, his hair was thinning, and the tight body he had in high school football was a little loose, especially around the waist.

His ex-wife? Exactly the same age as him and more beautiful than ever.

Her sleek brown hair fell to her shoulders and flipped up in some classy West-Coast style. Not the ponytail he remembered.

But her face, that face with those big brown eyes, was exactly the same as it had been those two years they dated in high school, exactly the same as the day they married. He sank into the photograph until his throat began to ache.

Fifteen years apart.

He'd tried to date other women, but they didn't have Stacey's spunk. Didn't have her looks. And didn't have that same pull on his heart.

But he needed to quit being a masochistic fool and focus on the picture of the house.

He scrolled across the screen until he no longer saw Stacey's photo and told Jack the price.

"Forget it," Jack said, low and flat, all hope gone.

"I know you got yourself out of debt. Sold that one painting for almost six figures. And you don't spend much, living out here as practically a hermit." Earl Ray gestured broadly to the rest of the house, then stopped, arm in mid-air. He pointed to the large painting on Jack's mantle. "You could sell that."

*"Ring-Necked Ducks in Flight?"*

"I know that picture means a lot to you, but it would be worth selling if you could keep the lake the way it is."

Jack scrunched up his face. "I don't think it would bring in enough to make a difference."

Earl Ray checked his phone once more, then looked Jack in the eye. Might as well get it over with. "You need to know the rest. This write-up reads like Stacey hopes to sell Leticia's place to some commercial developer."

Jack's eyes hardened, the hazel irises almost gray. "Exactly what I was afraid of." His words came out cold. "The construction noise will drive the waterfowl away. If the ducks and geese come back later, I can just see a bunch of drunk bozos in a pontoon boat using them as targets for empty beer bottles." He set his plate by the sink with a *thunk*. "Take the leftover brisket home. I don't want to eat." He strode toward his studio and slammed the door shut.

Earl Ray sat a while, looked again at Stacey's photo, then he scraped a bit of slaw from his plate into the trash and shoved the leftovers in Jack's fridge. Jack wasn't coming out of that studio any time soon. Just like after Kaitlyn died.

Earl Ray ran a hand over his stomach as he walked out to his truck. He never should have picked up dinner from Whole Hog Barbecue. Should have gotten something healthy and bland, like turkey subs on whole wheat. Because now dinner—and guilt—were stabbing him in the gut.

Even though it wasn't his fault. He had no control over his ex-wife, who waltzed into town, ready to make a commission off Jack's pain. Earl Ray climbed in and gunned the engine. It was almost as if Stacey took the listing as a way to hurt him, or at least his family.

He wouldn't put it past her.

And ever since she moved back to Abundance, people had been more than happy to point out the ad in the paper for her new business. Like he hadn't already seen it. Studied it. Yelled at it.

Earl Ray rounded the corner from Jack's long driveway onto Sunset Lake Lane and sent out a spray of gravel from beneath his tires.

Jack better call his gallery about that painting. If not, somehow Earl Ray had to find another way to help Jack, a way to protect him from Stacey.

☙

Tess took one more look in each bedroom. Nothing had changed. Boxes and boxes and boxes.

And trash.

And the smell. She didn't notice it downstairs. But up here? Clearly something had died.

There was no way she could deal with these bedrooms and be back in St. Louis tonight. The house would have to go on the market later.

She started to dial Stacey but another call came through—from a number she knew by heart.

"Tess?" The person on the other end of the line was sobbing.

"Mrs. Laudermilk? Are you okay?"

"Tess, I—I don't know how to say this. I've been planning for months and Christine seemed happy but…"

"Did they have a fight? Lots of couples do, but they still make up in time for the wedding." Tess walked down to the kitchen and got a glass of water. "I've seen it several times."

"No. No fight," Mrs. Laudermilk said with a whimper. "Christine said the wedding was all what I wanted and not what she wanted, and they eloped."

"I'm so sorry, ma'am." Tess braced herself and prepared to recite the section of the catering contract that held a client responsible for the entire bill for a cancellation within thirty days of an event.

"I know we have to pay the full amount. I just put the check in the mailbox. Would you possibly consider a discount for a reception later in the month, when they get back?"

Tess nearly choked on her water. A check for the full amount. Today. Most of the food was not even bought yet because she'd been here at the lake. Plus more business later? You bet she'd consider it. "Um, some of my costs are fixed—food and the wait staff, of course, but I would be happy to discount my services fifteen percent."

"That's very kind." Mrs. Laudermilk blew her nose. "Christine hasn't had the decency to...I mean, I don't know quite when to schedule until we hear more from her."

"No problem, Mrs. Laudermilk. You call me when you know your plans and I'll work you in."

"Thank you, dear," she said, sniffled, and hung up.

Tess set her glass on the counter. The words "full amount" echoed in her head. She lowered herself onto a stool by the breakfast bar and dialed Rose.

"Stop baking," Tess said, still numb, and told her the whole story.

"The poor woman. The hours she's spent planning."

"I know. She's heartbroken. We definitely have to make sure that reception is amazing. But"—Tess couldn't keep the delight out of her voice—"for us, it's fabulous." She drew in a breath, trying to get her thoughts in order. "I can't believe I hadn't bought most of the groceries, and she's already mailed us a check."

"And I can freeze these mini-cupcakes," Rose said. "We can easily use them later."

"Perfect." Tess visualized the work calendar. "I'll drive to St. Louis tonight, help you with the breakfast tomorrow morning, and we can drop off the van to get it repaired." The thought of a four-thousand-dollar repair bill was still scary, but Christine Laudermilk's elopement—and her mother's quick payment in full—would help.

"Getting it fixed would be good," Rose said. "I had to take it to the store, and I think it's worse."

Tess ran through the schedule again in her mind. "Except that small job next Monday, we had the rest of this week and all next week cleared for the wedding events."

"That's true," Rose said.

Tess sat back farther on the couch. "Oh. With all that free time, I can pack some clothes and come back here to get this place ready to sell. Not a quick cleanup, but clear out all Leticia's stuff." Tension she hadn't even known she'd been holding melted from her shoulders. "Perfect. The sooner this place sells, the sooner Silver Platter can expand."

Once her business was thriving, she could move forward and leave the past behind.

# Chapter Six

It was almost a vacation.

Granted, most people didn't spend their vacation sorting out a house after a loved one died, but Tess had lived and breathed catering for four years. She wouldn't admit it to anyone else, but sometimes Silver Platter was too much. If this was her time off, she'd take it. She'd even brought her favorite honeysuckle bath crystals and packed her special cooler with dry ice to bring a few samples of her latest ice cream flavors to have as a treat.

She turned off the state highway toward Abundance.

Late in the morning, while Rose had done the last of the dishes from the breakfast, Tess had gone over the prep she needed her to handle for the small event next Monday. Then Tess forwarded the business line to her personal cell and headed west.

Once she reached the little town, she parked near Antiques in Abundance, a shop she'd noticed when she visited Leticia's lawyer. C&K Tree Trimming was coming later to give an estimate, but she had enough time to check out the shop first.

If she did find Depression glass in one of Leticia's upstairs bedrooms, maybe the antique shop would buy it and she'd make enough to pay the tree service.

Tess walked up to the three-story, pale-yellow Victorian house and went inside. As she shut the door of the shop, a cowbell clanged on the inside doorknob.

"Be right there," a woman called from the back, over the sound of running water.

Tess looked around. The scarred hardwood floors and faded floral wallpaper looked old enough to be original. The room even sounded like an antique shop should, like the ticking of a grandfather clock. Most of the items—a wooden trunk with a curved lid, a chair with a woven hickory seat, a table with a marble top—were lovely. The wood gleamed and each piece was displayed with attractive accessories. A patchwork quilt folded across the trunk. A small china doll in the chair. A lace doily on the table. But there was a line that divided antiques and collectibles from the used-but-not-worth-saving. That green-and-brown-plaid recliner, front and center in the room with a huge stain on one armrest and a deep depression in the upholstered seat, definitely sat on the wrong side of the line.

If she found anything of value, she'd probably make more money if she took it to a shop in St. Louis. She turned toward the door.

And nearly bumped into Jack Hamlin, walking in tall, as if he owned the place.

Her heart sped and she stepped back.

"Sorry," he said. "I wasn't watching where I was going." Even as he spoke, his eyes focused beyond her, on the recliner. "Abby," he shouted. "That chair is hideous. What's it doing in your shop?" He cast a sharp look at Tess and continued yelling toward the back of the store. "It will drive away customers. Some of them are picky, you know, the kind of people who rearrange magazines in office lobbies."

Tess's cheeks grew warm. It was only one magazine.

"It's not staying." A young woman carrying a baby walked up behind Tess and gave the recliner a pained inspection. "The guy who brought it in should have taken it to the charity shop as a donation, but I didn't have the heart to tell him that. He seemed pretty desperate." She moved the baby's hands away from one of her earrings. "I gave him twenty bucks and called for pickup."

Tess kept her eyes averted from Jack and moved closer to the counter, her concerns with the shop gone.

Jack grunted and grabbed a stack of packages from the counter. Without a word, he left.

Tess struggled to keep the disapproval off her face. This Abby person couldn't help it if she had to do business with a jerk like Jack. "That was kind of you, helping the guy with the recliner."

The woman tipped her head in a nonchalant way that made Tess think he wasn't the first person she'd helped.

Then she turned the baby to face forward in her arms.

Tess's heart melted, and she forgot about the recliner. The little girl had porcelain skin, reddish-gold curls, and huge blue eyes. Too little to walk. Six months old, maybe.

And so incredibly cute. Tess stepped closer and patted the sleeve of the tiny pink polka-dotted sleeper.

The baby gave her a drooly smile.

"Sorry I took so long to come out to meet you. I had to deal with a diaper issue, Level One bio-hazard." The woman gave an exaggerated shudder. "And then the little stinker started pulling out the baby wipes and throwing them on the floor." She set the baby in a playpen in the corner and handed her a stuffed kangaroo. "But you gotta love 'em, even when they're a handful." She turned toward Tess. "I'm Abby Kincaid, by the way." She gestured to the baby. "And that's Emma." With Abby's short brown ponytail, white T-shirt, and white Keds, she didn't look old enough to have a baby or know about antiques. She had gentle eyes, though, and an easy air.

"Tess Palmer. Your daughter is beautiful."

Abby's face lit up. "Thanks. Are you Leticia's great-niece?"

"I am."

"I'm sorry for your loss. I really liked her."

"Thank you." Tess's words came out shaky. She'd thought accepting condolences would get easier. It hadn't.

"It's hard, I know." A wistful expression passed through Abby's eyes.

Tess looked at her.

Emotion filled Abby's voice. "My husband died four months ago. Sometimes it just..." She brought a hand to her collarbone and closed her eyes.

"I'm so sorry." Tess reached out, ready to touch Abby's arm, but something in the woman's rigid jaw stopped her and said Abby could only handle sympathy in small doses.

Tess ran her hands down the legs of her jeans, not sure what to say.

"I'm okay." Abby raised her chin. "I've been incredibly blessed with people who go out of their way to help me." She angled her head toward the door. "Like my cousin Jack, taking time away from his painting to pick up my packages and take them to the shipper. Sometimes they're really heavy. But after his own loss he knows what a loss like mine is like." She gave an almost imperceptible shake of her head, then gestured toward the store. "What can I do for you?"

Tess hesitated, putting the pieces together. The grumpiness. Living at the lake all alone. Jack Hamlin had lost his wife. Had loved so deeply that it still hurt. The poor man. "I didn't know," Tess said. She should be more understanding when Jack was irritating. "And I didn't realize he was a painter." That explained the streak on his shirt the other day. "I wish I could afford to hire him. Leticia's place might need some touchups before I put it on the market."

Abby waved a hand, dismissing the idea. "No, Jack's not that kind of a painter. He paints pictures of ducks. He's really good."

"Oh." Tess gave a slow nod. "A wildlife artist." No wonder he cared so much about the lake. And he couldn't be that horrible a person, not if he took time to help his cousin with her business. A lot of people wouldn't do that, even for family, because they were too wrapped up in their own world.

"How can I help you?" Abby said.

"I was wondering if you buy antiques and collectibles."

"Sometimes, if I think someone around here would buy them. Mostly I help people list stuff online and ask the right price. I have an online shop as part of a big antiques website that has lots of vendors."

"What do you charge?"

"Twenty to thirty percent, depending on how much you have."

A loud, plaintive *mrrroooooow* came from outside a screen door at the side of the building.

Abby walked near the door and her businesslike tone softened. "Look at her."

Tess moved to stand beside Abby.

Outside, in the shade of a wide awning, an orange tabby kitten with big green eyes chased a grasshopper. She was thin, but in a way that suggested a growth spurt, not starvation. Gangly, like a young teen. And the fur on her tail stuck out in all directions as if charged with static electricity.

"A stray," Abby said. "I put up signs, but I haven't had a single call."

"Are you going to keep her?" She could see why Abby might. The kitten was adorable, all big eyes, as though the whole world was an adventure.

"I can't. I'm terribly allergic. I picked her up once—she's very tame—and had to take so much antihistamine I fell asleep right there." Abby pointed at a pale-pink fainting couch. "I've been feeding her, but I'm worried. She's so little."

"Is there a cat shelter?"

"It's full. If I take her there, she'll be killed in three days."

"Three days?" Tess's chest tightened.

"It's a poor county and almost nobody adopts cats." Abby stepped back from the screen door and looked at Tess with a salesman's gleam in her eye. "What about you? Would you like a new pet?"

"I—I have so much on my plate already. Getting Leticia's house ready to sell, and taking care of my business in St. Louis." Tess looked back at the kitten.

"Seems to me like you need some fun in your life, something besides work. What could be better than a kitten?" Abby opened the door and angled her head in an invitation for Tess to walk into the side yard.

The kitten scampered over.

Tess looked out the door. A kitten would not help her efforts to clean the house and prepare it for sale. But even the thought of the little cutie in a cage at a shelter was horrible, not to mention the poor thing being put down. Her apartment did allow small pets, but the last thing in the world she needed was a kitten. She didn't have time for—

The kitten tilted her head and blinked like a contestant in a Little Miss contest.

Didn't have time for what? To pour some water and toss food in a bowl? It wasn't as though she'd have to walk the cat or anything. Was she too wrapped up in her own world to help an innocent animal?

She threw her hands up in surrender, stepped outside, and walked toward the kitten. Would she let Tess pick her up?

Yes.

The fuzzball even snuggled in close and began to purr. Pinpricks jabbed at the back of Tess's throat. The kitten knew as well as Tess did that they needed each other.

"I thought I had you." Abby's words held a trace of humor.

Tess turned to her. "I hope you're this good at selling stuff online."

"I am." Abby grinned and watched through the screen. "But I should warn you, even if you find something special, it can take a while before someone buys it."

Tess petted the kitten's head. She'd need to take it to the vet, another expense. And although the boxes in the bedrooms held promise, no matter what was in them, they weren't an instant source of cash to pay the tree service.

But looking at those fuzzy orange ears and big green eyes, she didn't care.

❧

*Ring-Necked Ducks in Flight* would never bring in enough.

Jack propped his feet on the coffee table and studied the painting over his mantle. A pair of ring-necked ducks, a drake and a hen, rose over a still pool that reflected fall foliage. His first work that had seemed, to him at least, that he'd really gotten it right.

In the beginning he'd kept the painting because he liked it and because no one was willing to pay much for his work. After it won a small contest, Kaitlyn died, and then he couldn't bear to part with it. He'd painted it with her beside him, asleep in her little pumpkin seat. She'd been such a beautiful baby. Those huge blue eyes, that later became hazel like his, with long lashes like her mother's.

And when Kaitlyn was older, she'd been so happy at the lake, delighted by the birds and the animals and the wildflowers. Even now, he could look at the shore and picture her, not long after her third birthday, showing off her ability to count by numbering the new ducklings.

He had loved being a dad. Losing his little girl had shattered him.

Before her death, if someone had told him the level of physical pain that a man could feel from grief, he would have dismissed it. Or said it might happen to other men, but not him. After the wreck, it took months before he even wanted to get out of bed.

Eventually he came to a guarded truce with his grief. He could get through the days—eat, shower, sit and watch television—and actually function. Nights were still ugly.

He wasn't happy, but he was alive.

And then he'd see a rabbit in the yard or hear a squirrel chattering in a tree and turn to point the animal out to Kaitlyn, sure that his little girl would be delighted to see it, only to remember she was gone. Pain would surge, crashing into him like an unexpected wave and knocking him to his knees.

He'd pull out every sketch he'd ever done of her, every photo he could find, and mourn his little girl all over again. Those sketches, those photos, were all he had left.

All he had except *Ring-Necked Ducks in Flight*. It, too, was a memory of Kaitlyn, a memory he didn't want to lose.

But Earl Ray thought it might save the lake.

Jack ran a hand over his chin. Even if he could bear to part with the painting, he had his doubts about Earl Ray's plan.

With Jack's credit history, he'd need a lot of cash to buy Leticia's place.

The time right after the wreck had been bad financially. Chloe had racked up huge debts he hadn't even known about. The interest on them spiraled out of control, and he was so depressed he didn't even care. And for three long years, every painting he started, he ended up destroying. Thanks to some big sales the past couple of years, he'd dug himself out of debt, but it had taken a while.

And he couldn't just whip off a painting in an afternoon. Often it took five or six months, going back again and again, to get a piece the way he wanted it. These days he was working steadily and had a good chunk of money in savings. Not enough to make him comfortable ordering those fancy delivered meals like Aunt Patsy suggested. And not enough to buy Leticia's house, but a solid amount of savings. Thanks to his debt disaster, though, a mortgage to buy the place across the lake was impossible.

All of which meant he'd need a lucrative sale of *Ring-Necked Ducks in Flight* if he wanted to buy her house. Really lucrative. That was never going to happen. With more experience, he could see flaws in the work, mistakes he'd never make today.

He should leave the painting where it was, a physical reminder that he needed to protect the lake.

Out of the corner of his eye, he saw movement on Leticia's porch.

Tess walked out the French doors. He could just make out her fair hair. It might be pulled back in a ponytail. At this distance he couldn't tell. Most likely though, she had it up in a knot on the top of her head again.

For a moment he envisioned what she might look like with her hair down, flowing over her shoulders and blowing across her blue-gray eyes, across her flawless skin.

She moved toward the deck rail.

A minuscule bubble of hope rose in Jack's chest. Something about the way she was standing, about the way she leaned toward the water, made him think he might be going about this all wrong.

Tess had come to the lake to say goodbye to her great-aunt and had understood Leticia's love of the lake. If she somehow shared that love, he might be able to get her to agree to limit a sale of the property to a private landowner, someone who would value the wetlands as much as he did, the same agreement he'd thought he had with Leticia.

With a sale like that, he could keep the lake the way it had been when Kaitlyn was alive.

Counting the funeral, two lawyer visits, and a stop at the diner, he'd spent more time with other people in the past two days than he usually did in a month. In his ideal world, he would spend all day painting the American black ducks. Alone.

Too bad. It was time for a conversation.

Half an hour later, teeth brushed and hair combed, Jack knocked on the front door of Leticia-uh-Tess's house.

Almost instantly, she swung the door open wide. Confusion flashed over her face. "Oh, good afternoon, Jack."

"Hi, Tess. Can we talk for a minute?" He gave her his best smile. He hadn't been his most charming self the other day.

"O-kaaay." She sounded as if she'd rather find an auditor on her doorstep.

Perhaps he hadn't been charming at all.

She gestured him in and led the way toward the living room.

A gangly orange kitten zipped across the hall and Tess tripped.

Jack leaned forward, arms out to steady her.

For a split second, she hung off-balance, so close that he could smell her light floral fragrance. And in that tiny slice of time, having her fall into his arms didn't seem like a bad idea.

She righted herself and chuckled, never noticing him behind her.

And he stopped short, surprised—almost intrigued—by his thoughts.

"Indy," she scolded the kitten. Her voice held amusement and only the mildest hint of censure. She turned and motioned for Jack to select a seat in the living room.

He sat in the recliner. "Indy?"

"I just got her. She zips around like an Indy 500 race car, then falls asleep in a heap."

"Oh." Jack watched the kitten chase its tail and looked back at Tess. In spite of her uptight hairdo, her face was soft with emotion, blue-gray eyes shining with love for the little animal. Warmth trickled around his heart.

She seemed nice enough. And he liked her hands. Short, unpolished nails and long, narrow fingers. Capable, honest hands. Earlier, he'd certainly appreciated the high heels, but he liked her better now in jeans and a turquoise T-shirt. The blue-green shade set off her pale complexion and highlighted the luminous quality of her skin. He didn't do much portraiture, but—

Her phone buzzed.

She jumped and grabbed it off an end table. "Excuse me, I should take this." She walked to the kitchen, keeping her voice low, but not low enough.

He could hear every word.

"They didn't get the check? It should be there tomor—"

She paused.

"Write another one and deliver it in person if we have to, so we can get the soft drinks for Monday. You'd think they could cut us a little slack." Tess sounded discouraged.

Another pause.

"Yeah, I guess they already did. Use one of the two signed checks I left. I'll call the bank and cancel the other one."

As Tess's footsteps came back toward the living room, he grabbed an old copy of National Geographic off the coffee table and flipped it open.

"Sorry." Tess sat back down. "I'm a caterer. Minor cash-flow problem."

He didn't say a word, but credit issues that impeded daily operations seemed pretty serious to him. From the tight set of Tess's jaw, serious to her as well.

None of his business. And not what he was here to discuss. Time to broach the subject. "Leticia really loved Sunset Lake."

"It's hard not to." Tess half-turned toward the windows, and her eyes narrowed in what looked like yearning.

His pulse ratcheted up. Exactly what he wanted. He slid forward in the recliner. "That's why I talked with her about a deed restriction, about only selling her land as a private home."

Tess looked confused. "The lawyer never mentioned a—"

"Leticia said she'd sign it, but she didn't."

An odd look flickered across Tess's face, something he couldn't read.

"So I came to ask if you might consider restricting the sale of the property to a residential buyer."

"Oh." Tess drew out the word and scrunched her brows together. "I think I have to assume Leticia changed her mind. And I can't rule out potential buyers. I mean, I see that you want it quiet for the ducks, but I need the property sold."

He sagged into the recliner. He'd really thought he had a shot at convincing her to sign a deed restriction.

Then she smiled, sweet and sudden, like a sunbeam bursting through a hole in the clouds. "You know, you should think about listing your place too."

His heart skipped a beat and...wait. What was she saying?

She leaned toward him, and he forced himself to focus on her words.

"I know it may be crazy," she said with a tiny shrug, "but if you listed your property too, we could sell the whole lake and cash in big."

His whole body stiffened and his fingers clawed into the arms of the recliner.

*Cash in big?*

Not. Happening.

"I don't think so." Earl Ray's suggestion of selling *Ring-Necked Ducks in Flight* was bad enough. Selling his part of the lake was out of the question. At least in the current situation, he had a chance that someone would buy Leticia's property for a private home. Slim, but a chance.

"We'd probably both make a lot more than selling individually." Tess's words came faster and she grew more animated, as if she believed more and more that her idea was fabulous. "Then you could buy another property, one where you could own a whole lake, maybe even one with more ducks."

Heat rose from his chest into his neck and face. He shook his head in stiff jerks. The woman had some nerve, assuming he'd go along with her idea. Which clearly was all about her making more money.

Like a fool, he'd been drawn in by her beauty. He should have seen the similarity to Chloe earlier. Should have known. Both were blondes with no respect for the lake.

And both were all about money.

"You won't even consider it?" Tess's voice rose and she sounded insulted that he wasn't going along with her plan.

"No."

She shrank back.

Okay, so that might have come out more forcefully than he'd thought.

"Fine. I think we've talked long enough." She rose from her chair and gave a pointed look at the front entrance.

He could take a hint.

He strode out the door and let it shut with a bang.

# Chapter Seven

Stacey rolled back in her office chair, reached deep in the bag from Whole Hog Barbecue, and pulled out the last of her not-so-low-cal afternoon snack, curly fries.

She had her first listing, her first step as a real estate agent in Abundance. She ought to be happy.

But if she was going to succeed, she needed more listings, as well as clients wanting to buy.

Other agents managed. They probably had advantages she didn't. Like, say, friends.

Despite being a hometown girl, she'd be hard-pressed to find a friend in Abundance, which made it downright foolish to start a real estate business here.

But foolish had never stopped her before. Take moving to California.

Stacey bit one ring off a curly fry and took stock of her office—two rooms and a tiny half bath, a block off the main drag, all carpeted in brown shag with a musty smell that no air freshener could hide. This place would never impress anyone. Neither would her credentials. Her real estate license had only arrived in the mail two weeks ago.

She polished off the fries and wiped the grease from her fingers. If only she could wipe away her past mistakes.

Or outrun them. If she started packing now, she could be in Kansas or Iowa or Illinois by dark. Somewhere far away from Abundance, Missouri, where she could start over.

But that would mean abandoning Dad. She was supposed to cook low-fat meals for him, encourage him to exercise, and help him get over the depression he'd been in since Mom died.

Leaving would also mean abandoning the money she'd put down for rent on this office and her dream of making it as a real estate agent in Abundance. And abandoning her dream of winning Earl Ray back.

But now those two dreams were in conflict. If push came to shove, Stacey knew that Earl Ray was her top priority. But talk about stuck. From what Mom had said while she was still alive, Stacey knew Jack Hamlin wouldn't want Sunset Lake developed. If she did her best as an agent and handled Leticia's property the way Tess wanted, it would upset Jack—and his friends and family, especially Earl Ray. That man would defend another Hamlin to the death.

Still, she had to do what was best for her client. And Earl Ray ought to be able to see that—if deep down he still loved her. Talk about a big "if." They'd only been married a few months.

She needed a second chance with Abundance. The odds of that were pretty low.

And she needed a second chance with Earl Ray. Those odds were even lower.

She'd dated other guys in California and felt next to nothing. A pale shadow of what she'd had with Earl Ray. Moving back to Abundance had to work.

Because she'd never forget that first day of her junior year of high school. Dad had just taken a job with the town fire department. She wandered through the unfamiliar school until she found her English class and took the only empty seat, behind the great-looking guy with light-brown hair, green eyes filled with mischief, and a friendly smile. A week later he'd given her her first kiss, slid his letterman's jacket around her shoulders, and told her they were meant to be together.

In spite of how she'd left, in spite of fifteen years apart, she still believed that. To someone else it might sound foolish, but she'd been there, heard his voice that day in the high school hall, heard the resolution in his tone two years later when they said their wedding vows, seen the love in his eyes. That love was too strong to be gone.

Thanks to pictures on social media, she knew Earl Ray was still as handsome as ever. And he'd picked a perfect career with an auction business. The man was so charming he could sell corn to farmers in Kansas, so full of life that all the men wanted to be his friend and all the women wanted his attention.

But Earl Ray was meant for her. And her alone.

She took a long, slow drink of Diet Pepsi.

Fake energy, fake sugar.

She'd take it, and she'd use it.

She sat up straighter in her chair.

Somehow she was going to win over Abundance and get more business.

And somehow she was going to win back Earl Ray.

First, her business. She pounded out an email to her landlord, a reminder to get cracking on that new carpet and fresh paint he'd agreed to. Then she picked up her purse, made sure she had a supply of her new business cards, and strolled toward Main Street.

Abby Hamlin—wait, she got married—Abby Kincaid might be Earl Ray's cousin, but she was the nicest person Stacey could think of. Even though Stacey was older and the two of them had never exactly been friends, they'd both sung soprano in the high school choir. Popping in on her was worth a try.

Stacey opened the door of Abby's shop. A cowbell on the inside doorknob clanged, an oddly restful sound. With the soft colors and the creative way Abby had things arranged, well, clearly Jack wasn't the only Hamlin with an artistic bent. The place was soothing.

Abby looked up from behind a cardboard box on the counter. She held up a length of packing tape just ripped off the roll. "Hi, Stacey. Welcome back." The tape tried to stick to itself, and she pulled it apart. "I heard you were in town. You're in real estate now, right?"

"I am. I got my first listing yesterday."

Abby's ponytail was shorter than in high school, and she had what looked like baby spit-up on the shoulder of her yellow T-shirt and dark circles under her eyes, but her tone was kind, almost as if her words of welcome were real.

Stacey ran a hand over the curved back of a rocker and walked toward the counter. "I had to stop by. My dad told me you have the cutest baby in the whole county."

Abby's face stretched into a wide smile. "Even if she did keep me up last night, I have to admit, your dad's right." She secured one end of the tape and tipped her head toward a playpen by a large window.

Stacey moved toward the playpen, careful not to let her heels clomp on the hardwood floor.

The baby was asleep on her side with a blanket pulled over her head so that only her button nose could be seen. Below the end of the blanket, two chubby legs stuck out.

"She's all covered up," Stacey said quietly. "I don't want to wake her. I'll have to see her another time. And hey, I wasn't around, but I heard about your husband. I'm really sorry."

"Thank you." Lines formed around Abby's eyes. "He was a good man."

"That's what my dad said." Stacey returned to the counter. Actually, Dad had said the man was a decorated war hero, barely back from Afghanistan a week when he was shot in Kansas City by some kid robbing a convenience store while high on drugs.

"You know you'll have an uphill battle with your business, right? Abundance has what, three other real estate agencies?" Abby spoke fast, as if trying to change the subject.

"Four." Stacey certainly wasn't going to force Abby to talk about her husband if it hurt. "A total of twenty-five agents, not counting me. And I know I need to make a new impression on this town."

Abby raised both eyebrows and ripped a second strip of tape off the dispenser.

"Let's say when I lived here before I wasn't the most...mature."

"I was younger, but I did hear a story or two." Abby paused. "The week you left town, at the carnival, did you really say on the loudspeaker that Abundance was full of inbred idiots? And give a top-ten list of people most likely to have parents that were first cousins?"

Stacey's cheeks grew hot. "Folks still remember that?"

"Oh, yeah. Especially the ones that made the list, like Louise Chambers."

Bad-mouthing Abundance had only been an excuse to leave—a way to save face instead of admitting that her marriage was crumbling—but clearly Stacey had gotten too carried away with it. "Count on Louise to still be mad," Stacey said as she toyed with a packing peanut that had escaped Abby. "What's she up to these days?"

"She works at the bank, processes loans."

Stacey could picture that. Louise had been good in math.

"Speaking of old times, have you seen Earl Ray?" Abby secured the tape, gave the package a pat, and set it to the side.

"Not yet." Stacey's stomach felt like a Mason jar full of live grasshoppers.

96

"He's still running his auction business. Doing really well." Abby's eyes gleamed. "And he's still single. You should call him."

The grasshoppers multiplied. Like a Biblical plague. Stacey gave a noncommittal shrug and studied the floor.

"Hey," Abby said. "I know how you might get back on Louise's good side."

Stacey raised her head, ready to discuss someone other than Earl Ray. Besides, she wanted her business to succeed, even if it meant buttering up Louise.

"She does a lot with the blood drive. You ought to sign up to donate."

Stacey flinched. Buttering up did not include giving blood. "Uh—" she struggled for how to respond.

The baby stirred, whimpered, and let out a shriek.

"I have to get her," Abby said.

Stacey followed her toward the playpen, letting out a long breath.

Abby picked up the baby and murmured and patted the little one's back.

Halfway across the room, Stacey stood up taller. Blood drives needed lots of help, not just donors. Maybe she could pass out juice afterward or call other people to get them to volunteer.

And then Abby turned, proudly displaying the baby.

A lump blocked Stacey's throat, like one of those packing peanuts wedged in sideways.

Abby came closer.

And swam before Stacey's eyes. Abby, the antiques, the package on the counter—everything swirled like a vortex around one spot in focus—the baby's face. Now that the little one was out from under her blanket—in spite of the difference in coloring—the resemblance was clear. Those eyes were Hamlin eyes.

She'd never thought that the baby might remind her of Earl Ray. Never thought—

She needed air, needed to leave. Her feet faltered. She sucked in a breath and bolted toward the door. "Thanks for the suggestion about Louise," she said, one hand on the doorknob. "Nice seeing you, Abby."

"Come by any time." Abby, her attention recaptured by the baby, carried the little girl toward the back of the store.

Outside, Stacey clutched the edge of a wooden bench for support and breathed deeply. She squeezed her eyes shut and forced thoughts of Hamlin babies out of her mind. After a minute, the dizziness passed.

She needed to focus on today, on getting her name out in Abundance in a positive light. Not on the past.

She'd call Louise about volunteering.

But as for giving blood, forget it.

## ❧

The smell could make a man gag.

Jack had definitely picked the wrong chore to do right after dinner. He held his breath, turned on the hose from the spigot by his back deck, and added just enough water to the fifty-gallon plastic drum to get the duck poop to dissolve. He tightly secured the lid. Aunt Patsy could add more water once he delivered the drum. Or maybe he could convince Earl Ray to drop it off. Patsy was his mother. Earl Ray ought to be the one to haul over the duck poop and water that she used for fertilizer in her organic gardening. Duck-poop tea, she called it.

If Earl Ray would haul the drum, Jack could escape, at least for today, Patsy's none-too-subtle hints that he was wrong to blame God for Kaitlyn's death. And it would leave him free to figure out how to protect Sunset Lake. Clearly, after his conversation with Tess last night, he couldn't count on her help.

In the distance, a vehicle approached on Sunset Lake Lane. Trees blocked Jack's view, but it had to be Earl Ray. No one else Jack knew blasted Guns N' Roses at quite that volume.

Poor Aunt Patsy. At fourteen, she'd told everyone to stop calling her Patty and instead, to call her Patsy, in honor of Patsy Cline. When her own dreams of a career in country music failed, she'd pinned her hopes on her kids, giving Earl Ray and Becky Jo and Hank names she thought perfect for country music stars. But Becky ditched "Jo" and preferred jazz, and Earl Ray rejected country music for hard rock and heavy metal. And he and Hank, who worked at the hardware store, didn't even pursue careers in music.

Jack sprayed water on his rubber gloves and shovel to rinse off any residual stench.

A couple of minutes later, Earl Ray rounded the corner of the house, wearing a Royals T-shirt and ball cap.

"What is that stink?" Earl Ray coughed and waved a hand in front of his face.

"Duck-poop tea. Can you take—?"

"No way."

"It's for your mother."

"You're the fool who built that little patio out there by the lake."

"I thought a concrete pad would make my easel more stable. How was I to know the ducks would use it as their personal toilet?"

"And you're the one who told my mom that you clean it off every spring."

"I didn't think she'd want duck poop."

"I don't care. That 'tea' is not going in my truck. The only thing that stinks worse than that stuff is having Stacey back in town." Earl Ray flopped down in a chair on the deck.

"She's not making my life any better." Jack turned off the water. "Neither is that great-niece of Leticia's. I went over there today to try to convince her to limit the sale of the house to someone who would keep the place for a private residence."

"Did you tell her about Kaitlyn?"

Jack's face and chest grew hot. Sometimes Earl Ray was bad for the blood pressure. "No way. I'm not using her memory like that." He peeled off his rubber gloves. "It wouldn't matter anyway. Tess Palmer is only interested in cash. She even had the nerve to suggest we sell the properties together, said that way we'd make more money."

"She's right."

Jack glared at him.

"Well, she is. Nobody around here is looking for a place like that as a home." Earl Ray cast a sorrowful eye at Jack, as if he pitied him his delusions. "If you can't buy it yourself, you'll have to accept that Sunset Lake will be developed. You'll end up moving later."

Jack ignored him.

Earl Ray raised his head. "Unless..." His voice held a note of glee and his eyes had a maniacal gleam. "Unless you sabotage things whenever the house is shown." He pointed at the drum of duck-poop tea. "Like throwing water balloons filled with that stuff."

Jack rolled his eyes. How did they let his cousin run around without a keeper? He wasn't any more mature now than when he was a teenager and convinced Jack to drive around town, so Earl Ray could throw lit firecrackers under passing cars. Lucky they hadn't gotten someone killed.

Lucky Jack's dad hadn't killed him.

At least these days Jack had enough brains to avoid Earl Ray's nonsense.

Should he point out the fact that once again, his cousin had crossed the line?

No, Earl Ray wouldn't care. Best to stick with an argument he might listen to. "There's no way to throw water balloons from this side of the lake, you moron. It's a quarter mile across."

"We'd need a high-powered catapult, like that trebuchet I made for the science fair in high school." Earl Ray ran his goatee between his fingers. "I think it's still in my mom's barn."

Jack picked up his shovel and gloves.

"We could call it the DDPL."

"The what?"

"The Dynamic Duck Poop Launcher."

"That's a horrible idea," Jack said. "Even your trebu-whatever-it's-called can't fling a water balloon a quarter mile. A better plan would be to make a bunch of noise during a showing, like you on the electric guitar."

Earl Ray stuck out his chest. "Only someone without appreciation for the finer things in life—such as hard rock and heavy metal—could call my musical stylings 'noise.'" His eyes narrowed. "But your idea is excellent. Noise during a showing could totally sabotage a deal. But even with an amp and the way sound carries across water, I don't think it would be loud enough."

"I was kidding!" Granted, the idea did have some appeal. Almost any plan to stop Tess from selling to a commercial buyer sounded good. *Almost.* But not one of Earl Ray's plans. "You are not coming out here with your guitar when Stacey shows the house. I don't care if you are still mad about your divorce."

"I think there's a way to make this idea work." Earl Ray's voice had the same tone as when he fantasized about another Royals World Series win.

Jack stomped into the garage, put away his tools, and used his heels to ease off his boots near the stairs into the house. He was desperate, sure, but not desperate enough to consider a plan that involved Earl Ray's music. Or the Dynamic Duck Poop Launcher.

He had lots of cousins. Why did Earl Ray have to be the one who stopped by all the time? Why couldn't it be some sane cousin, like Abby? Or her sister, Kristen? Or Becky? Sure, Becky would tell him she missed seeing him Sunday mornings. It was, after all, part of her job since she was the choir director at the Abundance Community

Church, but she was not nearly so in-your-face about it as her mother. And she was sane. Unlike Earl Ray.

The man was loony.

Loony.

Jack's breath caught and he stopped, halfway in the door to the house.

Leticia's cleaning woman and her husband had used that word. Thought Leticia had dementia. And Jack hadn't talked to his neighbor in a while.

Earl Ray, on the stairs behind him, nudged him in the back. "I thought we were watching the Royals."

Jack spun around. "Do you think Leticia Palmer had dementia?"

"How would I know? She was your neighbor, not mine."

Jack led the way into the living room. "Doesn't mean we talked much."

Earl Ray tilted his head in acknowledgment.

"You know how she said she'd sign the deed restriction and instead gave money to a conservation group? I heard Leticia's housekeeper talking," Jack spoke slowly as he thought it through. "In a lot of cases Leticia promised one thing and did something totally different."

Earl Ray held up his hands in a so-what gesture.

"So if Leticia had been suffering mental decline, wouldn't I actually be doing her a favor to get the court to see that things should be handled the way she had wanted it when she was fully capable?"

"That's never going to work. Old people say stuff like that all the time." Earl Ray sprawled on the couch and put his feet on the coffee table. "I see it at estate sales. The family hires me to sell stuff, and some guy complains that a chest of drawers or an antique table was promised to him and he shouldn't have to get out his wallet."

"Humph." Jack sat on the couch with an audible thump. Not the answer he wanted.

Earl Ray snagged the remote and flipped on the TV. "Those promises are a way to get attention. Not a sign of dementia."

Jack grabbed his phone off the end table. He could watch the game and surf the Internet at the same time. Maybe he could find something online to explain if it was possible, after Leticia's death, to prove she had suffered from dementia.

# Chapter Eight

Rain poured down in cold, steady sheets, almost obscuring Tess's view of Jack's house.

She still couldn't believe how upset he'd gotten yesterday when she suggested he sell his property. If he didn't want to move, fine. No need to get all huffy.

But he'd said that Leticia had agreed to a deed restriction and never signed it.

That bugged her.

She sat on the couch, watched the last ten minutes of her favorite cooking show, and finished her morning coffee. Then she picked up her phone and dialed her mother.

"Tess, hi. Did you find a real estate agent?"

"I did. I really like her. She seems like she'll work hard."

"That's perfect. I'm glad that for once you listened to me."

Tess pressed her lips together. Always such a pleasure to talk to her mom. "I'm staying a few days at the lake to get the house ready to sell. I had a big cancellation at work. Last minute, so I still get paid the full amount." She slid that part in quickly, before her mom could criticize her for neglecting her business. "Anyway, everywhere I go, people are talking about Leticia."

Seriously, everywhere. At the charity where she dropped off Leticia's clothes and linens, at the diner when she popped in for a piece of pie like Abby suggested, even at the grocery store.

"I keep hearing that she told people one thing and did another with her estate. Do you think she had dementia? That maybe her legal documents are invalid?"

"That your annoying Uncle Trevor should have gotten the house?" Mom's voice grew defensive. "Absolutely not."

"What about all these things people are saying?"

"Tess, no lawyer is going to make up a will for a client who isn't of sound mind. They could get disbarred. Besides, Leticia and Trevor had a fight over the last election. That's probably why she left you the house. If she made other changes, she probably had reasons for them too."

"Oh."

"Don't pay any attention to those people. Just get the house cleaned up so it will sell."

Mom veered off into talking about Patrick's career plans, and Tess tuned her out. Her older brother was a grown man, almost a doctor. If he wanted to work in primary care, not some specialized surgery like Mom preferred, that was his business. And Tess had heard enough from Mom about her brother's *career* in medicine when she was younger. Patrick was going to cure heart disease and cancer and the common cold, and she had "her little business."

But at least she didn't need to worry about Leticia having dementia.

Her phone beeped with another call. She pulled it from her ear to see who was calling and spoke into the phone. "Um, Mom, I've got to go. A client's on the other line."

Mom kept talking, faster than ever, but Tess hung up.

Luckily, the client only wanted a minor menu adjustment for an event in a couple of weeks.

But every time Tess turned around, she had another call from St. Louis. Mom was right. She needed to hurry up and get the house ready for sale. Then she could get back to her business.

On the carpet by the windows, Indy stretched, then strolled over and snuggled against Tess's leg, purring.

Tess scratched the soft, fluffy fur between the kitten's ears and reviewed her list of things to do. Today she had to clean out the freezer, ask the grocery store for boxes, and deal with Leticia's books. The books would be difficult, even more so than the linens and clothes she'd sorted yesterday. To Leticia, clothes had merely been a matter of modesty and warmth, selected for easy care and comfort. But to her great-aunt, books were different, each a personal friend. Tess would have to take them to a used bookstore that would find them good homes.

Once she did, she could check one item off her list. So far, she was right on schedule.

"There," she held the paper in the air, as if Indy might be impressed.

The kitten sprinted across the room and vaulted to the top of an upholstered chair with its back to the deck. She half-sat with every muscle aquiver, eyes fixed on a soggy sparrow.

"Not exactly volunteering to help, are you?"

Indy ignored her.

Tess grinned and opened the email app on her phone. Six work-related messages, each from a potential client.

Her smile flattened. She needed to talk to each person, schedule their event, and get all the details for the giant worksheet she'd created.

If the wedding hadn't canceled, she'd be preparing for the Laudermilk shower. She would have called each potential client and scheduled a time to talk to them next week. But being here at the lake, not focused on her business, made her feel guilty, made her feel those initial consultations should be handled today.

She read the next email.

From Rose.

Tess focused on the line at the bottom.

*If there is anything I can do, please let me know.*

Delegation. Far from Tess's strongest suit. Sure, if she'd found someone to clean out those rooms upstairs, she could have delegated that. But delegate client meetings, let someone else be the face of Silver Platter?

That was different.

She took her coffee mug to the kitchen. Standing by the sink, she rolled the mug back and forth between her hands. Rose was dependable. Anyone else would take her up on the offer in an instant. But Silver Platter was Tess's whole world. If Rose made a bad impression...

Rose was bright and good with people. She got a bit frazzled in a crisis but should be fine talking with a potential client.

Tess stuck the mug in the dishwasher. She simply needed to trust. Her chest felt jittery but she dialed Rose.

"Hi, Tess."

"Rose, how would you like to handle all the phone calls and that job on Monday? Be temporary assistant manager?"

"Seriously?" Rose shouted. "I thought you'd never ask. I wanted to offer, but I was afraid you'd say no." Her words came out so fast that Tess could barely keep up. "I know exactly how you want that giant form filled out for new clients. And that job Monday is a piece of cake."

Tess's jitters didn't go away, but they did subside a little. "You'll call if you have any questions?"

"Absolutely."

They discussed a temporary bump in Rose's pay, and Rose assured Tess three times that she would make her proud.

In spite of herself, Tess believed the assurances. She hung up—not just less stressed—but pleased. She was being a good manager. Letting Rose grow as an employee. Maybe even taking her own step toward growth.

And Tess could focus on moving forward with things at the lake, like cleaning out the freezer, so she could be back on the job sooner.

She yanked open the door and counted twenty-two bags of frozen peas. From different stores. With different sell-by dates. And no other vegetables.

Twenty-two bags?

Something twisted in the middle of her chest, and cold air from the freezer settled on her shoulders.

ය

Lightning streaked down from the charcoal clouds outside Jack's studio, followed by a boom of thunder that jarred his house.

He scooted back from his easel, studied his work, and added another wake line behind the female duck, listening for his package to be delivered. The tracking information said the new lens should arrive any time.

He needed to paint something new, something different. Maybe the better super telephoto lens that he'd ordered would help.

Someone knocked insistently on his door.

Jack set down his brush. That had to be the delivery guy.

It wasn't.

Tess waited on his front porch, her kelly-green raincoat and jeans spotted with rain. She carried an umbrella printed with Monet's *Water Lilies*, and a few loose tendrils of hair hung near her cheeks.

He'd bet his favorite round brush that those tendrils had been secured before she went out in the storm.

From under her jacket she pulled out a wet cardboard box with a return address of Plackett's Camera Shop.

Jack took the package. "My new lens."

"I saw the return address. I picked up some empty boxes in town during a lull in the storm, and when I came back, it was on my porch, totally soaked." There was a worried note in Tess's tone, as if she felt it was her fault. "I thought maybe if I rushed right over, you could open it and whatever it is might be okay." She leaned in as if she wanted to see for herself. The woman gave all the vibes of one of those uber-responsible types.

He motioned her into the kitchen and cut the packing tape with a knife.

A fresh torrent of rain coursed down, and another bolt of lightning hit the earth with a crack.

From the outer package, he withdrew a smaller, cardboard box. Also damp. "I can't believe they left it out in the rain."

Tess lurked behind him, moving to one side to watch.

"Is it a camera?" she asked.

Jack unfolded the tabs that held the smaller box closed. "Super telephoto lens. Used. Hard to find. New ones are almost nine thousand."

"Dollars?" Her voice squeaked at the end of the word.

"Yeah." He shrugged. "I need it for work. A lot of times I paint from images I shoot. This has more magnification than my old lens." He slid the lens out of the smaller box.

It was wrapped in two layers of plastic, but the outer layer was speckled with water. And the guy who sold the lens didn't have another used one. If this one was ruined, there was no replacement.

Tess snatched a paper towel from the roll on the counter. "Here." She handed it to him and hovered, looking as nervous as if the lens was hers.

Jack wiped his fingers and dried the outer bag, then unwrapped the lens and examined it. He let out a sigh of relief. "It's dry." He looked up at her. "It probably wouldn't have been if it stayed out much longer. Thank you."

"You're welcome." Her eyes shone with sincerity. A moment later she peered out the windows toward Leticia's. "I better head out. I've got a lot to do before I go back to St. Louis next week."

The sky lit again and a tremendous boom jolted the earth.

Her shoulders tensed. "Did that hit your house?"

"I don't think so. Power's still on."

She said nothing and, though she'd sounded like she was leaving, she just stood there, looking toward the windows with an uneasy expression on her face.

The silence grew between them and settled on his shoulders like an icy, wet towel. She'd gone out of her way to help him. He ought to make some effort to be polite, at least for a couple of minutes, until the worst of the storm passed. "So, you're a caterer." There, people liked to talk about their work.

"Yeah. I'd never be able to stay away this long except a client canceled a wedding so late that they still had to pay the full amount."

"Does that happen often? Getting paid without doing the work?"

She moved toward the door. "Second time in four years," she said lightly and let out a laugh.

A kooky, infectious laugh that ever so slowly uncurled something in his heart. Like a seed, long-dormant, warming in the first thaw.

The woman probably alphabetized her spices. She pulled her hair up tight, almost every wisp controlled. She tucked in her T-shirt like a soldier awaiting inspection. Everything about her was rigid.

Except that laugh.

He followed her toward the door. In spite of her plan to sell Leticia's place, he wanted to hear her laugh again.

She angled her body to halfway face him. "This is going to sound weird, but do you think Leticia showed signs of dementia?"

Adrenaline hit Jack's veins. He straightened bolt upright, all thoughts of Tess's laugh forgotten. "Uh, why do you ask?" Earl Ray had made him doubt his theory, but if Tess thought Leticia had been slipping mentally, maybe he'd been right.

"She was almost ninety. And you said she was going to sign that deed restriction but didn't. And people keep telling me she made other promises. And—" The skin around Tess's eyes tightened as though she were assessing whether or not to continue.

He moved nearer. If Tess believed Leticia had dementia, he might be able to convince her to sign the deed restriction.

"I mean she may have simply changed her mind." She twisted her hands in front of her. "I did learn she had a reason for leaving me the house instead of Trevor. But I found all these peas in the freezer. Bag after bag. Like she kept forgetting she bought them."

He ran a hand over his mouth. Those peas didn't mean Leticia's mind was slipping, but no one else would understand. This was his chance.

"I know I should have come to visit her more." Tess's eyes filled with anguish. "I was caught up in my business and didn't take the time."

Guilt kicked him in the stomach. "It wasn't dementia. Leticia bought the peas to feed the ducks. Stocked up whenever they came on sale."

"I thought you fed ducks breadcrumbs," Tess said slowly.

"Breadcrumbs are terrible for them. It's better if you don't feed wildlife at all, but she read somewhere online that peas aren't quite as bad."

"Oh." The distress melted from Tess's eyes, and her face brightened. "Thank you. That makes sense." She opened the door.

Jack gave a silent wave and watched her tromp out into the rain.

He was a fool.

If there was a prize—chosen by a jury of curators, critics, and collectors of fools— he'd win hands-down. In fact, when his name appeared on the list of finalists for World's Biggest Fool, the other finalists would politely decline from proceeding to the next round, knowing full well they wouldn't stand a chance.

Because with one simple sentence or maybe a sad nod, acknowledging Leticia's dementia, he could have saved Sunset Lake.

But had he done it?

No, he had to tell the truth. He simply couldn't bring himself to say that Leticia had dementia when—on the rare occasion he talked with her—he had to admit she had seemed fully mentally competent, probably more so than him. He envisioned her doing crossword puzzles in Latin—in pen—while he vegged out watching TV.

Okay, so there was a part of him that was proud, that knew he'd done the right thing by telling the truth, that never would have been happy at the lake if he'd lied. But why did honesty have to cost so much? Why did it have to mean that his beautiful lake and his memories of Kaitlyn might be ruined? That they might be transformed into some hotel that would cater to people who wouldn't know a wood duck or a red-tailed hawk or a whippoorwill if it laid an egg on their beautifully turned-down bed?

So unfair.

But the bottom line was he couldn't do it. Couldn't lie.

Not even to save the lake and his memories of Kaitlyn.

# Chapter Nine

The flavor was mid-way between fake marshmallow and chalk.

Earl Ray screwed the cap back on the heartburn medicine, shook the bottle, and took another swig. He shoved the bottle back in his medicine cabinet. He wasn't even sure the vile stuff helped.

The torment was pretty much on schedule. He'd been asleep maybe half an hour. And it was all his own fault. He knew he shouldn't have microwaved that frozen French bread pepperoni pizza before bed. There was a reason it was still in the fridge after he'd eaten most everything else. In spite of his stomach, in spite of his efforts to stay on the low-fat, healthy track, he'd gone off the rails again.

And the face staring back at him in the bathroom mirror looked awful. His eyes were bloodshot, his skin pale.

He trudged to the living room, flipped on the TV, and tried to care about soccer.

Hopeless. They could have been talking about the Royals and all he'd be able to think about was the pain and nausea in his gut.

And Stacey. For some dumb reason, he wanted to call and tell her about the crazy lawsuit that his cousin was considering, wanted to warn her of the mess it could bring for her new business. Wanted to protect her.

Talk about ridiculous. He'd be the last person she'd want help from. Just because he still had dreams where he ran his fingers through her soft brown hair and gazed into those big brown eyes didn't mean she'd forgiven him. Because in hindsight, he saw that their door-slamming, wake-the-neighbors-screaming fights were over insignificant issues. The real problem was the night he wasn't there for her, the night he'd failed her when she needed him the most.

A couple of months later, when he'd stormed off on his motorcycle, he never imagined she'd be gone when he got back. Never imagined what his lack of courage would cost him. Never imagined she'd ask for a divorce.

Now with her back in town, he couldn't get her out of his mind.

If he went in the kitchen, he pictured how fast she'd start cleaning. In the dining room, he saw the dartboard, where for two years after their divorce he'd pinned her photo on the bull's-eye. Worst of all, whenever he sat on this couch, he remembered lying on it with her, kissing her senseless and—

He balled his hands into fists. He needed to buy a new couch.

Because even if Stacey was back in town, he wasn't getting a second chance. Not with her looking like some classy TV news anchor.

So telling her about Jack's crazy ramblings would be a mistake.

Besides, by this time Jack must have realized that the lawsuit was a ridiculous idea. And Jack was family. Family mattered. If Jack *was* filing his crazy lawsuit, he wouldn't want Earl Ray giving Stacey a heads-up. That would be betrayal.

What he needed was a better solution for Jack. He'd failed Stacey. He wasn't failing Jack too.

He shoved aside a pile of papers on his desk and booted up his computer, so he could scan the local property listings. In a perfect world, Jack would realize that this Tess woman was right and would sell his place at Sunset Lake now instead of holding out hope that it would stay undeveloped. Maybe if Earl Ray could find the right house, he could convince Jack.

He searched for several minutes but found nothing his cousin would even consider.

The cramp in his stomach twisted and sharpened, worse than he ever remembered.

With a grunt, he typed "abdominal pain" in the search engine and scrolled down the selections until he found one site that sounded good. Not some hoodoo voodoo quack, but a legitimate resource.

He read the possible diagnoses and ruled them out one by one. No, he didn't have food poisoning. He'd thought that the first time he felt like this, but no one else he'd eaten with had been sick.

And no, he didn't have an ovarian cyst.

No. No—

This one. It sounded like what he had. Almost every single symptom.

A cold sweat came over him. Earl Ray pulled back in his chair, back from the words on the screen.

"No." The word came out hoarse.

If this website was right, he didn't have heartburn.

He had stomach cancer, like what killed his mom's brother, Uncle Lou.

Earl Ray crossed his arms over his stomach and let out a shaky breath. Lou had lived in Seattle. Earl Ray had barely known him. But he'd seen his best friend's mom battle cancer when he was a kid. How she wore that bandanna on her head and got thinner and thinner, so weak from the treatments she could barely stand. And none of those treatments helped. In less than a year, his folks took him to her funeral.

He sat for a moment, not sure what to do, then he clicked back to his property search. One way or another, he was going to help Jack through this property mess.

Easier than thinking about cancer.

And maybe he didn't have cancer. Maybe using the Internet when he was half-asleep wasn't the way to get a correct diagnosis. Maybe the symptoms would go away.

Or maybe he simply needed a different heartburn medicine, one that didn't taste like marshmallows and ground-up chalk.

CB

Louise Chambers sputtered when Stacey called Friday morning and volunteered to help with the blood drive, but she didn't say no.

Ten minutes later Stacey opened an email message from Louise, including a list of the names of twenty-five people who had donated blood in the past.

Stacey scrolled down to the list. The plan was perfect. All she needed to do was sign people up to donate. She'd do valuable community service, get her name out in the best possible way, and perhaps even overcome her high school reputation for being a tad self-absorbed.

She read the list, and her shoulders sank. Maybe Louise hadn't been so eager for her help after all. There was one name on the list that she wanted to call, number twenty-five, Earl Ray Hamlin. The rest? Top prospective members for the "We Still Hate Stacey" Club.

She slid down in her chair. Why had she ever thought she could be a real estate agent in Abundance?

Back in California three years ago, she'd taken a job at a real estate agency, working as an office manager for Delia St. James. Delia had changed Stacey's life— encouraged her in every way possible. To take classes in community college, to come to church, to see the past clearly, and to really think about her dreams. Two months ago, when Delia retired and gave Stacey a very generous bonus just as it became clear that Dad needed help, Stacey decided it was time to pursue those dreams, a career in real estate and Earl Ray's love. Those dreams were supposed to work together. Real estate would pay the bills so she could live in Abundance and win back Earl Ray without mooching off Dad.

But what if the two years of community college she'd taken at night and the online real estate class she did last month weren't enough? What if she really needed a four-year degree? Or she just wasn't smart enough?

Finding business seemed impossible.

And her landlord hadn't done a thing. No new wall color. No new carpet.

No new clients.

She looked back at the computer, at the screensaver her online teacher had insisted they install. In big letters, it read "Real Estate Requires Persistence."

Stacey glared at it but, bit by bit, straightened her shoulders. The teacher didn't say a person had to be brilliant, didn't say anyone had to have a four-year degree, didn't even say people had to like the agent. He said persistence. That was all. Persistence.

If it meant reaching her dreams—Earl Ray and her career, she could do it.

Stacey dialed the first number, a mousy girl she remembered from English class. Louise had given a work number.

These days Miss Mousy sold insurance. And—wonder of wonders, she seemed to have forgotten how Stacey snubbed her in high school. She was eager to give blood, thanked Stacey for her call, and told her to stop in to talk about an umbrella policy for her agency.

Stacey moved on to the next name. Allison Kendall. She and Stacey had cheered together.

"Kendall Realty. This is Allison."

Kendall Realty? The business name tripped Stacey up, but only for a second. "Ally? Stacey Gilcroft. I'm back in town, and I'm signing up donors for the Abundance blood drive. I wanted to get you on the list. Louise Chambers tells me you've given for years."

"Are you kidding?" Allison's tone was icy. "If you're the one asking, I wouldn't donate the baggie we pick up after our labradoodle. I can't believe you'd even ask, after you snuck that photo of me in the senior yearbook. It was the worst moment of my life, and it's there in print forever." She huffed out a breath.

This conversation was surreal on so many levels. "I'm sure no one ever opens our high school yearbook anymore," Stacey mumbled. Truly, if a dress tail caught in the waistband of her underwear was the worst moment of Allison's life, Stacey could tell her a story or two. Like about when she first got to California and had to sleep in her car at a campground because—even though she found a job right away cleaning houses—she couldn't afford a security deposit for an apartment. About how she went to sleep each night clutching her pepper spray, half afraid she might accidentally spray herself in the middle of the night, but more afraid one of the creeps from two campsites over might break into her car.

"If that wasn't enough—" Allison's words came faster and less distinct. "You come back into town and open a real estate business two weeks after I open mine."

"Allison, I had no idea you were in real estate until I got here. By then, my business was already set up."

"Liar." Allison made that word distinct.

And loud.

123

Stacey held the phone away from her ear.

The next moment the line went dead.

She set the phone on the desk and ran her hands through her hair. At least that conversation was over. The rest had to be better.

They weren't. After two hours of calls, Stacey had signed up the mousy insurance agent, a former classmate who sounded like his blood donation might be at the 0.3 alcohol level, and a casual acquaintance of her mother's, who didn't remember her. She'd been hit on by two guys she knew were married and cussed out by another former cheerleader, still Allison's best friend.

At last Stacey had come to Number 25.

She pulled out her purse, checked her makeup in her compact, and touched up her lipstick. Silly. Earl Ray couldn't actually see her. But it gave her a little more confidence.

She pushed her hair back from her forehead and dialed.

"Hello?"

Her pulse did a shuffle step and she pressed the phone more closely against her ear. It was him. "Earl Ray?" She could picture him, leaning against that ancient red Ford truck he'd had in high school, green eyes shining while he tried to convince her that no one would catch them if they went skinny dipping—in the quarry right next to the sheriff's office.

"Stace. How are you?"

His words wrapped around her heart like hot fudge around soft serve. He cared. She could hear it. He'd even recognized her voice. "Good," she said. "And you?"

"Doing great. I heard you were back in town. We ought to get together sometime, catch up."

Another shuffle step of her heart. She'd love to see his grin, to watch his eyes light up as he told some wild tale, to maybe even find a spark of interest in them.

"I'd love to see you. I guess I should get you signed up first, though." She clicked over to the signup screen. "I'm working with Louise Chambers on the local blood drive. Tuesday or Wednesday, the twenty-fourth or twenty-fifth. What looks good?"

"Oh." Earl Ray's voice dropped. "Not really my thing."

"The record says you've given in the past, a total of two gallons."

"Last time made me, uh, woozy. You know what I mean."

Stacey's chest suddenly felt empty, as though her heart and lungs had been surgically removed. Did she know what he meant? "But—"

The line went dead. He'd hung up. Just like Allison.

Stacey plastered her arms around her chest, as if she might protect her heart from any more pain. Because, yeah, she knew what he meant, knew all about passing out while having blood drawn.

She'd passed out twice with that needle.

Two months before her graduation from Abundance High, when she learned she was pregnant. And that night in late June, less than a month after her wedding, when she'd gone to the hospital in an ambulance.

The night she'd lost Earl Ray's baby.

# Chapter Ten

Earl Ray pulled up outside Jack's house Friday afternoon and laid on the horn.

What was taking so long? He couldn't wait to show Jack the house he'd found. If Jack saw that he had the option to move, it might make changes at Sunset Lake less painful.

Over the lake, the clouds hung low, contemplating another downpour.

Earl Ray honked again, long and loud.

At last Jack appeared from around back and climbed in.

"Would you hurry up?" Earl Ray peeled out of Jack's driveway and turned at the dam onto Sunset Lake Lane. At the intersection with County Road 28, he hit a pothole squarely with the front passenger-side tire.

Rainwater splashed out and Jack bounced as hard as a test dummy.

He jabbed a fist at Earl Ray's upper arm and made an elaborate production of putting on his seatbelt and securing his hoodie in his lap.

Earl Ray rolled his eyes. "Wimp."

"Death wish. You should have let me drive."

"And risk your SUV breaking down? No way."

Jack scowled at the road.

There wasn't much the guy could say in defense of his SUV. It had already been in the shop twice this year. Earl Ray swerved to avoid a dead skunk.

"What are you so all-fired-up to show me?"

Earl Ray drove even faster. This next part might get a bit dicey. "A house. On a lake."

Jack's mouth tightened and his chin jutted out.

Earl Ray wasn't giving up. "I talked to a guy I know just over the county line. He's selling his house himself. He's leaving to see his grandkid in a school play in Kansas City, but if we get there in the next"—he glanced at the clock on the dash—"forty minutes, we can see it."

Jack's eyes grew hard. "I do not want to see some house."

"You're not still thinking about that lame-brained lawsuit, are you?"

"No."

Earl Ray almost congratulated Jack for coming to his senses, but... Best to make sure first that he didn't have another equally bad idea. "Well, you sure won't be happy at Sunset Lake with a hotel on the far shore."

Jack grunted and folded his arms over his chest. "No. It will be a disaster. They'll probably build right up to the setback line. And I can just see teenagers on personal watercraft racing near the wetland fringe, disrupting the waterfowl. The hotel will have big asphalt parking lots funneling drips of motor oil and antifreeze into the lake whenever it rains." Jack jutted his chin toward Earl Ray. "And a manicured lawn that some idiot will accidentally treat with chemicals that will leach into the lake and spawn algal blooms and—"

"Hey." Earl Ray raised both hands in an I'm-unarmed gesture. "I'm on your side, remember. You gotta trust someone." He grabbed back ahold of the wheel. "I'm the one."

A few miles and a couple of turns later, he got on the highway. He pushed his speed close to eighty, took a swig from the paper cup in the console, and forced the drink down. The taste and the smell of boiled weeds. Absolute swill. He must have been crazy, thinking that herbal tea might solve his stomach troubles. He needed to find out if it really was cancer. At least he hadn't been brainless enough to give blood. Doctors had that doctor-patient confidentiality thing. Folks who worked a blood drive? In this town? He wasn't sure. If he did have cancer, could be that about ten minutes after some screening, his parents would hear about it.

And so would every other Hamlin in the county.

And Stacey.

"I can't believe your ex is involved in this." Jack sounded like the whole situation was Stacey's fault.

"Don't blame me. I can't control the woman," Earl Ray said. "But I kind of doubt the hotel was Stacey's idea."

"Yeah. I think Tess really needs money. Her business sounds shaky."

Jack's voice held a note Earl Ray hadn't heard in a long time. He shot him a look and exited the highway. "You *are* interested in her." He took a sip of his repulsive tea. "I knew you noticed those high heels."

"I am not interested in Tess Palmer."

Earl Ray slowed to fifty and swung right through a light. "So you say."

Jack gathered up his hoodie. "Slow down at that stop sign up ahead and I'll get out. The last thing I need is an afternoon listening to your mouth."

"Not a chance. We're almost to the house."

A minute later he parked in the driveway. They hadn't passed a single house since they left the highway. Jack had to like that. And he had to like the front of this place.

Jack turned to Earl Ray, an unsettled expression on his face. "You're not a total idiot."

Earl Ray grinned.

The house was gray, stone and stucco, dreary in the overcast day. But his experience with furniture had given him a good eye. The place had impeccable lines. It fit into the landscape like an outcrop of exposed limestone. According to the owner, the design echoed Frank Lloyd Wright.

Jack was already out, walking toward the house, spellbound.

The owner waved them in, told them to explore, and returned to searching for his video camera.

Jack wandered toward the living room.

Earl Ray trailed behind.

The room had a high ceiling and three huge windows that faced a lake. Not one as big as Sunset Lake, but not a pond, and not another house in sight. Three ducks sat on the water.

Earl Ray gave them approving nod. He'd really nailed it with this place. Even the air coming in the one partly open window smelled right.

"It's bigger than I need," Jack mumbled.

"Yeah, but look." Earl Ray pointed at the view.

Jack moved closer to the wall of glass.

A flock of Canada geese—fifteen, maybe twenty— flew over the trees and landed on the lake, honking and chatting like a bus tour checking into a hotel.

Jack drew in a breath and his jaw relaxed.

Earl Ray kept silent. His plan might work.

Ten minutes later, hugely apologetic, the owner gave Jack a paper with details about the house and his number, and hustled them out, eager to drive to Kansas City.

"Well, what do you think?" Earl Ray put the truck in gear. He'd turn nice and slow so Jack could get a good last look.

"I like it." Jack read the paper from the homeowner, even flipped it over to see the back. "I like it a lot." But his words were too flat, too dead.

Earl Ray turned the truck at his regular speed. A slow view of the house apparently wouldn't help.

"Doesn't matter," Jack said. "I can't move. Because of Kaitlyn."

☙

Tess opened the front door. A cry, somewhere between a hoarse meow and a howl of distress, echoed through Leticia's house.

She tossed her purse at the hall table and ran into the living room. "Indy?" She scanned the room and the adjoining dining room.

No kitten.

No kitten in the kitchen. Or Leticia's bedroom. Or the study.

Another cry, more desperate, pierced the air.

Tess's heart tightened. She raced upstairs. What if—while she'd made that last trip to the used bookstore in the next town—the kitten had played with one of those mousetraps?

No. Wait. Here the cries were fainter.

She drew in a ragged breath, dashed back down the stairs, and crept through room by room, straining to hear.

In the master bathroom, she paused. The cries were loudest here. She yanked open the doors of the cabinet beneath the sink and got down on her hands and knees.

No Indy. Where—

She turned and froze.

Under the window, set in the baseboard, was a heat return. The metal grill was only partly attached and one side tilted up—enough to allow a small kitten to fit through.

"Indy!" She scrambled across the floor and wrenched the grill up farther. She squeezed her arm in but felt nothing but the metal walls of the duct.

"Hold on, Indy!" Tess ran to the kitchen, returned with a flashlight, and trained it into the opening.

The silver duct went back, turned ninety degrees, and went straight down.

But down where?

℃

Home from his trip with Earl Ray, Jack unlocked his back door and trudged inside.

His landline rang, cutting through the silence.

Jack jumped. Probably some telemarketer. He checked the phone in the kitchen.

The caller ID said *Silver Platter Catering*.

"Tess?"

"Jack, I need help. Indy's inside—" She broke off for a second. "Inside the ductwork."

"The what?"

"The ductwork. I tried to call a heating and air conditioning place, but it's after five. The only one that answered was a recording that said weekend calls start at a hundred and fifty dollars, and they haven't called back." Tess's voice got higher at the end.

And was that a sob?

"The screws that hold the ducts up in the basement are so rusted that even after I finally found a Phillip's head screwdriver, I can't get it to work."

A sniffly sound. No doubt about it. Tess was crying.

"Hold on. I'll get some tools and be right over." No matter what she might do to Sunset Lake, he couldn't ignore a woman in tears.

Five minutes later, Jack shifted his cordless drill and toolbox to one hand and raised the other hand toward Leticia's door.

133

It swung open before he could knock.

"Thank you. I didn't know who else to call." Tess's words spilled out, frantic. Her nose was pink and her light green T-shirt was rumpled and untucked.

He followed her down the hall and studied the long lock of blonde hair that had escaped her bun and hung down her back. He didn't know much about women's hairstyles, but if he had to guess, he'd say the rest of the bun was precarious. It was off center and lopsided, as if all her hair would come down if he removed one hairpin.

A whiny meow echoed through the house and drew Jack back to the job at hand.

"I think she fell in here," Tess said. She entered a room on the left, the master bedroom, and pointed to the heat register in the master bath.

The grate over it sat askew.

"I turned the heat off."

The kitten cried out again, and Tess's frame stiffened.

Jack raised his toolbox. "Let's go downstairs."

She led the way into Leticia's unfinished basement. Like at his place, the builder had cheated a little and made the basement ceiling seven and half feet.

"I think she's in there." Tess pointed a flashlight at a metal duct between two joists.

The duct looked like it came from the master bath. And the meows were louder.

She had picked a good joint to try to separate. He could see where she'd cut the tape around the duct, but the screws that held up the strap to support the duct were completely rusted. No wonder a screwdriver was useless.

Well, maybe he wouldn't need to worry about the screws.

Jack slid the step stool Tess had used out of the way and took hold of the duct with both hands. If he could bend it enough to separate the two sections, maybe he could make a hole big enough to free the kitten.

He tugged and tugged and tugged.

Tess circled him, angling her head to one side, then the other, to see.

The duct didn't budge.

Tess stopped circling and the tension around her eyes grew more pronounced.

"Don't worry. I can handle this," he said. Using pliers, he got a firm grip on one of the screws that held the strap and twisted.

The screw loosened. Excellent.

He squeezed the pliers tight around the screw on the other side of the strap and twisted.

The rust held like Super Glue.

A single screw was not stopping him. He re-gripped the pliers, clenched his back teeth together, and tried again.

The head of the screw broke off.

Not exactly what he'd hoped for, but it would work.

Tess leaned closer.

A few seconds later he removed the strap. "Almost there." He separated the sections of metal, pointing one down toward him. Dust trickled down the duct, but no kitten.

He angled the duct lower.

A small glob of dust rolled out, followed by a yowl and the scratching of tiny claws against sheet metal. Dust and grime poured onto Jack, and then the kitten thumped against his chest.

Needle-like claws pierced his favorite flannel shirt. Jack bit back a yelp, caught the creature around the middle, and peeled it off his chest.

"You did it!" Tess's words bubbled out, high-pitched and happy. Her eyes were fixed on the kitten. Her hair was even more disheveled, her cheeks pink. And her lips looked so soft.

Jack coughed dust out of his lungs. "Nothing but trouble," he said to himself.

Tess raised her head, eyes narrowed.

Had he said that out loud? "Not you," he lied. He held the kitten toward Tess. "This thing."

She scooped the kitten from his hands and stepped back. "He doesn't mean it, Indy." She cuddled the little animal against her chest and murmured endearments.

He fished in his tool box for new screws and reattached the ductwork. "You hang onto her a minute longer, and I'll fix that register." He dashed upstairs, brushing off dust. Far better than hanging out with Tess and thinking about kissing—uh, thinking about kittens.

The repair only took a moment and a couple more replacement screws. "I'm done," he called into the basement.

He was almost out the front door when Tess raced up the stairs, holding the kitten.

She released Indy, came closer, and wrapped her arms around him.

His mouth went dry. Softness and warmth surrounded him, and she smelled like his grandmother's flower garden, like summer and happiness. And she felt like...like he wanted to stay next to her forever.

As if pulled, he moved closer to her, his tool box in one hand, his cordless drill in the other, his brain unplugged.

As quickly as she'd embraced him, she moved back.

A cool breeze blew in the door and whirled around him, making the loss of her warm body even more noticeable.

"Thank you for rescuing Indy."

"You're welcome," he muttered. "She is kind of cute."

Tess beamed as if the kitten were her firstborn.

Jack backed out the door and escaped before he said another word. Because someone else was cute.

And way too appealing.

Almost appealing enough to make him think about how much his house echoed at night. And how lonely it was. And how good it would be to laugh with her and feel truly happy and alive again.

But all that would come at a price, a price he couldn't bear to pay.

Being lied to again, being hurt.

No, he did not need to get involved with another woman, especially not one who was set on destroying Sunset Lake.

# *Chapter Eleven*

The morning sun sparkled on the water, and a female wood duck rounded Kaitlyn's Point. If a hen was on the water—

Jack walked closer to the French doors that led to his deck and picked up his binoculars.

Yes. There they were. Six, no eight, brand-new ducklings, brown-and-yellow bits of fluff, following their mother toward the north branch of the lake, gliding along as smoothly as if they'd been swimming in Sunset Lake for years. Just as cute as could be.

He ought to show Tess.

Tess? He set down his binoculars. What was he thinking?

His brain was still frazzled from watching her with that kitten.

A lesser man would use those ducklings to convince her to protect the lake. Babies, puppies, ducklings. All the same idea. Play on that maternal instinct. Very useful in marketing, as he'd learned when he worked at the ad agency in Chicago.

But this wasn't marketing. This was Tess.

Back in the kitchen, he picked up his new camera lens. She had been beautiful when she'd brought it over. And beautiful last night when she'd hugged him.

He was an artist. He was supposed to appreciate beauty.

But he needed to let it go at that, needed to focus on the fact that he'd blabbed about the peas and ruined his best chance to save the lake. Sure, telling Tess the truth had been ethical and moral, all well and good. It still meant he had no way to stop her from selling Leticia's property to a developer.

He dumped his dirty cereal bowl in the sink and refilled his coffee mug.

The back door squeaked open, and Earl Ray walked in, wearing another of his many Royals shirts and carrying a Styrofoam box.

"Cinnamon rolls from Cassidy's Diner." Earl Ray popped the lid. "I still let myself have them once a week."

An amazing aroma wafted through the room, and Jack's mouth watered. He poured coffee for Earl Ray, set it on the table, and snagged a roll.

Earl Ray opened the fridge, pulled out the skim milk, and added a glug to his coffee.

Jack took a bite of the roll. Butter, yeast, cinnamon, and creamy vanilla frosting. Cassidy's rolls were just as delicious as their pies.

But in spite of the amazing flavor, his mind returned to Tess. He'd thought, at first, that she was like Chloe. Both blonde, both city women.

He'd been wrong. Even externally, they were different. Tess had clear skin, undisguised by makeup, and hands with short, unpolished fingernails. Chloe started every day in front of the makeup mirror and scheduled sacred time each week for a manicure.

There was something else about Tess, not only her looks. It was how she'd been worried about his UPS package. How her face had softened when he explained about the peas and she knew Leticia had been all right. How she worried over a silly orange kitten. The problem was, Tess Palmer wasn't simply gorgeous. She was kind. And authentic.

Earl Ray sat across from him and picked up the biggest remaining roll, the one with the extra frosting.

Jack took a drink of coffee. A second later, as though his brain had been activated by the caffeine, he turned toward Leticia's house and sat up taller.

"What?" Earl Ray peered at Jack as if he were a piece of furniture he was assessing before auction.

"I realized that I haven't seen anyone across the lake except Tess. Maybe no one's interested in Leticia's place."

Earl Ray rubbed his goatee, then ate part of his roll, almost losing a dollop of frosting.

"All my worry might be for nothing. I'm going to stop by sometime when I see her outside and ask."

"You've been watching this woman Tess out your windows, and now you—the official hermit of Abundance—are going over to chat?"

"She's a pleasant person. It won't kill me."

"Right." Earl Ray stretched the word into three syllables. "I think you must have spent last night staring at the moonlight."

Jack ignored him and took another cinnamon roll from the box.

"Be sure you give me plenty of notice." Earl Ray smirked and ran his fingers over the hair near his temples. "I'll need a trim to make sure I look good. When I'm your best man."

"Out," Jack said, the word garbled from his mouthful of cinnamon roll. He marched to his back door and swung it open. "I've got to work."

Earl Ray took a swig of coffee and ambled out the door, laughing.

Jack slammed the door behind him. His cousin was a moron.

If Jack saw Tess outside, he was going over to ask one question, one simple question.

Nothing more.

ॐ

Tess ripped off the yellowed packing tape and peered into the large cardboard box.

Her heart shot into her throat. What had once been old magazines was now shredded paper, arranged into a mouse-sized nest. She dropped the flap of the box like a pan she'd grabbed without a hot pad.

The flap fell shut.

With her arms fully extended, she picked up the box and carried it out to the sidewalk, well away from the house. She opened the flaps with her fingertips and tipped over the box with her foot. The mouse's nest fell out and—before she could catch them—a few bits of newspaper swirled off in the wind.

She didn't see any mice, but if there were any hiding in the box, hopefully they would exit. Honestly, Indy should have scared them away by now. Still, before Tess had made dinner, she'd wipe the kitchen counters with disinfectant. Because mice in the pet store were cute. Mice, loose, in a place where she prepared food, were vermin.

She gave the box one last glance, shuddered, and turned away.

And saw Jack's house.

He'd been so kind last night, rescuing Indy. She knew he was unhappy with the idea that she might sell to a developer, that she was probably the last person he wanted to help. But Abby had been unavailable, and Stacey, skilled as she was at arranging pillows, had that perfect manicure and did not seem like she'd be handy with a wrench. So Tess had taken a chance and called Jack.

And then she'd hugged him.

And felt a connection.

The man was definitely attractive, that was a given. Rugged and outdoorsy in a way she never expected a painter to be. But there was something more, a sense that his emotions—his love—ran deep, like one of those nineteenth-century poets she'd studied in school.

A brisk breeze hit her, and she scurried to the house. Most likely, she was just romanticizing things *because* he was an artist. Any connection between them was probably all in her mind.

Besides, she needed to be careful when it came to men. It was too easy to make major mistakes. And she lived three hours away, too far away to think about Jack Hamlin. What she needed to think about was Depression glass.

As she opened the door, her phone rang from upstairs, where she'd left it.

Tess sprinted to grab it.

*Rose.*

Tess picked up.

"How's the cleaning going?" Rose asked.

"Pretty good on the first floor, but upstairs I've barely made a dent. The boxes are piled so high in these bedrooms that I can't even see the windows." She positioned another box on a chair where she could easily open it. "But I really think there's Depression glass up here. It could be valuable."

"Absolutely. People collect it."

"I haven't found any yet. Just trash and some old Avon perfume bottles, thimbles, and weird spoons, like you'd buy to commemorate visiting different states."

"Those are probably collectibles too."

"I wouldn't collect them, but I hope so. They were wrapped up really carefully. It looked like a whole box of each, but I didn't unpack them very far."

"Well, maybe they'll be worth a lot. That would be good. Because I heard from the mechanic." Rose sounded nervous.

"Uh-oh. What did he say?"

"It's not just the engine. The van also needs a new transmission. Fixing it is a waste of money. It's ready for the junkyard."

Tess's legs grew weak and wobbly. "He said it would be ready at the end of the day."

"I reminded him of that."

"Couldn't he have figured this out sooner?"

"He didn't know how bad it was until he opened it up. We can drive it, and if we're lucky, it might last another month."

Tess turned and rested a hip on the edge of the box. "A month?" That was all? "Don't drive it unless you have to. It sounds iffy."

"Okay."

The van wasn't the only thing that sounded iffy. How on earth was Silver Platter going to stay in business if she had to buy a van? But she didn't want to worry Rose. She tried to sound as if everything was under control. "I'll figure out something."

So much for the everything's-under-control tone. The quaver in her voice was all too apparent. As was the truth about her business. Silver Platter wasn't any more stable than that mouse's nest, scattering in the breeze.

# Chapter Twelve

Unless Dad was already dying, Stacey was going to kill him.

She couldn't believe he'd called while she was talking to a client.

Again.

She climbed down the front steps of a thirty-five-hundred-square-foot recent build in one of the two upscale neighborhoods in Abundance. Then she turned and gave the homeowners in the doorway a confident smile. She fought the need to shiver in the early afternoon breeze and headed to her car, smile slipping.

She really wanted this listing. The middle-aged couple had only lived in Abundance two years, so they hadn't known her in high school. And they were desperate to buy once they got back East, so they wanted to price the house very competitively. If she could list their house and sell it quickly, she could show Abundance how capable she was. People would be more than willing to overlook the past if she could make them money today.

She wrapped her arms around herself. Like the rest of her nicer clothes, her navy sweater was made for warmer weather. Too bad. She didn't have money left from the bonus Delia had given her.

If she sold this house, she could definitely go shopping. And she'd gotten a good vibe from the husband. The wife, not so much.

And that was before the interruption.

Two minutes later, three blocks away, she pulled into the parking lot of the grocery store and called her dad back.

"Where's my bowling shirt?" Dad came on at top volume, as if at any minute he might have that coronary the doctor had warned of.

"I told you I'd be with a client for forty-five minutes, and you call four times about a shirt? I don't know where it is. Did you look in your closet?"

"Twice. It's not in there. You know I bowl every Saturday afternoon. The doctor even said it's good exercise."

Stacey wasn't touching that one. Maybe bowling was good exercise compared to sitting on the couch, watching TV, and eating junk food. But it wasn't the half-hour daily walk the doctor suggested. Besides, it was all too easy at the bowling alley to wander over to the concession stand and buy a hot dog and nachos.

"Stacey, pay attention. I can't bowl without my blue plaid shirt."

"Blue plaid? Did you check in the washer?"

No answer, just the squeak of the laundry room door and the washer lid slamming shut.

"It's soaking wet," Dad yelled. "How am I supposed to dry it in fifteen minutes?"

She'd thought she was helping, putting in a load of laundry. "Wear a different shirt."

He let out a sharp grunt. "Stacey Lynn, we're a team. We're supposed to match. And if I wear some other shirt, it will affect my score."

"Dad, you're such a good bowler. The shirt won't matter."

"Humph."

He probably saw right through that one. But he stopped yelling.

"I'll have supper ready after the game. I'm making that turkey chili." Healthy, high-fiber, like the nutritionist at the doctor's office had suggested. Stacey even bought the pricy ground turkey breast with practically no fat at all.

"Turkey goes with mashed potatoes and gravy, not chili," Dad said. He began his tirade about how in everything she cooked, she replaced "the good stuff" with "pathetic substitutes."

She stared out the car windows, mostly ignoring him.

In the parking lot, a shopper rolled a laden cart to a nearby black Audi, not a car seen every day in Abundance. But an Audi sure would be a fine vehicle to drive once her business was booming.

Her other line beeped. "Got to go, Dad. I have a call on the other line. I think it's the potential client."

"Just don't do this again—"

"I won't." He could do his own laundry.

She switched lines, took a calming breath, and counted to three as she exhaled. "Hello."

It was the client. Luckily, the husband.

"Did you have additional questions I could help you with?" she said, exactly like she'd learned in her online class. Her words even came out with the same cadence as the woman on the videos.

"I'm sorry, Stacey, we've decided to go with someone else, a woman who's been in real estate longer here in Abundance."

The rejection sank into Stacey's stomach as fast as a boulder dropped into a pond. What was it she was supposed to say? Oh— "The fact that my agency is new means I have more time to devote to selling your house." There, the perfect line, memorized word for word, delivered without a hint of desperation.

"My wife really wants to go with a friend of hers, Allison Kendall."

"Allison only opened her agency two weeks ago." The comment slipped out before Stacey could stop it. And it sounded more than a little bitter.

"For the past three years, she's been with Abundance Realty. She knows the market. Sorry." He clicked off.

Of course Allison knew the market. She also knew all kinds of stories she'd probably told the wife.

Stacey threw the phone in her purse.

In the parking lot, the black Audi drove away, her dream speeding toward someone else's garage.

How was she ever going to make it in real estate in Abundance when the past kept showing up like a set-in stain?

❧

Tess dashed into Abby's shop and glanced around.

Abby looked up from where she and a dark-haired woman were unpacking a small wooden trunk. "Hi. Did you bring in some collectibles?"

"Well, I hope someone collects this stuff besides Leticia's sister," Tess said.

"Why don't you put your box on the counter, and I'll take a look."

Abby and the other woman met her at the counter.

"Tess, this is my cousin Becky." Abby gestured. "She teaches music down in Columbia, but she's off for spring break this week and is helping me with stuff I bought at an estate sale."

The dark-haired woman smiled. "Hi. I'm sorry for your loss. Leticia was a real sweetie. I knew her from church, of course. And she always came to my community youth concerts here in town and spoke to the kids afterward, telling them what a good job they did. You could just see that she'd been a great teacher, that she really cared about her students."

"Thank you." Somehow Tess got the feeling that Becky was a pretty good teacher herself. She looked back and forth between the two women.

They were close to the same age, but didn't look alike and didn't give off the same vibe. Abby, with her T-shirt, Keds, light-brown ponytail, and hazel eyes, looked like she might never have left the little town of Abundance. Becky, even casually dressed in leggings and a long denim shirt with the logo of a jazz festival, seemed more sophisticated. Her makeup was flawless, drawing attention to her dark eyes, and her lipstick was a rich red that perfectly complimented her dark hair.

"You two are cousins?" Tess turned to Becky. "So are you my neighbor Jack's sister?"

"No," Becky said. "Jack's dad and my dad and Abby's dad are brothers."

"Jack has a sister, Samantha, but she's lived in Dallas since high school. And his folks don't live here either. He bought that house from them when they retired early to Florida."

"But lots of the rest of the Hamlins live in Abundance," Becky said.

Tess looked away. Extended family was fine, but poor Jack. When he'd lost his wife, his parents and sister lived so far away. They'd probably come for the funeral, but even so...

"What did you bring?" Abby leaned toward the box.

Tess unfolded the top flaps and pulled out an Avon aftershave bottle shaped like a car. "What do you think? Is this worth listing on the Internet?"

Now that she looked at it more closely, she noticed that the bottle had a chip and the label was partly missing. Even so, a tiny wisp of hope formed in her chest. Maybe Abby would know something that made it priceless, like maybe Avon only made a few in this color.

Because Tess had to buy a new, at least new-to-her, van immediately. And even if she bought it on credit, she'd need it customized to haul food and dishes.

Abby gave her a look of regret and handed Emma to Becky. "Let's see what else you have."

Tess unpacked the rest of her samples—three thimbles, two more Avon bottles, and three teaspoons that were souvenirs from Ohio, North Dakota, and the Statue of Liberty.

"That's pretty," Becky said in an encouraging tone. She pointed to a silver thimble edged with flowers.

Abby glanced at it but didn't seem impressed.

Emma gurgled and kicked her feet toward Tess.

She patted the sleeve of the baby's pink sleeper with frogs on it and watched as Abby picked up each item and examined it. If there wasn't Depression glass in any of the remaining boxes and this stuff was worthless, what was Tess going to do?

"Not bad," Abby said at last. "Do you have more?"

"From what I can tell, possibly boxes and boxes. Is stuff like this valuable?"

Abby picked up a thimble. "Some of it."

Emma pulled a drooly hand from her mouth and tried to snag the thimble, but Abby moved it away. "This thimble is the best of the lot, might bring twenty dollars."

"For one thimble?" Becky said.

A tingle ran through Tess's veins. She took the thimble from Abby, stuck it on her forefinger, and twisted her hand to study it from all directions.

"Remember," Abby said. "I get part of that for commission, and you have to pay for shipping. Still, you ought to clear about twelve dollars."

"This could work." Tess put the thimble on the counter, ready to ship it off. What if that whole box was full of thimbles? What if all the boxes were? "I could make enough off these collectibles to outfit a new van."

"If you want to get the best money, you need to bring it all in so I can check for sets. But take a picture of everything first for your records. And remember it can take a while to sell." Her voice had that don't-get-too-excited tone.

Perfectly logical, but the words didn't slow the adrenaline in Tess's veins. If the boxes were all collectibles, even if only a fraction of the items sold quickly, she'd make enough to pay the tree trimmer and outfit a van. On the other hand, the boxes might all be filled with nests of mice. "I'd better go see what I've got," she said. "Thanks, Abby. Nice meeting you, Becky." She waved at Emma and sped out the door.

Twenty minutes later she ran upstairs at Leticia's. Two entire bedrooms. Piles and piles of boxes. Good, in the sense that it could mean piles and piles of money. But so much to photograph. And the upstairs still smelled like dead mouse.

Time to get started.

She carried the box that had held the $20 thimble down to the dining room table, opened it, and began to unwrap the balls of newspaper. One after another, she unwrapped thimbles. Silver thimbles, gold thimbles, thimbles with flowers and houses and birds worked into the patterns of the metal. She dug to the very bottom and found porcelain thimbles decorated with flowers.

Tess lined up the thimbles on the table and opened the camera app on her phone.

Then, near the top of one side of the box, in faint ball point pen, she spotted "T 1/10" in Leticia's tidy handwriting.

Her heart rate kicked up a notch. Could the notation mean Thimbles, box one of ten? Mean the collectibles were already completely sorted by type in the boxes?

Tess ran upstairs and scanned the boxes. She found another box with the letter T on it—T 4/10. She ripped off the tape, whipped back the flaps, and found thimbles.

Yes. Ten boxes full of thimbles.

One by one she read Leticia's labels. Some boxes she had to twist. Some she had to squeeze to get to. Eventually she checked them all. Nine boxes of spoons marked S, seven boxes of Avon bottles marked A, and five big boxes marked D, all at the bottom of the stacks, contents unknown. She'd lay good money that those held Depression glass.

She hefted three boxes out of the way and opened a box marked D 2/5. She carefully unwrapped the first item, a blue plate made for serving deviled eggs. Next she found a green punch cup and a pretty pink vase. All glass.

She thrust both arms in the air and danced about as if her team had scored the winning touchdown.

She still had to unwrap it all, take photos, rewrap things and haul them to Abby. A big job ahead. Huge. But if she kept finding things as pretty as that vase, it would be almost like Christmas.

# Chapter Thirteen

Stacey drained the last of the Diet Pepsi out of a two-liter from the fridge and studied the nail polish she'd just applied. The red was bright, but she liked it. Careful not to smudge, she sorted through a pile of recipes on the kitchen table, looking for the one for turkey chili.

She absent-mindedly rubbed a burned dent on the table top, the spot where her brother had set a pan straight out of the oven almost twenty years ago.

Boy, Mom had not been happy about that.

Overall, though, the room held wonderful memories of Mom, memories that seemed to slam into Stacey whenever she was in the kitchen alone. If the kitchen affected Dad the same way, no wonder he was depressed. All those meals here alone. All the while knowing he'd retired early from the fire station so he and Mom could travel, and a month later they learned she was dying.

So unfair.

"I got a two ten." Dad burst in, face lit with a joy Stacey hadn't seen since the first day she arrived back. "My best day in months. I may never wear the team shirt again."

"Congratulations." She worked at a smile but couldn't quite pull it off.

Dad leaned back against the green Formica countertop. "You didn't get the listing, did you?"

"No." She studied her Pepsi. No need to mention she'd also been missing Mom.

"I forgot when I called that you were talking with a client." His words were tinged with guilt, as if he thought her lost client was all his fault.

Not only had she failed to celebrate his great score, but she was making him feel bad. "It didn't make a bit of difference, Dad, not in the end. The wife is friends with Allison Kendall, and they went with her agency."

Dad sat down across from her. "You've only been back a few weeks, sweetheart. You've got to give it time."

If people in Abundance were all like Allison, Stacey wouldn't live long enough to give it time. And if she couldn't get either the locals or the newcomers to work with her, her business was doomed. With one finger, she traced the pattern of bubbles on the inside of her glass. "Not one single person has asked me to help them find a house."

There, she'd said it. Admitted to Dad how bad things were. She raised her eyes.

He steepled his fingers in front of him, elbows on the table, and his bushy eyebrows closed ranks. He leaned forward. "You've got that listing on Leticia's place. If you sell it, won't you make both parts of the commission?"

"Ye-ess." Although that house didn't seem like the type to move fast.

"All you need to do is to sell that house. Once you do, folks will come around." Dad sounded excited, the way he used to on the days he trained new firefighters.

"I'm trying, Dad."

"What about advertising? Something people would see in Kansas City and St. Louis?"

She bit her lip. She'd thought of advertising, of course. The problem was how to afford it. But she didn't need to go into that with Dad. She hadn't told him she'd already spent all her start-up capital. He'd just worry. "I could do a bit more," she said. "I'll work on it, then start the chili."

"That's my girl."

Stacey stood up. She was supposed to be giving him support, not the other way around.

But he could be right. If she advertised—more than simply listing on MLS—she might sell Leticia's house, maybe even to someone who would keep the lake as it was.

If she didn't, she'd have even more problems. The kind that charged exorbitant interest.

A tiny claw of worry pricked at the top of her spine.

She hurried to her bedroom—to hide like she had when she got that C- in geometry on her report card.

Because Dad wouldn't like how she planned to pay for the ads. And she wasn't telling him. She didn't need a lecture on the evils of a credit card.

159

Especially not when that credit card was her only hope.

CB

Tess came out of Leticia's front door, carrying what appeared to be a box.

Strolling along the lakefront path after lunch on Sunday, Jack squinted across the lake. Yes. Definitely a cardboard box. Probably stuff of Leticia's she planned to take back to St. Louis.

But this was just the opportunity he'd been waiting for since yesterday morning. If she was outside loading her car, he could easily stop by to ask if developers were interested in the property. Maybe they'd found some problem—like a stray sinkhole—that would scuttle the whole idea.

A squirrel scampered in front of him, climbed a few feet up a tree trunk, and turned to chatter at Jack with a who-are-you-kidding expression on its face.

Jack glared at the squirrel. Okay, so a sinkhole was unlikely, but a guy could dream.

Tess loaded the box in her car, went back in the house, and emerged with another, this one larger.

Jack dodged a patch of mud, then scrambled up the hill and met her at the driveway. "Let me help you with that. You want it in your car?"

"Oh." She startled and backed away. "I didn't see you."

He hadn't meant to scare her. He gave a friendly smile.

"Thanks," she said. "That would be great." A wisp of hair that had worked its way out of her uptight hairdo brushed her cheek. She wore jeans and a blue St. Louis Zoo sweatshirt that heightened the color in her eyes.

He took the box and carried it toward her car. "Taking home some mementos?"

"No. These are collectibles. Thimbles and spoons. They were in boxes upstairs, belonged to Leticia's sister. Abby's selling them for me on the Internet."

"Ahh, my enterprising cousin. It amazes me the junk people will buy. Uh, I mean…"

Tess's shoulders shook with suppressed laughter. "Don't worry about it. Some of it seems like junk to me too." Her lips quirked up on one side, transforming his awkward comment into a shared joke. "And it's not super-valuable. But with so much of it, it adds up."

"You've got more?"

"Boxes and boxes. There's other stuff too, but I haven't gone through it all yet. But Abby said that even though she's not open, I could drop some off today since she lives upstairs."

Jack slid the box into her tiny hatchback. "So, uh, has anybody expressed interest in this place?" he asked in a casual tone.

"No. I think Stacey would have told me if someone called."

Not one single call? Perfect. "That's too bad." He tried—really tried—to sound disappointed, then turned around.

Her face was drawn in as though worry pressed in at each temple.

Guilt uncoiled in his stomach. He knew from that phone call he overheard that her business was in trouble. She probably thought selling Leticia's house was the answer to all her problems.

Only a heel would be happy in this situation. He straightened the boxes in her car, just as neatly as she'd arranged those magazines at the lawyer's.

It didn't allay his guilt.

He turned around and pointed a thumb over his shoulder at her hatchback. "You probably get great gas mileage, but your car won't hold many more boxes. We could use my SUV, and I could help you load."

Tess's eyes grew wide. "You'd do that?"

He was as surprised as she was that he'd made the offer. But now that he had, his stomach felt better. "Why not? I'm done for the day. I was working outside, playing with some ideas, but it got too cloudy."

The worry melted from her face, and her eyes shone. "That would be fabulous."

"I'll be right back." He waved and took the lakeside path at a brisk pace.

Ten minutes later, after he moved junk from the back of his SUV to his garage floor, he parked at Leticia's.

Tess had stacked four more boxes on the sidewalk.

As she turned to face him, a shaft of sunlight shimmered through the clouds and illuminated her cheeks and fair hair.

His heartbeats leapfrogged over each other.

She was stunning. Like one of Raphael's Madonnas. That same glow. He slid out of the vehicle.

"This is so nice of you," she said. "I tried to hire someone to help, but one woman's out of town, and I never could get ahold of the other one."

Jack shrugged. Helping her out would be no hardship.

"If I can sell this stuff, it would be wonderful," Tess's words rushed out. "The van I use for my business is shot. I need to buy a new—well, used—commercial van and have it outfitted for hauling my catering stuff."

"Ah, I see." Jack trailed after Tess into Leticia's house. He understood some of what she said—certainly the part about a vehicle needing repair. But he couldn't see how a few boxes of spoons and thimbles could finance a van. Pointing that out, though, seemed mean.

Tess stopped in the dining room.

She wasn't kidding about a lot of boxes. He pointed to the stacks on the floor. "All of these are collectibles?

Her face fell. "I understand if you don't have time."

"No, no, not a problem," he said. It wouldn't take more than an hour. Surely he could spare an hour to help a neighbor.

Afterward he could go home and savor the fact that no one was interested in Leticia's house and that her property could—for now at least—stay undeveloped. Exactly the news he'd hoped for.

And exactly the news that ought to make him happy.

And it might.

As long as he wasn't seeing how hard Tess was working to sell a bunch of thimbles to finance a van for her business.

Or thinking about that phone call he'd overheard.

Or looking at her face.

163

# Chapter Fourteen

Tess peeked at Jack out of the corner of her eye as he parallel parked in front of Abby's shop.

Why was he helping her? Was he simply a nice guy? Did he possibly want to buy Leticia's house himself and think he could get her to give him a good deal? Clearly he didn't drive people around much. He'd tossed three wadded-up drive-thru bags off the passenger seat and into the back before she got in.

She allowed herself a second, quick glimpse in his direction. Halfway through loading, he'd taken off his hoodie, revealing a faded black T-shirt. Now, with one hand on the steering wheel, the other arm propped on the seat back, he twisted to see behind him. The muscles in his arms tightened.

Earlier, when he'd seemed embarrassed about calling the collectibles junk, he looked like a little boy.

Now he looked like a man, a very attractive man.

Not that she noticed.

Or had any interest in feeling that bicep ripple under her touch.

They were here to drop off collectibles. Nothing more.

"Ready?" Jack nudged her elbow.

"Y-yeah." She stammered and fumbled for her purse. Good grief. How long had he been waiting while she was daydreaming? "Let's see where Abby wants the boxes." Tess bolted out of the SUV and into the shop.

"Hey," Abby whispered. "Emma's asleep." She held a dust cloth and used it to point to the playpen, where a little head peeped out from beneath a blanket covered in pink pigs.

"Hey, Abby." Jack's voice boomed through the quiet.

"Shh," Tess said, finger to her lips. "The baby is—"

Emma let out a howl like she'd been pinched.

Abby started toward her.

Jack waved Abby away and scooped Emma out of her playpen. He lifted her high in the air until she giggled.

"Good thing babies like you, loudmouth." Abby took Emma from him. "What brings you in this afternoon?"

"He's helping me," Tess said.

"Really?" Abby dipped her chin and widened her eyes.

Tess scanned the store. "Where should we put the thimbles and spoons?"

"Over there." Abby pointed near a dressmaker's dummy. "I'll be right back. Someone needs a fresh diaper and a teething ring." She settled Emma on her shoulder and carried her toward the back of the shop.

Tess propped the door open.

Jack had already opened the rear hatch of his car and taken a box inside.

She picked up another and backed away from the vehicle, closer to the silver sedan parked behind it. She turned to move toward the sidewalk.

Jack blocked her path.

She walked more slowly, giving him time to get out of the way. She was carrying a box, after all, and his arms were empty.

But he didn't move. He stayed there, inches away, with a teasing look in his eyes, a look that made her think he would have preferred they were even closer, without the box between them.

Her heart sped.

She took a half-step forward, and the edge of the box bumped his chest.

He reached to steady it. His hand grazed her arm, and an electric current zipped through her.

She moved back. Heat rushed to her cheeks and suddenly she was thirteen, gawky and self-conscious. She turned around, checked for oncoming cars, then scurried into the street and around the front of the SUV. Inside the shop, she drew in a deep breath.

So she'd acted a little weird when he touched her arm. He probably didn't notice, right? She arranged her face into a calm, sophisticated expression and returned for another box.

Jack was stacking the remaining boxes on the curb— as if he didn't want to risk sending her into the street again.

Fine. He'd noticed her gawky moment.

Tess wrapped her arms around the top box and lugged it inside, head down.

The man was helping her, for pity's sake. She needed to act normal, but she couldn't. She wanted distance between them, so she could process the electricity she'd felt. Because that wasn't normal. At least not for her.

Finally, the boxes were unloaded.

Tess stood—four feet away from Jack—in front of Abby's counter.

"I got the photos you texted. Those will be a big help. There are a few items I know I want to see. I'll give you a call after I check on them."

"Thanks." Tess edged toward the door. "We'd better go. I don't want to take all of Jack's afternoon."

"Bye, Tess. Bye, Jack. You two have fun." She drew the last word out. Fu-uhn. Like she'd seen Tess's gawky moment. And been amused.

Back in the SUV, Tess settled herself safely, but not obviously, away from the console.

Jack started the engine.

Silence stretched.

She arranged her purse on her lap. "Thanks for helping me." She should say more, apologize for how weird she'd been, but that would only draw attention to it.

"No big deal." The silence returned, now palpable, like tiny insects skittering down her arms. She needed to say something, anything. The weather—she could talk about the—

Jack turned on the radio. An ad finished, and an announcer began a newscast.

Tess sank against the seat and pretended to be engrossed in current events until Jack pulled into Leticia's driveway.

A text dinged on her phone. From Abby.

Six spoons are a rare sterling set. Ought to bring about $2,000 total.

Tess moved the phone closer and reread the text.

"You all right?" Jack asked.

"Six of those spoons are a set worth almost two thousand dollars."

He slid the gearshift into park. "Wow." He sounded as shocked as she felt.

She turned to him.

He glanced down.

Without realizing it, she'd rested a hand on his forearm.

His hazel eyes met hers, and the electric current was back, zipping through Tess's veins.

His eyes grew serious and he spoke again, this time barely audible. "Wow."

Heat rushed to her cheeks. Embarrassment. Delight that he felt it too. And awareness of the warmth of his skin.

Casually, oh-so-casually, she pulled her hand back. As if the electric charge that had now reached her heart was no big deal at all.

CB

"Can I show you something?" Jack asked as he undid his seatbelt. "On the other side of the lake?" He glanced at her.

Tess turned toward him. "What?"

"One of the mother wood ducks brought her ducklings out on the water this morning."

Tess's forehead crinkled, as though that was not what she'd been expecting.

"Eight of them. They're pretty cute." But she wouldn't want to see them. And even if they were wildlife painters, men didn't admit they liked baby duck—

"Ohhhh. Okay." Her voice held surprise. And interest.

So maybe his invitation wasn't totally insane. He hadn't meant to invite her, like he hadn't planned to help with the boxes, but the woman seemed to override his good sense. And when she touched his arm—

"C'mon," he said. "We'd better hurry, before it gets dark."

Tess put her purse inside the house and joined Jack in the backyard. She pulled on a jacket. "Which ones are the wood ducks?"

"The drake has a greenish-purple head with a red eye. The hen is brown with a white eye patch. Do you know the ones I mean?"

"Not really." She scrunched up her face.

He walked beside her to the path that circled the lake, telling her about the different species of waterfowl that visited Sunset Lake each year. They progressed northwest around the lake, and he identified the ducks that swam past, a blue heron in the reeds across the water, a red-tailed hawk that dipped and soared overhead.

They rounded a bend in the shoreline, and Tess pointed. "Is that another of those blue-winged teals?"

"It is." She was smart, quickly picking up the differences among the species.

"A drake, right?" She turned to him, face lit with expectation, like the girl in the front row who always knew the right answer, who always wanted affirmation. A few strands of her blonde hair blew across her face, and she veered from the path, closer to the water.

"Yes, but be careful. I know from when I was a kid that those reeds are always—"

Tess's feet slid out from under her. She landed with a yelp, backside in the mud.

Jack rushed to help her up, but by the time he got to her, she was on her feet.

"I should have watched where I was going." She twisted from one side to the other, trying to see down the back of her legs. "How bad is it?"

Mud covered the seat of her jeans and brown splotches spattered her legs. If he told her the truth, she'd want to head back.

"That bad, huh?" She gave a soft laugh, that same kooky laugh he'd heard before. "My own fault, too. C'mon. I want to see the ducklings." She tromped toward the path with a determination that brought a grin to his face.

Chloe hated everything about the lake, would never have hiked through the mud to see ducklings. Tess was actually having fun.

And so was he.

Jack tipped the idea from side to side in his head, searching for a defect in his thought processes. No, no defect. He *was* having fun.

"You grew up here?"

"Yeah," he said. "I lived here until I started college, then came back after I worked in Chicago awhile, bought the place from my parents."

"Oh, that makes sense. I guess when I came here, when I was in high school, you were away."

He nodded. He'd thought she was about five years younger than him. And he hadn't come home much in college.

They passed a clump of trees and reached the northern tip of the lake. He led her off the path, closer to the water, but to a spot he knew would be dry. A narrow cove stretched before them, and the water reflected the orange and russet and violet of the sky. About ten feet out, a mother wood duck glided through the water, and eight ducklings followed in her wake, fluffy brown-and-yellow adventurers, each marked with a dark cap and stripes drawn back from its eyes.

"Oh." Tess's word floated out on a sigh. She raised her hand toward her chest and watched the little family. "They're darling."

For at least five minutes the family of wood ducks played in the cove until at last Mama Duck led her babies farther out.

Tess looked up at Jack, her eyes soft and luminous. "I've been so caught up with the collectibles, I never noticed them on the lake. Thank you."

Without thinking, he reached out and ran a finger down her cheek.

Her eyes widened and grew bluer, but she didn't move away.

With his other hand, unable to stop, he drew one pin from her hair.

A tendril burst free and feathered against his fingers in the breeze. Pale silk, teasing against his hand.

His whole body ached to touch her again. Should he? Did she want him to?

A slight color rose in her cheeks.

He pulled out another hairpin.

Her breathing grew deeper.

Pin after pin after pin, he freed each tendril until her hair tumbled down over her shoulders. That sweet floral fragrance surrounded him, reminding him once more of his grandmother's garden. Of honeysuckle and happiness.

He shoved the hairpins in a pocket of his jeans, and then, slowly, savoring the softness, he threaded his fingers into her hair until they met at the nape of her neck.

She dropped her eyes to his mouth and slid one arm around his waist, and he lowered his lips to hers.

His heart pounded. He deepened the kiss and tasted strawberries and something else, something intoxicating.

He pulled her closer.

And then a Canada goose honked, almost on top of them.

He moved back, startled.

His breathing came heavy, and Tess's cheeks were flushed.

Alarms rang in his brain, and he took a step back. What had he done? He'd avoided women for five years and then kissed Tess Palmer, a woman he'd only met six days ago, a woman who could destroy his whole world.

Confusion flashed through her eyes.

"Uh, I'm glad you liked the ducklings. I need to see my painting now that it's dry. I've got to go." He awkwardly handed back her hairpins. Then he hurried away, headed for home.

Headed for sanity.

# *Chapter Fifteen*

"Dad, I'm getting ready to show Leticia's property. The ad only began yesterday, and the guy called a couple of hours ago." Stacey turned off County Road 38 onto Sunset Lake Lane.

"Sweetheart, that's wonderful." Pride filled his every word.

She had the best dad. "It's a guy out of St. Louis, wants the site for a hotel," she said as she parked at Leticia's.

The client, Jeremy Seasky, pulled in behind her and gave a quick wave.

"I'll tell you more later, Dad. I've got to go."

"Not a problem, I'm heading out to the drug store to get my refills. Bye, Stacey."

Finally. Dad was getting his refills, taking more interest in his health. He'd get better. And she would make it in real estate. Her Monday was starting great.

She ran her hands over her dark jeans. No sweaty palms. Despite her misgivings about the development of Sunset Lake, she needed to make this sale.

So far, so good. Tess's car was gone. From the outside, the property looked fabulous. Bright sunshine sparkled off the water, the hills were awash with spring color, and two pots of yellow pansies gleamed on the porch. Everything perfect, as if she'd had days to prepare for this showing, instead of two hours. Because either this Jeremy guy had been cocky enough to leave St. Louis before he even talked with her or he'd broken every speed record set on I-70.

Jeremy climbed out of his Lexus and reached back in for something. Oh, yes, his notebook. His uncle was the real potential buyer. When she first met Jeremy outside her office, she'd had a pretty good idea that he'd merely been sent to gather information. Despite the fancy car, he didn't seem like a man who could afford Leticia's place. People with that much money wore better cologne.

Stacey slid out of her car.

The air was warm and still, and ducks and geese jabbered quietly on the water.

She welcomed Jeremy to the property and handed him a packet of information. "As you can see, the place is beautiful. Such a lovely, restful setting." She gestured to the lake and the woods beyond. "Dogwood, redbud, and just as nice in the summer when the oaks leaf out. So green. You don't get that in the city." Certainly not in Los Angeles, she could assure him.

Jeremy walked to the edge of the drive and faced the lake, then turned back to her and gave a tight nod, like royalty approving her feudal offering. But he liked it. She could tell. His eyes had become a little less beady.

Stacey led him toward the porch stairs. She could do this. She could get this guy to make an offer.

Although he said his uncle would probably tear the house down, she showed him the first floor, then Leticia's deck.

"Imagine your resort facing southwest like this deck." Stacey forced herself to slow down, to stop her nerves from running away with her words. "The view from your lobby, particularly at sunset, would be spectacular. A wonderful place for destination weddings." She'd thought of the wedding idea while driving out. Downright brilliant, if she did say so.

Jeremy took four photos from the deck with his phone. "This property is county, correct? No zoning?"

"No zoning. Only state laws about wetlands."

He waved a hand to dismiss the state. "Seasky Enterprises is a huge conglomerate. We have lawyers and engineers to deal with issues like those."

She kept her expression solemn, as if she was impressed, and led him around the property. Eventually they returned to the driveway.

Seasky edged closer. "I have to say, Miss Gilcroft, we might be interested in this property."

Bursts of adrenaline ricocheted through her veins. An offer was right around the corner. Her first commission. The respect of folks in Abundance. "That's great to hear. Will your uncle also want to see the property?" She pulled a business card from the side of her purse. There was one in the packet she'd made, but an extra couldn't hurt.

Jeremy sniffed. "No need. He trusts me implicitly. We're family."

The bubbles of excitement fizzled in Stacey's chest, and she looked across the water at Jack's house. She knew all about family connections.

"Tell me about the area," Jeremy said. "Guests at Seasky properties expect high-quality dining and some shopping." His tone implied that little in Abundance would be good enough. "Sitting out here staring at the water will get dull fast."

The beautiful Missouri countryside could never get dull for Stacey. She'd missed it terribly while she was out west. "Uh…"

"I realize you won't have upscale shopping like our guests are used to." He tipped his head as if acknowledging that the people of Abundance did the best they could.

Her mouth grew as dry as central California. Mostly, if folks in Abundance wanted real shopping, they drove to Columbia. "Both Miller's Junction and Prattsville are a bit of a drive, but they have some places."

"What about here in Abundance? Someplace for little excursions. Homemade candles, a farmer's market with fresh bouquets, a craft fair?"

"There's a nice antique place and…" That was all she could think of. Seasky's rich city clientele wouldn't be interested in finding bargains at the discount place or picking up poultry grit at the feed store. Really, all Abundance had was the county hospital, and it only had that because it was halfway between the two bigger towns.

"What about restaurants?"

"The best place around is Cassidy's Diner. It's delicious. Let me take you there for lunch, and we can discuss the property."

Jeremy's lips curled like she'd offered him a place in the line at a soup kitchen. He closed his notebook. "Thank you, but I'm not interested in a diner. I'll do further research online." He moved toward his car.

Her throat tightened. "I'm sure I could think of some place."

He opened the door of the Lexus.

She rested one hand on the hood of the vehicle. She had to come up with something. She was losing a sale. "There's a barbecue place—"

He gave a slow shake of his head. Once left, once right. He got in his car, backed, turned, and sped off, leaving her with one hand in mid-air, where it had rested on his hood.

The sun slid behind a cloud.

Stacey looked at her business card, still in her hand, and folded it over and over, smaller and smaller, until it became a tiny rectangle.

CB

Tess fidgeted in her car outside the lawyer's office. She'd gone to the store for more packing tape. She'd given the lawyer's secretary the jewelry, books, and the small painting that Leticia had left to other family members. And now she didn't have any more errands, but she couldn't go back to Leticia's. Stacey hadn't texted that the showing was done.

If the guy liked the property, if he made an offer—

She lowered her head onto the steering wheel. Who was she kidding? She couldn't focus on her list of things to do or even on the possible sale of the house. Jack still filled her mind, even after she'd lain awake for hours, trying desperately not to think about him.

Trying not to think about that kiss.

She let out a sigh. She couldn't just sit here, head down on the steering wheel. People would think she was having some sort of a breakdown right in the middle of Abundance.

She sat up and checked her list once more. No. Nothing more she could do until she could go back to Leticia's and photograph the collectibles. She'd started on the Depression glass, which she really liked. She might even keep a piece or two, if they weren't too valuable. But she was more than happy to let the other stuff go, like the spoons. Especially since they were turning out to be so profitable...

Ten minutes later she entered Abby's shop, carrying a Styrofoam box that smelled fabulous and contained three cinnamon rolls, the diner's specialty. Even if it was getting close to lunchtime, a little celebration for the two-thousand-dollar spoons was in order, plus it might take her mind off the showing.

And Jack.

Abby looked up from where she sat on the floor with Emma, building a tower of plastic blocks.

Emma whacked the tower, scattered the blocks, and laughed with delight.

Tess held up the box. "I brought cinnamon rolls. I thought maybe you could take a break for a snack. A little thank-you for your help with the spoons." She looked around the store. "I got an extra for Becky. Is she...?"

"How sweet of you. Sit. Becky should be here any minute." Abby angled her head toward a nearby pair of green upholstered chairs, a loveseat, and a small table. "I'll make tea to go with the rolls and tell you about the sale."

"Sounds great."

Abby gave Emma a rattle and set her in her playpen, then went to the back room.

Tess settled into a chair and listened to the grandfather clock as it ticked, slow and comforting. Maybe if she got up her nerve, she would ask Abby about Jack.

A few minutes later, Abby returned with a tray holding a little china teapot covered in violets, matching cups and saucers, three lavender plates, and a crystal sugar bowl. She set the tray on the table, put Emma on the floor beside her with a caterpillar that made a crinkling sound when touched, then poured the tea and curled up on the loveseat.

"What a sweet tea set," Tess said.

"Thanks. I fell in love with it at a flea market. Anyway, I haven't found anything else so far in your boxes that's worth nearly as much," Abby said. "But that spoon set already sold for $2,199. I can write you a check next week." She opened the rolls and released more of the spicy, buttery aroma. "You know," she said with a twinkle in her eye, "Jack almost never leaves the lake if he can help it. If people saw the two of you together, you're already famous."

Tess's cheeks grew hot.

Abby served them each a roll. "I think it's sweet. He needs some romance."

Tess sputtered, unable to get a word out. How did Abby know?

"I could hardly believe it, though," Abby said. "I can't count the women who've tried to get his attention. Here you are, barely in town for a week, and he's helping you haul boxes."

Tess exhaled and took a bite. Abby didn't know. Not about the kiss. And these rolls tasted even better than they smelled. "Jack was simply being neighborly. My car is so small it can only hold about four boxes at a time. He's got that big SUV."

Abby lowered her chin and looked Tess in the eye. "Then why are you blushing?"

"Um, well..." She let out a nervous laugh. "Is this what you do all day? Give advice to the lovelorn?"

The cowbell clanked as Becky shut the front door. "The lovelorn?" she cried. She dashed across the room and took the other chair.

The two cousins looked at Tess with the exact same gleam in their eye. There was a family resemblance after all.

"I knew there was more to it than boxes." Abby jabbed a finger toward Tess. "Talk. Every single detail."

"Who?" Becky interrupted.

"Jack," Abby said.

"Our cousin Jack?" Becky's voice shot up.

Abby gave a knowing nod.

"He helped me haul in a bunch of boxes of collectibles," Tess said.

Becky crossed her arms and narrowed her eyes. "Hauling boxes is no cause for the way you're blushing. Abby's right. Talk." She reached for a plate and took the last cinnamon roll. "You know you want to. And who better to talk to than the two of us? We've known him all our lives."

Tess caught her tongue between her teeth for a second, then spoke, halting frequently. "He did, sort of, kiss me."

Becky nearly choked on her roll.

Abby chewed dramatically, as if to show her mouth was full, and waved a hand in a keep-going gesture.

Becky gulped some tea and leaned closer. "This is huge. Where? When?"

"After he took me home yesterday, we took a walk by the lake." Now that Tess had started talking, the words seemed to rush out. "He showed me these darling baby ducks—Emma should see them—and the sun was setting and it was so gorgeous and—and he kissed me. But then he got all weird and left—" She shook her head violently, trying to get her brain to reset. "And I have no interest in getting involved." She took another bite of her roll.

"Obviously you do or you wouldn't be talking about him," Becky said.

Abby nodded. "You're interested. At least sub-consciously. And you know why he got nervous and left. I mean, I told you he's been through a lot of loss."

Tess shrugged. "I live three hours away and…"

"And what?" Becky said.

"I'm crazy going on and on about this because it was just one kiss." But even thinking about it filled her chest with warmth. The gentle touch of his lips to hers. His hands buried in her hair. Her heart filled with starbursts of joy. "But it was amazing," she mumbled to the floor.

"And you say you're not interested," Abby said with a laugh.

Tess shifted in her chair. No way she could admit the truth out loud. Admit how she'd thought about Jack for hours last night as she tossed and turned and stared at the ceiling.

Could she take the risk? Take the chance that Jack might love her enough to move beyond the loss of his wife? Take the chance that she might be loved, in spite of her mistakes in the past?

Some people loved unconditionally—the way Abby seemed to love Emma. But not everyone. Not Tess's mother. Not her old boyfriend at the bank, the man she'd thought was the love of her life. And not God.

"Long-distance relationships are hard," Tess said, wavering. She studied the scratched, scarred hardwood floor, then glanced up.

"Long distance isn't impossible." Becky gave her a look that said she knew Tess was weakening.

An odd sensation ran down her neck and along her arms, as if invisible goose bumps had appeared. She set her cup and plate on the table. "No. Not impossible."

"He's a really good guy," Abby said, in the same tone she'd used when she talked Tess into taking Indy. "He's just been through a lot of pain."

"And it's been five years. Time for him to move on." Becky leaned in.

Tess looked from Becky to Abby and back again. What were they, used car salesmen? She scooted back in her seat.

And then her phone chimed with a text.

We're gone. I'll call in ten minutes.

Stacey. Perfect. An excuse to leave. "Sorry, but I have to go. Stacey needs to talk with me about Leticia's place." Tess finished her cinnamon roll in one bite, slipped to the door, and waved goodbye.

☙

Jack scowled at his computer. Still loading updates. What a joy on a Monday.

He glanced back at his sketchpad.

There, staring up at him, was a sketch of Tess, looking just as she had after he kissed her, soft lips tilted up at the ends and a hint of rose blooming on her creamy cheeks.

Jack shoved his notepad and watercolor pencils far back on the desk. The last time he'd drawn sketches of a woman without thinking, he'd married her.

Trouble. Nothing but trouble.

He needed to remember how he'd felt when he learned that Chloe had cheated on him for the last two years of their marriage. Needed to remember how much he could be hurt.

He hadn't remembered it yesterday. No, he'd kissed Tess like he'd found the soul mate his wife only pretended to be.

And Tess had kissed him back. Tentatively and then sweetly. Like it mattered. Like it really meant something to her.

He ripped the sketch off the pad of paper, crumpled it, and lobbed it into the trashcan. He needed to be careful, to avoid getting hurt.

And he didn't want to hurt her either. With the way he'd left, he might have.

What they needed was a sensible, logical conversation. He'd simply explain that St. Louis was too far away for them to get involved. She could go back to her big-city life, and he could stay at the lake, hoping no one ever bought Leticia's house.

Definitely the right approach.

He looked at the trashcan.

Quickly, as if someone might come in and catch him, he plucked out the sketch, laid it on the desk, and smoothed out the creases.

Then he pulled a large book about Michelangelo from his shelves and slid the sketch inside.

There was no reason to throw away a perfectly good piece of art. He could keep it and still have that logical conversation.

# Chapter Sixteen

"This is Bud Blake. I'm interested in a quiet retirement place and I'd like to take a look at a property you're offering."

Adrenaline surged through Stacey, and she sat bolt-upright at her desk.

Bud Blake? *The* Bud Blake who owned a chain of barbecue places around Kansas City, who could more than afford Leticia's property? It had to be. The voice sounded exactly like the man on the TV commercials.

She fumbled for the notepad on the edge of the desk, knocked her pen on the floor, and yanked a new one out of the drawer. "I'd be happy to help you, sir." She was talking too fast. She needed to slow down. "Which property are you interested in?"

As if she didn't know. She only had one listing, the one she'd shown Jeremy this morning. But Bud Blake didn't need to know that.

She played it cool for the rest of the conversation and set up an appointment. "I look forward to showing you the house and grounds next week. I think you'll love it." She hung up and gave a quick prayer of thanksgiving.

If he made an offer, Sunset Lake would stay undeveloped. She'd show Abundance she was a mature professional and earn her first commission, a big one. And if Earl Ray happened to notice she made the sale that kept his cousin happy, all the better.

Finally, things were looking up. Even the smell in her office seemed a little more pleasant. She'd run over to Cassidy's Diner, get an iced tea, and give Tess a call to update her.

She took her purse out of the bottom drawer of her desk and her phone rang again. "Hello, this is Stacey Gilcroft."

"Stacey, Jeremy Seasky here."

A shudder ran through her.

Over the phone, he sounded even slicker than he did in person.

"Jeremy, how wonderful to hear from you," she lied.

"I talked to my uncle. He says the local restaurants won't matter. We can put a bistro on site, tell the guests the price is all-inclusive except for alcohol, and rake in the money." He chuckled. "I'm sending you an offer."

"Wow, that was fast." She felt like she'd been hit with a skillet. He'd only seen the place this morning. "I mean, uh…"

"Once you've been in the business as long as I have, you'll know that this is where you close the deal, not slow things down."

"I, uh, I don't want to slow—"

"Just kidding. Seriously, my uncle has been considering buying lake property for more than a year. Once he saw the photos of that place, it was weird—I don't know—like he'd seen it in a dream or something. He wanted it. We spent the whole weekend checking details online."

"I'm so glad you both like it." Still numb, she pulled the proper phrasing from her memory. "I'll watch for your offer, discuss it with the owner, and get back with you." She hung up. The numbness faded and the reality of the phone call trickled through her veins. Bit by bit, her stomach tightened like the time she'd eaten some bad shrimp.

She ought to be excited.

This would be her first sale, a huge sale. She'd thought she could do this, thought somehow it would be okay. But now that it was actually happening, it made her feel sick. If this sale went through, Jack Hamlin would be miserable. And if she made Jack miserable, she'd never have a chance with Earl Ray.

She checked her email. Nothing yet.

If only Bud had seen the property, had made an offer first.

Hold on.

She could still show Bud the house. She just had to follow those rules about multiple offers she'd learned in Lesson 8. It might even mean more money for Tess.

Her fingers flew as she punched in Bud's number. Then she channeled the professional demeanor of the teacher on the class videos, hinted at the urgency to act quickly, and repeated the selling points of the property.

"Well." Bud drew the word out as though he was leaning back in some pricey leather desk chair. "I can't get down there today or tomorrow, back-to-back meetings."

Her throat narrowed.

"You mentioned some other properties I might like, right?"

Wrong. When they'd been on the phone before, she'd said something vague about other properties, but only because her mouth worked faster than her brain.

"To be honest," she said, her voice unsteady, "none are anywhere near as nice."

"It can't be helped. Keep me posted."

An email arrived with a ding.

Her stomach twisted. "I will, sir." She hung up.

Easy for Bud to be so casual about the whole deal.

If Seasky Enterprises bought that property, she was the one who'd lose all hope of getting back with Earl Ray.

⊰

Half an hour later Stacey pulled onto Sunset Lake Lane and shoved another curly fry in her mouth. An iced tea, all by itself, seemed ridiculous after the call from Jeremy.

The offer from Seasky Enterprises was low—really low—and stated rather rudely that no counteroffers would be accepted. Surely Tess would reject it. But Stacey had overheard Tess on the phone. Her business was in trouble. She might think some money now was better than more later.

The decision was up to Tess, not Stacey.

At least she could present it in person, pick up on those non-verbals they talked about in class. That way if Tess seemed like she had doubts, they could discuss them. Stacey could give her best advice as a professional real estate agent.

Which would be to reject this offer. Today.

Then Stacey could get Bud to see the house, convince him to buy, and win back Earl Ray.

She wiped the grease from her fingers onto a napkin, careful to protect her nice sweater and favorite jeans, got out, and knocked on the front door.

Tess opened it, wearing yoga pants and a faded sweatshirt that was ripped near the waistband. Even in her jeans and boots—perfect for showing rural property according to her online real estate class—Stacey felt overdressed. Or at least like she should have called. She hadn't even thought of it.

"Hi. Sorry to drop by unannounced."

"Not a problem. I was just calling Abby about these three spoons." Tess waved her in and set the spoons and her phone on the breakfast bar.

"I have an offer for you."

A smile burst across Tess's face. "Oh, that's fabulous." She led Stacey past the dining room, where the table was buried in pink and blue and green glass dishes, and into the living room.

Stacey sat on the couch, her weight barely on the seat. If Tess took this offer, if Stacey was responsible for causing Jack pain, she could say goodbye to Earl Ray forever.

She swallowed and plunged in. "So, it's a developer. He wants to build a hotel, like you pictured."

Excitement flashed across Tess's eyes.

That bad-shrimp feeling erupted again in Stacey's stomach. "But the offer is rather low, and no counteroffers are accepted." She tried to keep her voice calm, but that part was so Jeremy, so high-handed, that it would have bugged her no matter what property was involved. Her annoyance might have slipped into her tone.

Stacey quoted the offer and watched Tess's eyes widen.

Dutifully Stacey explained the pros and cons of the offer. She mentioned the barbecue guy and how he wanted the house for a retirement place, but made it clear how nonchalant he seemed, how they couldn't count on him to buy.

"It never seemed real before, but now it's cold, hard cash." Tess sounded more and more interested. "I could have it in hand, what, next week?"

"Probably the week after," Stacey said, and she bit the inside of her lower lip. Once they had the closing, Earl Ray would...

Tess glanced toward the table full of glass dishes, then looked out the French doors at the lake, half-squinting, as if the answer was written on the water.

Stacey was afraid to say anything more. She'd done her best to be a good agent, which was all she could do.

"That is a lot of money," Tess said slowly. "But it's so far below the listing price. And below the assessed property value." Her voice became firmer, more certain. "Tell the buyer no."

Stacey looked down at her notepad, exhaled, and pretended to make meaningful notes. She couldn't let Tess see her relief.

"See if you can get the guy from Kansas City to make a better offer. If not, I'll wait."

"That's very smart." Stacey gave Tess an approving smile, a smile that hopefully hid any conflict of interest.

ᘓ

Jack closed his sketchpad.

Tess walked straight toward where he sat at the north end of the lake, as if she wanted to relive last night, wanted to rush headlong into romance.

Her hair was knotted up again, but looser this time, and she wore yoga pants and a green sweatshirt. The setting sun lit her face. Her eyes focused on the water, and she seemed peaceful.

He'd come over to do some quick sketches of the ducklings, just for fun. He hadn't come to see Tess.

But maybe it was for the best. He could have that logical conversation with her, get it over with.

A breeze stirred the water, and tiny waves lapped against the shore. In the middle of the cove, the mother wood duck led her brood on a walk along a dead log that rested half in, half out of the water. Her little ones followed along, willing, but not exactly marching in formation.

Tess stopped beside him. "You came to see the ducklings too?"

"Yeah." No need to point to his sketchbook. Nothing he'd done was for public view.

"I ought to be dealing with those collectibles, but I decided to take a break. I didn't even bring my cell."

"Good for you." He still didn't buy into being at the world's beck and call 24/7. His phone had been dead all day yesterday, and he hadn't missed it.

"They love it here, don't they?" She angled her head toward the wood duck family.

"They do. This wetland fringe at Sunset Lake is perfect for wood ducks, for lots of waterfowl. That's why commercial development is such a bad idea. The habitat is fragile."

One of the ducklings leapt from the log, landed with a splash, and turned toward them, peeping loudly, as though he had something important to say.

Tess put one hand over her heart, the other on Jack's arm. Her lips fell slightly open and she leaned forward. "Hello, little one."

The duckling peeped more, swam toward them, and stopped three feet away.

Tess squeezed Jack's arm.

A zing of awareness ran through him. He glanced at her and drew in an audible breath. His lungs filled with her faint, floral fragrance.

She turned to face him.

So beautiful. So kissable.

Every impulse drew him toward her. But he took a step back, behind a rotting branch that lay on the ground. Two inches in diameter, maybe three feet long, the branch was little protection. But if he thought of it as a barrier, maybe he could keep from compounding the problem, keep from kissing her again.

Because this was the perfect opportunity for that logical conversation he'd planned.

"Sometimes," he said, "I get caught up in the moment when I'm out here by the lake and I don't think. Like the other day..."

Her mouth tightened, and her lips shrank in.

A quiver ran through Jack's gut, the same quiver he'd felt at advertising presentations that didn't go well. But he couldn't stop. He forged ahead and blurted out the next line he'd practiced. "I think kissing you was a mistake."

She crossed her arms over her chest, and her eyes hardened.

Uh-oh. It had sounded way better in his head.

"So why exactly did you bring me to see the ducklings?" Tess's words were laced with anger and suspicion.

He mumbled a few syllables, not even forming words.

Color rose in her cheeks. "Did you think if you got me to like the ducklings, you could convince me to keep the lake the way it is? Protect that fragile habitat?"

"No—"

"The thought never crossed your mind?"

His stomach twisted. The idea had come to mind, but not that way. Unless—had he done it subconsciously? "I, uh..."

"That's why you helped me move those boxes." Her voice grew louder, and she sharply enunciated each word.

The ducklings peeped, and all of them, even the one with so much to say, moved closer to their mother.

"Tess, I..." Jack raised his hands, palms up. He'd helped with the boxes because he'd felt guilty for being so happy that no one was interested in Leticia's house. He couldn't say that.

She leaned toward him and her jaw tightened. "And that's why"—her voice grew even more strident—"you kissed me."

Mama Wood Duck led her babies out of the cove.

Jack's heart beat faster and he wished he could leave too. "No, really—"

"Forget it. The ducklings are cute, but they can fly to some other lake." Tess thrust her hands on her hips. "I thought we had some sweet, magical moment, and you were simply trying to manipulate me."

"Tess." He reached both hands toward her, hit an invisible wall, and dropped them to his sides. "I kissed you because I couldn't help myself. It's like...like I'm drawn to you." There, he'd said it, bared his soul, but at least she would understand.

Her face contorted, and she let out a single syllable of a laugh. "Right. As if I would ever believe that. Or anything else you say." She spun and picked her way back to the path.

Two seconds later she disappeared behind some trees on the way to Leticia's.

Jack stomped down on the rotting branch and crunched it flat.

No need to worry about romantic entanglements with Tess Palmer.

The woman hated his guts.

# *Chapter Seventeen*

Twenty minutes later, Tess dashed into the study at Leticia's and pulled the accordion folder from her suitcase. First Jack and his "mistake" of kissing her, and now she'd lost her list of things to do to get the house ready for sale.

What a horrible, horrible day.

She searched through the folder. No list. What could she have done with it?

She strode into the kitchen and slid Indy off the breakfast bar with a swoop of her hand. Earlier, right before she found those three spoons in the box of Depression glass, she'd spilled her coffee. She'd taken the list off her clipboard, dried it with a paper towel, and set it on the breakfast bar.

The spoons had looked like they might be sterling, so she'd called Abby. Then Stacey came over. But what had happened to the list?

The doorbell rang.

Outside, Abby held a squirming Emma propped on her hip.

Tess opened the door.

"I was out running errands after supper and thought maybe I could see those other spoons you found. And I wanted to tell you in person—you've got four thimbles that are worth at least a hundred dollars each." Abby moved Emma to the other hip. "And I still have tons more things to list. Your relative who collected this stuff really found some great pieces."

"Wow. Thank you. Finally something good happening today."

Abby raised one eyebrow.

"I've lost my list of things to do. I spilled coffee on it, and I put it right here to dry." She pointed to the bar. "Next to my clipboard. At least I thought I did. And your stupid cousin…"

"What's that sticking out from under the fridge?" Abby asked.

Tess rounded the breakfast bar into the kitchen. She snagged the corner of the paper and pulled it out. Coffee stains. "Thank you."

"Not a problem. Finding lost things is one of those super powers you get when you become a mom."

"I think I know exactly how it got 'lost'." Tess glared at Indy, who was back on the breakfast bar, toying with a twist tie.

The kitten hopped off the bar, rubbed her fuzzy head against Tess's leg as if no further apology was needed, and scampered upstairs.

Tess handed Abby the spoons. "What do you think?"

"They definitely might be worth something, but what did Jack do?"

Tess gestured toward the living room.

Abby peered at the Depression glass as she passed the dining room table, smiled appreciatively, then sank onto the couch. She sat Emma on the floor with her legs spread wide to steady her.

Tess's words spilled out, fast and angry. "I know he's your cousin, but I can't believe I thought for one second that I liked him. The kiss was just a ploy. He was trying to get me to sell the property only as a residence, not for development. And to make matters worse, it worked." She picked up a throw pillow and scrunched it into a ball. "I had a commercial offer—granted it was really, really low—but I could have taken it, and at least part of the reason I didn't was because I thought of those ducklings and—"

Abby held up both hands. "Slow down. If you take the first offer, one that's super low, you're only hurting yourself. And Jack may act a little out of sorts sometimes, but manipulation does not sound like him. Not at all."

Tess turned the pillow ninety degrees and scrunched it up again. She should have expected Abby to defend Jack. "But he got so mad a few days ago when I suggested that he sell his place too. And it was a good idea. Then he could buy property somewhere else where he could own a whole lake." She spread her arms wide, as if to indicate a lake from shore to shore. "But no, he wants to act like he owns all of this lake, like he alone can determine what happens to it."

"Oh." Abby dragged the one syllable into three.

"What? If he won't be happy with a hotel built here, he ought to move now. I bet the properties would bring the best price for both of us if they were sold together."

"Tess, I should have told you." Abby laid a hand on her forearm. "Jack's never going to move."

"I see that. The man is impossible."

"His daughter's ashes were scattered over Sunset Lake."

Tess's mouth went dry and her hands fell to the couch, limp. "Daugh—?" Her voice cracked. "Daughter?"

"I thought you knew. Kaitlyn was five. Jack's wife, Chloe, was driving. There was a huge wreck and they both died."

Tiny rainbows flashed in front of Tess and swam before her eyes. Jack wasn't stubborn. Or simply worried about the ducks. The poor man had lost his wife and a child, a child whose resting place was Sunset Lake.

And she'd suggested he sell that resting place.

&#9043;

Stacey stopped outside the post office to tuck her stamps in her purse, looked down at her feet, and twisted her mouth in disgust.

What had she been thinking, wearing these brown-and-cream spectator pumps this morning? She'd wanted to look good at the Chamber of Commerce breakfast, but she hadn't thought about the rest of her Tuesday. The minute she got home, she was taking these shoes off and writing on the lid of the box that she should only wear them to church. They were too cute to get rid of, but after a couple of hours, boy, did they hurt her feet.

And foolishly, with it being such a beautiful day, she'd walked over to buy stamps. How ridiculous was it that a person couldn't pay a City of Abundance utility bill online? Not even for a commercial account like her real estate office. Would this town ever move into the twenty-first century?

She, for one, had no desire to live in the past.

She stepped away from the door, looked down Main Street, and almost lost her balance on a crack in the sidewalk.

Half a block past the diner, Earl Ray had stepped out of the insurance agent's and started toward her.

All right, she'd admit it. She did want to live in the past, at least in a past romance.

This was her chance. Before she left her office, she'd fixed her hair and redone her lipstick. These shoes, torture though they were, went perfectly with her cream dress and her leopard-print scarf. If she happened to run into Earl Ray, she might get a date.

Ignoring the burning sensation at the base of her toes, Stacey strolled to meet him—the consummate relaxed, professional real estate agent. She patted the outside pocket on her purse. If need be, she even had business cards at the ready. Perhaps Earl Ray would offer to hand out a few at auctions. Because if someone had an estate sale after a death, they probably needed to get the house on the market, maybe even sell their own home and use the money from both to upgrade to a bigger place. Three real estate transactions. She and Earl Ray could be the perfect team—romantically and professionally.

Once she'd crossed the street, she passed the bank and waved to an older gentleman driving a truck that needed a new muffler. Then she slid a glance toward Earl Ray. He'd stopped to talk to someone, was farther away from the diner than she was, and hadn't even noticed she was there. She pretended to check a text, made sure her most alluring smile was in place, and resumed walking.

A few feet closer and she could see that his green button-down had the logo for his auction business embroidered on the pocket. He would never buy that shirt. Probably something his mom ordered him for a Christmas present. It sure looked good with his green eyes.

He looked up. "Hi, Stacey."

Two words, two simple words, but that voice of his still touched her. Maybe to other people, it was nothing special. To her, it was the voice that echoed in her heart. The voice she'd been so desperate to hear in California that she'd called on Sunday mornings when she knew he'd be at church, just to hear the answering machine for his business. The voice that pulled her fifteen years into the past, when they'd been young and in love and newly married, expecting a baby. The voice that made her long to rush into his arms.

His gaze met hers, and he joined her in front of the diner, where stairs and a ramp led to the door. His gaze flicked down to her high heels, came back up, and lingered at the hem of her dress.

Her plan was going to work. "Earl Ray, fancy running into you here. Heading in for lunch?" Because she was available, if he wanted to invite her to join him.

"No, I met Becky here for lunch an hour ago. I just ran in to check on some insurance before my appointment out east of town."

Stacey gave a nonchalant shrug. So he was in a hurry and had already eaten. Maybe he'd ask her for dinner.

"How's your dad doing?"

"Not bad." He wouldn't ask about her dad if he hated her, would he? "But he needs better test results if he wants to avoid bypass surgery. I've been trying to keep his spirits up and serving as the junk food police."

Earl Ray laughed. "Now that sounds like a challenge."

Her chest swelled. She'd made him laugh. Oh, she'd missed that laugh. "It has its moments."

He gave her that wide, wild grin she'd seen so many times before, the grin that said, no matter what, the two of them would have fun.

"How's auctioneering?" She stood up straighter, stomach in, chest out. Earl Ray was a sucker for curves. She edged closer to him and smelled a faint hint of his aftershave, spices and musk and memories.

"I can't complain. How's your new business?"

He was so close that she could shift her weight and their arms would touch.

"Wonderful." She laid a hand on his arm. "I'd love to tell you all about it."

A pained expression flashed across Earl Ray's face, and he stepped back.

She drew her hand away from his arm as if she'd been stung. She'd been too pushy, assuming he'd want to hear about her plan to sell Leticia's place to the barbecue guy, assuming he'd want to get back together immediately. And now he looked even more uncomfortable, desperate to change the subject.

"Maybe another time. Good to know you're doing well, though," he said. "I've seen you driving around town."

But his voice was tight, and his words were clearly a jab, his not-so-cute little way of saying that if she really was doing well, she wouldn't be driving an eight-year-old economy car. If he planned to ask her to dinner, he wouldn't say things like that, wouldn't back away, wouldn't look at her like he wanted to escape.

Like he never wanted to get back together.

Ever.

"Nice talking with you," she mumbled, scrambling to think of an excuse for why she'd walked toward him. "I'm in a bit of a rush to talk to a client. I better get my iced tea."

"Bye." His single word came out clipped, as if he wanted her gone.

Her heart constricted, barely letting blood through. She twisted her lips into her best fake smile and went up the diner stairs in front of him, putting a bit more sway in her hips than necessary. If he still couldn't forgive her, after all this time, she'd make him regret it.

But darned if adding that extra sway didn't seem to tighten the pinch of her shoes.

# Chapter Eighteen

Earl Ray hurried to his truck, trying to look as if he had pressing business.

Because he had to look good, in case Stacey glanced out the diner windows.

And he had to sit down.

The hurt in his stomach was horrific. He'd been in heaven, talking with her, asking about her new business and then, in a single second, his stomach had started acting up. Big time, like he'd taken an ice pick to the gut.

At last, he reached his truck. He slid inside, drove out of downtown, and pulled into a parking lot.

He grabbed a bottle of water out of the back seat. Anything to take the edge off the stabbing in his gut. He hadn't thought his lunch was that greasy. And it wasn't spicy at all. But he never should have agreed when Becky suggested the diner.

He slumped down, rested his head on the steering wheel, and rubbed a hand over his stomach. He had read more on the Internet. No matter how much he wanted to avoid it, he was going to have to call for a doctor's appointment to find out if it really was cancer.

He took deep breaths and—though he still felt like he might lose his lunch—gradually the pain eased.

At least the ache in his gut. The ache in his chest stayed the same. Guilt at how he'd failed Stacey. Longing for what he'd lost.

How was it possible his ex-wife hadn't aged a day? Seeing those legs again, that swoop of hair that brushed across her cheek, that dress that clung to her curves, nearly killed him. When she climbed those stairs, if it hadn't been for the pain in his gut, he'd have heaved her over his shoulder and hauled her off to the minister to have him remarry them.

Sure, her dad was doing well, and her business was great. Jack should just give up on saving Sunset Lake. No red-blooded man could refuse to buy a house if Stacey was selling it. She'd find some big developer and make a killing on the commission.

Yep, her life was right on track, and she had everything she needed to live in Abundance.

Without him.

His throat constricted. Every day he walked this earth he'd regret his mistake.

Of course, God might put him out of his misery pretty soon.

Without question, the last thing Stacey needed was a dying ex-husband chasing after her, expecting her to play nursemaid. As if she would. Wouldn't that be the ultimate agony? If he told her about the cancer and she didn't even care?

Nope. He couldn't face that. And he wouldn't have to.

As long as he stayed away from Stacey Gilcroft. Far, far away.

ೞ

Every eye in Cassidy's was on her. As though right before she came in, they'd all been talking about her.

Stacey would bet her first commission on it.

She forced her shoulders to relax and turned to give a quick wave goodbye to the lunch crowd, focusing on no one, then left.

It took every ounce of acting skill she had.

Outside, heart still tight, she kept her head high and carried her iced tea around the corner. By the town library, she sank onto a bench and took a long drink. She ignored the smell from the dog poop on the sidewalk and slid off her shoes.

Ugly red dents came into view, one on each foot, at the base of her big toes.

Those red places paled next to the wounds on her heart.

How on earth could she live here?

If she had the sense God gave a goat, she'd have thought this through. But no, she'd told her brother and sister she could help Dad, then moved home and opened a business. And she'd spent every penny of her bonus to pay six months' rent on an office.

Had she considered what Abundance would be like if Earl Ray didn't want her back? If everyone saw that she was in love with him? If they laughed behind her back, thrilled to see her taken down a notch?

No.

She hadn't given it a thought, just let her yearning for Earl Ray overpower her brain.

Abby said he wasn't seeing anyone. Which meant that he even thought being alone was better than being with her.

Anguish washed through her chest, and her throat burned. Stacey slid her shoes back on. Better to think about her sore feet than about Earl Ray. She was not going to cry, not out here in front of the library.

Was there anything that might help?

She took a long drink of tea, then drew in a ragged breath and released it, bit by bit.

One thing might help.

A new man.

☙

By five o'clock, the dead oak was gone and the tree trimmers' truck rumbled down Leticia's driveway toward Sunset Lake Lane.

Jack peered through his living room window.

The house did look better without the dead tree. And, thanks to his good advice, Tess had used C&K, instead of Lou's.

One more thing she could check off that list he'd seen on her clipboard. One more step toward the day when she'd be gone, when he could sketch the ducklings at the north end of the lake in peace.

But he didn't want her to leave. Not like this.

He shoved a frozen pizza in the oven and let the door slam shut.

She'd been so excited when she saw the ducklings for the first time—her eyes wide and filled with wonder, her cheeks pink. So beautiful when he pulled the pins from her hair, and it fell in a wave of pale golden silk over her shoulders. And so perfect in his arms when he kissed her.

For a moment there, hope had filled his heart.

And then fear rushed in. Fear of losing Sunset Lake, fear of getting hurt.

But he didn't want to live that way, didn't want to act out of fear. And what he'd done had hurt her. He'd made her feel used, made her feel their kiss was part of a scheme. Guilt slithered into his stomach like a centipede heading under a rock.

Soon she'd be gone. After she went back to St. Louis, he'd probably never see her again. If only there was a way he could fix things.

He wandered into the living room and flopped down in the recliner. Minutes passed. Brilliant solutions eluded him. He couldn't even imagine how another conversation might begin. She'd open the door, see him, and slam it in his face.

He turned on the Royals game. No Earl Ray to watch it with tonight. He was packing and going to bed early, headed to Hannibal tomorrow for a huge two-day auction.

The ballgame was delayed by rain. And the commercials were obnoxious.

Jack hit Mute and flipped to the weather. Based on the radar, the game might never start.

Jack ate his pizza and thought about Tess.

And still felt guilty.

He ought to apologize, but words seemed so insignificant. And words were what got him in trouble in the first place. If only there were a way to show her, something more meaningful than flowers.

In the middle of a commercial, in one quick movement, he leapt up from the couch. He grabbed a sketch pad and his favorite watercolor pencils and began to draw.

After an hour, he erased a bit of shading, added another ripple to the water, and ran a finger down the spiral of the sketchpad. Done. Ready to take to Tess.

The small drawing was nothing fancy and far more whimsical than his paintings, but it captured the duckling well. He'd drawn the little fellow swimming from the left. His fuzzy-topped head was turned, facing straight out, and angled slightly. If he had a cartoon bubble, he'd say "Did you notice that I'm cute?"

With luck, Tess would look at it.

Long enough for Jack to apologize.

# Chapter Nineteen

Even if Tess gave the sketch one look, she still might not talk with him. But he was already here. He would try. He knocked on her door.

Tess opened it. Surprise—and something softer—flashed through her eyes.

"Here." He held out the sketch. Best to offer it before those eyes changed over to anger.

"What—?"

"I made you a present." He moved the drawing closer to her. What if she saw this as manipulation too? He didn't mean it to be. He pulled it back a fraction. He just wanted her to remember the ducklings, just wanted her to go back to St. Louis without feeling used.

Just wanted...her.

She looked down at the sketch. "Oh." Her voice quavered with emotion. "Thank you." An early mosquito buzzed past her head, and she brushed it away, loosening a tendril of hair from her bun. She waved him inside.

"Come in for a moment." She raised the sketch. "This is lovely. I didn't know you could draw too."

Jack walked into her front hall and shrugged. "It kind of goes with painting."

"Yeah, I guess it would." She sounded embarrassed. "I was so caught up in the picture that I didn't think." She tugged at the hem of her pink T-shirt.

His nerve endings tingled. The perfect opening.

As long as he didn't mess it up.

"That was me," he said. "When I kissed you. I was so caught up in how beautiful you are that I didn't think straight."

She raised her eyes. Her face softened, and her lips curved into the sweetest little smile.

"I admit that after I saw how much you love your kitten, I did think about the fact that I could use the ducklings to sway you. But I also thought about the fact that it would be wrong." He paused to let the word sink in. Somehow he had to make her see he was telling the truth. "I would never do that. I showed them to you because I wanted to share them. And that kiss..." He shifted his weight. "I never meant to hurt you."

"Jack." She angled her head toward the living room and walked down the hall.

He hesitated, then followed her.

She sat at the far end of the couch, face narrowed as if she had big news.

He lowered himself to the other end and ran his fingers over the contours of the fabric. Had the house sold?

"I know," she said gently. "About your wife and daughter. I'm sorry."

He stiffened like he'd taken a punch to the solar plexus. "Who told you?"

"Abby." Tess spread her hands in front of her, palms up, in a helpless gesture, then slid them under her thighs. "I feel so bad that I ever suggested you sell."

"I understand why. Your idea makes sense."

"I didn't know about your daughter's ashes." Her face tensed and pain filled her eyes.

"I know." He looked out the French doors at the water and then back at Tess. "It's not so much her ashes. It's having the lake the way it was when she was alive. It makes me feel like she's still here. At least a little." The idea made sense in his brain, in his heart, but out loud it sounded ridiculous. And his grief was none of Tess's business.

She pressed her lips together, moved closer, and laid a soft hand on his arm. "Do you have any pictures of her on your phone?"

Of course. And—granted, he didn't spend that much time around people, but even when he did—no one ever asked. Like they thought he'd try to forget about Kaitlyn. He pulled his phone from his pocket and opened his favorite.

Kaitlyn stood at the edge of the lake, laughing, a three-foot-long fishing rod in her hand and a tiny sunfish dangling from the line. Chloe had taken the picture back when things still seemed good, back when they really were a family. Pride and wonder shone in Kaitlyn's eyes, and light reflected off her sun-streaked hair.

He held the phone toward Tess.

"Oh." She let out a soft breath and raised a hand to her heart. "She was darling. How old was she when she died?"

He ran a finger along the side of the phone. What he wouldn't give to be able to reach into that photo and brush his fingers across his little girl's hair once more. "Just turned five." He looked away and blinked.

"What was she like?"

Something in Tess's tone—something that said she was truly interested, that Kaitlyn was still real to her—eased the tightness in his throat and loosened his tongue. One by one, he shared memories of Kaitlyn. The way he'd felt painting *Ring-Necked Ducks in Flight* with her in that pumpkin seat beside him. The way she played beside him in a plastic turtle sandbox when he painted by the lake so often that they named the spot Kaitlyn's Point. The way she snuggled closer the instant a bedtime story ended and bargained for another. And the way she'd named every duckling the spring before she died, even made Chloe write down all the names on a list.

When he finished, Tess spoke. "What a perfect life she had while she was here."

He nodded. "Chloe wanted me to stay in advertising in Chicago, but when my folks decided to move to Florida, I wanted to buy this place from them and paint full time. She finally gave in, but she hated it. Then the money started coming in from painting. She said she could handle living here if she could go to Chicago once a month to shop."

214

The rest was harder to tell. But part of him—the part that wouldn't shut up—found comfort in talking to Tess and was willing to risk it.

"She was happy for a while, when Kaitlyn was a baby, but then once a month to Chicago became twice, sometimes more. Eventually I realized there was more drawing her to the city than Nordstrom."

Tess's jaw tightened and she shook her head, chin lowered.

At least she got it, didn't make him say it out loud. Even now, he hated to admit that his wife had cheated on him. That was part of the reason he didn't like church, didn't like the diner. It was the first thing people thought of when he walked in the door. He knew. He saw it in their faces.

"Anyway," he shifted his weight on the couch, "one day when I went to run some errands, Chloe packed up Kaitlyn without even telling me. By the time I got home and found a note asking for a divorce, Chloe's car had been hit by a semi. They were both already dead."

He looked at Tess, half-afraid that, like everyone else, she would offer the unhelpful platitudes, the uncomfortable expressions of sympathy that made him feel guilty for sharing his grief and made the unspoken assumption he'd somehow caused his marriage to fail.

She sat silent a moment, then scooted right beside him, reached for both his hands, and squeezed them together. "I'm so, so sorry." Moisture shimmered in her eyes, and the scent of honeysuckle surrounded him.

Warmth radiated from their joined hands all the way to his heart. Tension drained from his shoulders. He glanced away and blinked. "Thank you."

Somehow, she made him feel better.

A minute passed and the impact of all he'd said hit him. He rose from the couch. "I should go."

Tess followed him to the door. "I'm going to Columbia tomorrow to check out a commercial van. After I get back, would you like to come over for dinner? Say, seven? It's the least I can do, to kind of apologize for the house and all."

Jack turned. Dinner? He didn't want pity.

But she wasn't looking at him with pity. She looked sincere. And beautiful. And nice.

She gave a half-shrug and spread her hands wide, as if to say "no pressure."

"I'd like that," he said. "See you tomorrow."

&#x2683;

This was not a romantic dinner.

Tess shoved the candles back in the bottom drawer of Leticia's hutch. There was no reason to put them on the table. Candles meant romance.

The fact that her hair was down, like when Jack had taken the pins out of her bun and kissed her, was a coincidence. She was wearing a nice shirt and pants—instead of jeans and a T-shirt—because she'd been to Columbia. And tonight's dinner was simply a small way to make up for the pain that her decision to sell Leticia's house was causing Jack.

She was not reading too much into the way he'd squeezed her hand before he left last night, not thinking about that kiss by the lake in the sunset, not wishing for anything more.

The scallops began to sizzle.

She popped into the kitchen, flipped them, and heard a knock.

Jack stood on the porch, wearing khaki pants and a polo that made his hazel eyes almost green. His hair was still damp and his beard neatly trimmed. He held a bouquet of Siberian iris, a burst of bright yellow and indigo.

Flowers? Her heart gave a tiny jump.

No. She was not getting carried away. They were a hostess gift, nothing more.

Once inside, he handed the bouquet to her and slapped a hand against his chest as if he was having a heart attack. "What is that amazing smell?"

"Dinner," she said and chuckled.

"What is dinner?"

"A chopped salad, some bread from the bakery at the market, and pappardelle pasta with scallops and asparagus, carrots, and peas in a béchamel sauce."

Jack's mouth dropped open. He seemed to approach the kitchen with reverence and inhaled deeply, as if trying to taste the food through the aroma.

Tess put the flowers in the pink Depression glass vase she'd kept as a memento and took the bread out of the oven, where it had been warming. Its yeasty fragrance mingled with the smell of the scallops and the sauce.

"Do you know what I usually eat?" Jack asked. "Carryout, frozen pizza, and canned soup." His tone made it sound like the food was fed to him at gunpoint. "Can I do anything to help?"

"Fill those with water?" She tilted her head toward glasses on the counter.

"Done." He gave her a smile that sent tingles through her veins.

She took two salads from the fridge and carefully carried them around him, all too aware of his presence.

Her skin felt charged with electricity. She shared a kitchen all the time—with Rose. But this was different. Distracting. Delicious.

She put the salads on the table in the dining room. Then she returned to the stovetop and peeked at Jack as he got ice out of the freezer. He was just so hard to ignore.

Somehow, in spite of having him in the kitchen, she arranged the scallops on top of the pasta in a serving bowl, fixed a tiny sample for Indy, drizzled some sauce over the kitten's kibble, and served the meal.

At his first bite, Jack's eyes grew round. His face lit like a man so happy he might float off the ground.

Tess hid her expression of pride behind her napkin.

"This is incredible." He scooped up another, larger bite. "You must be an excellent caterer."

She gave a modest shrug.

"How did you get started in the business?"

A ripple of unease passed through her, and she paused with a forkful of salad halfway to her mouth. "Um, I got fired. And while I was trying to figure out how to handle that on my résumé, I did a couple of events for friends for the cost of the food. I got other jobs through word of mouth."

He piled more on his plate, and his eyes narrowed as if he wanted the whole story.

That wasn't happening. Not the whole story of the day she got fired. But she could tell him part of it. "I worked for a big bank in special events, had been there six months. I dated a guy in the marketing department, and he was the one who originally suggested I apply."

Jack took a bite of salad but kept his eyes on her.

"One day my boss had the stomach flu, and I ended up in charge of a huge special event to commemorate the fiftieth anniversary of the bank. Everything was going perfectly, and my boyfriend kept catching my eye and grinning at me. I actually wondered if after work he might propose. We'd sort of talked about the future. And I felt like a special-events superhero." She paused. "Then it was time for the honored guests to be recognized."

He leaned forward.

She ate a bite of pasta, then said, "A girl who'd started a savings account there when she was six and then given her money to charity when she turned twelve, a woman who invested twenty-five dollars a month with the financial services department back in the seventies and ended up a millionaire, a former bank president who was ninety-five—there were eight of them to be honored in all. Only they weren't there."

Jack's face scrunched up. "None of them?"

"I was supposed to send drivers to pick them up, but I didn't do it. I got so caught up with making the food perfect and thinking about how awesome I was that I never made the call."

"Oh." Jack sounded as if he didn't know what to say.

"That was my last day at the bank. And my last day talking about a future with my boyfriend."

"You got fired, and he broke up with you?" Jack's voice held disbelief.

"Didn't want to be associated with me. Afraid it would affect his career."

He set down his fork. "What a creep."

"Yeah. Too bad I didn't see that sooner." Jack's words helped, but they didn't stop the heavy feeling that was sinking into her stomach. She'd been so arrogant—and so devastated.

And then so stupid. So very, very stupid.

She looked away.

"Is there more?"

She shifted in her chair. There was, but she'd never told anyone. Without meeting his eyes, she skimmed her gaze past him.

He sat, calmly eating another piece of bread.

He'd bared his soul about what he'd gone through. To be fair, she ought to tell him all of her story.

Besides, what would it hurt to tell him everything? The two of them had no future. After tonight, she might never see him again, except maybe to wave across the lake if she stopped by Leticia's when she came back to close on the house.

And maybe…maybe it would feel good to let it out.

"There's more. And it's awful." She studied her plate and rolled the edge of the paper napkin on her lap between the fingers and thumb of her left hand. "That evening a friend was trying to make me feel better and took me to this Mexican restaurant. We had to wait for a table, so we sat in the bar and started drinking sangria. A lot of sangria. And then these guys started talking to us." She glanced up at Jack.

Something in his eyes said he had a pretty good idea what happened next.

Under the table, she held her napkin in both hands and ripped tiny, parallel tears in it like a fringe. "Long story short, I got drunk and had sex with this guy that I just met." She stared at her napkin and ripped three more tears. She was just going to say it, get it over with. "And then—I can't believe I'm telling you this. I still can't believe it even happened." She drew in a deep breath. "Then his phone rang. I was still drunk and thought I was being funny. I picked it up and said 'Nick's answering service. Can I help you?'"

"And?"

Her stomach tightened, forming one of those little Civil War cannon balls she'd seen as a kid on a school trip. "And this woman's voice came over the line, tight and panicked and like she might be crying. She said, 'Tell Nick his wife called and that she's going into labor.'" Tess looked back at Jack, ready for the disapproval and disgust to appear in his eyes.

He sat silent. Emotions rolled through his eyes, like blurry images on an out-of-focus movie screen, images she couldn't read because she didn't know him well enough to tell what he was thinking. But it couldn't be good.

The cannonball in her stomach tripled in size. What had she done? She'd been thinking of herself, wanting to get things off her chest, maybe feel a little better about herself in spite of her one-night stand with a married man. And she'd poured out her story to a man whose wife had cheated on him, a man who had suffered incredible pain because of infidelity.

She wanted to look away, but couldn't. She didn't deserve to. She was dirt. Worse than dirt. She was inconsiderate and insensitive and heartless.

She swallowed hard.

"That's...quite a story." Jack spoke like it took effort to squeeze out each word. "And you're right. It is awful."

"I know. It makes me about the lowest of the low." She blinked and wadded her shredded napkin into a ball.

"I didn't say that. You were really drunk, right?"

"Yeah."

"You made some bad choices, but you were also a victim."

She shut her eyes. It would be so easy to let him think that. To blame it all on Nick Whatever-His-Last-Name was.

But she couldn't.

"Not really," she said, in a thin, scared-little-kid voice that echoed in her head. She opened her eyes, but didn't look up. "There was a point where I saw what was happening. I knew what I was doing was wrong. And I didn't care. I went into—I don't know—catastrophe mode or something. Everything was ruined. It could never be fixed. And nothing mattered. I just wanted to feel better somehow. And I stupidly thought that this guy might help."

"Tess," Jack said quietly.

"No, a one-night stand was bad enough." The words poured out of her. "But he was married, and his wife was pregnant. What kind of effect did that night have on his wife? On their marriage? On their child's life? And I'll never even know. I don't even know his last name."

"He was the one with the marriage vows."

Her chest felt tight. A wall around it blocked Jack's understanding from reaching her heart.

But, little by little, it did.

Her shoulders sagged. "Thank you. You're very kind." She looked up at him. "Maybe we should, uh, talk about something else."

"Sure," Jack glanced around as if looking for a billboard that might suggest a topic. "Um, how was van shopping in Columbia?"

She took a deep breath and exhaled, trying to let the tightness subside from her body. "I saw one that isn't bad. But I'm really excited about one I found online in Kansas City. They emailed me a price, and it's way better than I expected. And it's silver."

His forehead wrinkled.

"Silver Platter Catering. Most commercial vans are white, and I can't afford to have the whole thing painted. If I find one that's silver and add a logo, it will look really good."

"That sounds ideal." He smiled, slow and easy, and that smile removed the last remains of the wall around her heart. It made her feel that, in spite of what she'd done, he didn't think she was worthless and despicable.

Somehow, after that smile, the rest of the meal flew by, as though she had never mentioned her past. Jack told her about the contest win that had launched his career and about how he needed a new project, a new challenge. He raved about the Peanut Butter Banana Split ice cream. She admitted that she'd made it and told him about her passion for creating gourmet ice cream flavors.

Eventually, they moved to the kitchen, working companionably to clean up.

And then, suddenly, she'd washed the last dish.

He hung up the dishtowel. "It's after ten. I guess I should head home."

She reluctantly led the way toward the front door. Except for her ugly confession, she'd enjoyed the evening.

In the hall, Jack took both her hands in one of his and, with his other hand, made an elaborate X over his heart. "This is me promising that the fact that you made one of the best meals I've ever eaten has nothing to do with what I'm about to say."

One of the best meals he'd ever eaten, and this was something she whipped up after being gone most of the day. He should try her cannelloni with homemade pasta, or her beef tenderloin medallions with red wine reduction sauce and oven-roasted root vegetables, or—

"Tess Palmer." Jack's voice was low. His fingers enclosed hers in warmth. "Your boyfriend at the bank was not only totally without class, he had no brains at all. You are an amazing woman. And"—he squeezed her hands—"the guy in the bar didn't change that."

She stared up at him.

"I mean it."

Her heart tingled. In spite of what she'd told him, it seemed that he liked her. And not in some tawdry way like the guy in the bar, but like he really cared, like he was solid and honest and sincere. Like he was a man she could trust.

He looked down at her, then gently slid his fingers up her arms, over her shoulders, and into the hair at the nape of her neck.

Her pulse sped. Hesitantly, she wrapped her arms around his waist.

He moved closer, until there were only inches between them.

Her breathing grew shallow and the air, thick.

He lowered his lips to hers and kissed her—slowly, as if he treasured her more than anything in the world.

Then he drew her body against his and held her.

Emotion rippled through her heart.

At last he stepped back, his hazel eyes filled with tenderness. "I should go," he said in a husky voice.

She nodded, unable to speak. Because for the first time in four years, she felt worth loving.

And because she'd dated her boyfriend at the bank for fourteen months—and never felt a connection like this.

# Chapter Twenty

The next morning Tess tucked cash in her back pocket and watched the used-furniture dealer drive toward Sunset Lake Lane. The sun cut through the trees and glinted off a mirror that had hung in Leticia's study and was now strapped in the back of the rusty truck.

Except for the couch, the dining room furniture and Leticia's china, all of which Tess had decided to move to her apartment, the house was almost empty. Even the TV was gone. No more watching cooking shows while she ate her meals on the couch. Today, according to her list, she'd work on items marked in teal gel pen—packing the dishes and small kitchen appliances for the resale store and making a couple of trips to Abby's shop to drop off the boxes of Avon decanters. She could ask Jack for help again, but she didn't want to pester him.

The sun climbed another degree higher and reflected off the lake in front of his house.

She stared at the door that led from his back deck to his living room and wished he'd step outside, even for a moment, so she could see him, see that it all wasn't just a dream. It felt like one. Or like a fairytale with Leticia as the fairy godmother. Had she meant all along for Tess to meet Jack? Was that why she'd hoped Tess would move her business to Abundance? So she could find love at Sunset Lake?

She wasn't moving Silver Platter. But she could consider a long-distance relationship, if she was brave enough.

Was she?

She went inside, sat on the couch, now dwarfed by the otherwise empty living room, and pushed her hair back over her shoulders. Could she risk a relationship? For a second, she closed her eyes and remembered the tender expression on his face after he'd kissed her.

Call her crazy, but she was not running away from a chance of a future with him. Long-distance relationships could work.

She opened her eyes. Now that she knew why the lake mattered to Jack, she had to talk to Stacey. Surely the collectibles could tide her over. Selling Leticia's property to a developer felt wrong.

Tess reached for her phone and dialed.

After three rings, Stacey picked up.

"Hey, Stacey, it's Tess. If I limit the sale of Leticia's house to only residential buyers, would I make a lot less money?"

"Well, if you want to do that, you'd have to add a deed restriction. The way things are now, a buyer can do anything they want to with the property. As your agent, I've got to tell you that this decision would not be in your best interest."

"A commercial developer would pay more."

"Not so much that," Stacey said. "You'd be ruling out a big chunk of potential buyers right off the bat. It may take you longer to sell. For a private residence in this area, the property is in the upper end of the market. I've done some research. Those houses sometimes sit for a year before they sell."

A year? That was a long time. Tess rubbed at a thin place in one knee of her jeans. What if the collectibles didn't sell? What if she couldn't afford to outfit the van and pay the tree trimmer and the property taxes?

She'd have to borrow against the house. More debt. Just thinking about it made her shoulders tighten.

"You know—" Stacey stopped short. She sounded strained.

The situation was probably hard for her too. A delayed sale for Tess meant a delayed commission for Stacey. She was probably counting on the money.

"Real estate aside," Stacey said, "as a friend, I'd say to do what you think is right. I know there's more than finances to consider in your decision."

Tess hadn't even thought about the small-town factor. Stacey was from Abundance. She'd probably heard all about Kaitlyn. "Thank you. You're right. There is more to think about than money."

"I don't know you very well, but I had an amazing boss, Delia, out in California. The wisest woman. She got me started going to church again. I'm still kind of finding my way, but I know Delia would tell you to pray about it."

Tess glanced at the deck, where Leticia had read her Bible. "Not really my thing anymore." Not for the past four years.

"At least think about it a day," Stacey said.

"Okay." Tess clicked off.

Her phone dinged with a text. Rose needed approval for some estimates.

An hour later, Tess set her laptop beside her on the couch and leaned back. Rose had done a great job. Delegation was working out better than Tess could have ever dreamed.

Her phone rang.

"Tess? Are you sitting down?" Stacey's words came out so fast that Tess almost couldn't understand them. "I can't believe it. After we talked, that guy who sells barbecue called and asked if the place was still available. He had an appointment for next week, but now he's coming tomorrow."

Tess's heart leapt. "Tomorrow?" If he made an offer, she could sell the house, plow plenty of money into her business to get it on solid footing, and have the lake stay the way it was when Kaitlyn was alive.

"At eight thirty. He's an early riser. You need to have that place looking perfect." Stacey started listing tasks Tess needed to accomplish.

"Hold on, let me write these down." She found her clipboard and a teal gel pen.

"This is it, Tess, I can feel it. Your house is going to sell. I'll talk to you after I email the client some more information. I tell you, you must have said some prayer."

Tess's chest tingled. She hadn't prayed at all. But maybe God was taking care of her anyway.

A couple of minutes later she pulled into Jack's driveway and dashed to his door.

He opened it, holding a paintbrush and wearing a splotched sweatshirt and ripped jeans. His hair was tousled, his eyes lit with an appreciative gleam.

Tess drew in a breath, then reminded herself why she drove over. "Stacey's got a client coming to see Leticia's house—and he wants to keep it the way it is."

"Really? That's great." He grinned so wide that the corners of his eyes crinkled.

"A guy from Kansas City who owns barbecue restaurants. She says he's really interested, wants a quiet place to retire."

"That would be perfect." He stepped back, inviting her in.

"Oh, I can't stay. I've got a list a mile long to do today. I just wanted to tell you. I should have called but…" But she'd wanted to see him again.

"Hey, thank you. It's wonderful news." He moved forward and touched her elbow. His gaze caught hers. "And wonderful to see you."

Warmth swirled through her. If she spoke, she'd babble. She forced herself to turn, give a little wave, and go to her car.

Everything could work out. The house could sell, her catering business could thrive, and her relationship with

Jack—a relationship that he seemed to want as much as she did—could grow.

She really could have it all.

☙

Jack couldn't remember the last time he was so happy.

He finished his work on a tail feather, set down his brush, and drank the last of his coffee. Then he looked out the window of his study.

At the edge of the water, sunlight filtered down through the trees in bursts of gold that shimmered on the surface. Canada geese swam in the middle of the lake. Closer, in the quiet cove by his house, a family of wood ducks sunned themselves—Mama, Papa, and at least a dozen ducklings. And though he couldn't see them, his favorite family of wood ducks was probably soaking up the sun at the north end of the lake.

Right where he'd first kissed Tess.

The woman had delighted him. And surprised him.

Kind. Capable of appreciating what the lake—and Kaitlyn—meant to him. Easy to be with. An amazing cook. Gorgeous.

Definitely gorgeous. Those blue-gray eyes, that flawless skin—how could he not have kissed her last night? Any man would have wanted to kiss her.

And would want to do it again.

But what about the things she'd told him? The one-night stand? He stared across the water and saw her climb the steps to Leticia's house and go inside. He'd meant what he said. She was an amazing woman. And she shouldn't be beating herself up for something that happened four years ago, especially something that wasn't completely her fault. But that poor pregnant woman on the other end of the phone...

He leaned back and studied the painting on his easel. It had flaws, things he would fix in the weeks ahead. And people had flaws too...and made mistakes. He certainly had. Yes, Tess had made bad decisions under stress. But if he wanted a future with her, he needed to forget about her past. Besides, if she was still miserable about that one-night stand four years later, it wasn't something she'd repeat.

Not like his wife, who had an affair that went on for two years and who had only cared about her own happiness—

He let out a long breath.

Actually, Chloe hadn't seemed very happy at the end, not even times when he'd been pretty sure she was on her way to see her lover. Had she regretted her choices?

He glanced at his palette and picked up a tube of Burnt Umber.

Should he have made more of an effort to save his marriage instead of just being angry?

Frankly, he liked blaming every bit of what happened on her. Because...

The paint shifted inside the tube.

He looked down at his hands. He'd squeezed the tube so hard that he was lucky it hadn't burst.

Okay, he'd admit it. He knew why he liked blaming Chloe for everything that had gone wrong. Because he hadn't wanted any responsibility for Kaitlyn's death.

He set the tube down.

Was her death his fault? In any way?

His chest tightened. He crossed his arms and forced himself to relive that day. After a moment, he exhaled.

He wasn't responsible. He hadn't been the one who drove off with Kaitlyn in the car. And he hadn't fought with Chloe that morning, hadn't done anything to prompt her to leave. But the trooper had said the trucker caused the wreck, that Chloe couldn't have avoided it.

Kaitlyn's death wasn't his fault—or Chloe's.

Bit by bit, his chest eased. The wreck was simply an accident. And Chloe's affair had been wrong. But he should have worked harder at his marriage. And like Tess, Chloe deserved understanding. Maybe it was time to give that understanding, that forgiveness, and move on.

After a moment, across the water over at Leticia's, Tess came back outside and began sweeping the front porch.

Maybe he'd been wrong to give up on women and think God was always against him.

There was no reason he couldn't kiss Tess again. No reason they couldn't see each other. St. Louis wasn't that far away.

A tingly feeling spread over his shoulders and down his arms. Feeling a little dazed, he walked toward the kitchen to get more coffee.

But as he passed through the living room, the house darkened. He went out on his deck and looked at the sky. No rain, but a mass of storm clouds was piling up in the southwest.

He put his mug on the coffee table, opened the garage door, and dashed back out to bring in his empty trashcan from the end of the driveway. Already the wind had started to pick up. And he'd planned to work outside this afternoon. Not happening. He'd be back in his study, at his easel. Good thing he had a Plan B. Life was full of curve balls.

Like...

Like what if that barbecue guy wasn't interested in Leticia's property?

He rolled the trashcan in front of his SUV, came back inside, and shut the garage door. He refilled his coffee and sat on his couch, still thinking about what could happen.

If the barbecue guy didn't buy the house, Tess might feel she had to sell to a developer. Her business might not succeed without an influx of cash. If a hotel was built at Sunset Lake, he'd be miserable. But if she had an offer and rejected it because of him, then lost her business, she'd be miserable. Either way, the two of them wouldn't have a chance. The obstacle was too big for a relationship just starting out.

He took a drink of coffee. Logically, his "relationship" with Tess shouldn't matter. But he felt a connection to her, way more of a connection than made sense. Crazy.

And the only Plan B for them, the only way he could ensure that things would work out, was if he bought Leticia's place himself, as Earl Ray had suggested.

He looked up at *Ring-Necked Ducks in Flight* on the mantle. Maybe it *had* gone up in value. He'd become fairly successful these past few years. And even when he'd first painted it, it had won that small contest. And maybe there was a way to get a smaller loan, just until his current painting sold. With what he had in savings, the proceeds from his current work and *Ring-Necked Ducks in Flight* might be enough.

What would it hurt to talk to Mort? If the barbecue guy bought Leticia's place, Jack could keep the painting. If not, and if it could bring in enough, he'd sell it.

He had to protect the lake.

And, crazy as it seemed, he had to protect his relationship with Tess.

# Chapter Twenty-one

The curly fries sat in a waxed paper bag on Stacey's desk, all too sure of their power.

She glared at the bag. Those fries, and the fact that she'd made a trip out of her office to get them as soon as Whole Hog Barbecue opened, were Earl Ray's fault.

Thanks to her ex and the drive-thru window at the barbecue place, her favorite jeans wouldn't zip.

If only she could get over him. She hadn't seen him for days and had been reduced to driving around town, hoping to see his truck, like she'd done when she was sixteen.

She reached for the fries. Time for some changes.

Big changes.

For a moment, her hand hovered over the bag. She could always eat the fries first, then start eating better. A viable option. No need to rush into things.

The blend of spices and grease wafted toward her through the air, a guarantee of yumminess. Even after the drive across town, the fry on top looked especially crispy.

She inhaled. Maybe she should just eat that one fry. She'd paid good money for them.

No!

She grabbed the bag, smashed it between her hands, and slammed it into the trash. Things were changing.

Her diet, her business, and her fixation on Earl Ray.

No more fries. No more worrying about what her ex would think if she sold Leticia's house to a developer. This was her career. And no more pretending she was looking for clients when she was really looking for Earl Ray.

Time to get down to basics.

According to her class, she needed to make a dozen contacts every day if she wanted to keep listings rolling in. Those contacts were good in theory, but she'd been avoiding them.

She added a handful of business cards to her purse, stood, and brushed some lint off the hem of her long, coral-colored cardigan. Not everyone in Abundance knew her from high school. She'd ignore the rain, introduce herself at every business in town, find something positive to say about each place, and ask people to keep her in mind if they needed a real estate agent.

If one of those business people happened to be a handsome, single man who asked her out, she'd accept.

An hour later, she'd visited five businesses. None of the encounters had seemed that promising, but they hadn't killed her. She pulled into the lot of the new car dealership, checked her lipstick, then popped open her umbrella and headed for the door.

At first, everyone seemed busy with customers, so she admired a shiny red sports car parked in the showroom, even opened the door a crack to caress the leather seats and drink in the new-car smell.

"Hi there. Want to take her for a spin?" A young guy in twill pants and a blue polo approached. His mouth quirked up on one side as if he knew the line was corny.

She shut the car door. "I'd love to, but I'm not really shopping." Not yet. After the showing tomorrow—maybe. Today she needed to stay on task. She pulled out a business card, introduced herself, and explained the reason for her visit.

The salesman, Brad, took the card. "My sister might be moving out of town. If she does, I'll give her your name."

Stacey beamed at him. She'd done it! Found a potential listing. "Thank you."

"You know, beautiful women don't come in here every day." He motioned to the door and led her out toward the rows of shiny new vehicles. The rain, at least for the moment, had let up. "Would you be interested in dinner tonight?"

Her stomach tensed, and she ran a hand across the hem of her sweater. Exactly what she'd told herself she wanted. Although she hadn't expected to get asked out by someone she'd only known a few minutes. Here, though, among all the fancy cars, something new looked good. New might help her forget Earl Ray.

Brad gave her a melt-your-heart grin. "We could go to Whole Hog," he said, as if he somehow knew how much she loved their fries.

He was cute. Dark hair, dark eyes, and muscular arms. He gave a vibe that said reliable, said he paid his bills on time, mowed his elderly neighbor's yard, and thought rebellion was ordering root beer instead of Diet Coke.

And he looked about ten years younger than her.

She pulled her cardigan tighter around her. What was she waiting for? "That would be real nice," she said with a nervous smile.

�❧

This time tomorrow her life could be golden.

Tess set down the sweeper at the top of the stairs and rolled it into the larger bedroom, now cleared of boxes and trash and dead rodents. Her lunch break was over, and it was time to get that fuzz off the baseboards.

All she needed to do was finish the items on Stacey's list and make sure the house sparkled. The place could sell, she'd have plenty of cash to invest in her business, and nothing would stand in the way of a relationship with Jack.

Her phone dinged with a text and she pulled it from her back pocket.

I need to talk to you. I've taken a position with Head Chef Catering.

She re-read the text.

Very funny. Rose would never quit. Especially not for Head Chef. Their food was so boring, it was one notch above trays from the grocery store.

She dialed Rose.

"Hey, Tess, thanks for calling. Listen, I'm really sorry to give you such short notice, but I got the most amazing offer."

Rose was playing it really well, with exactly the right apologetic tone.

"Very funny," Tess said. "I know you'd never work for Head Chef. But you're late. It's been a while since April Fool's."

Rose didn't answer.

Tess's heartbeat grew slow and erratic. "You're kidding, right?"

"I'm not." Rose's words were faint, as though her phone had suddenly gone out of range.

Numbness started inside Tess's ears and spread through her brain. She must have heard wrong. "But Head Chef is the opposite of everything we believe about food. Their menu reads like it came from 1974. You said that yourself."

"They offered me a nine-to-five position. Twenty percent more than you're paying, even with the raise as temporary assistant manager."

Tess staggered into the hall, clutched the rail, and lowered herself onto the top stair with a thump.

"I can be home with Charlie every evening and put him in regular day care. Mom's getting older and having trouble with her hip and—" Rose broke off, crying.

"Don't cry. It's okay." For a few seconds, guilt overpowered Tess's panic. "I, um, I understand."

But she didn't. Rose wasn't only her employee. She was her friend. How could she leave, right when Silver Platter could really take off?

"I feel terrible. But it's such a good offer."

Tess swallowed hard. Even if Leticia's house sold tomorrow, even if Silver Platter was on the cusp of huge success, Tess was a long way from being able to guarantee Rose evenings off. She had to be a grownup about this. "It's a great offer. You have to think of Charlie. You have to take it. Con—" Her voice caught. "Congratulations."

She could handle this, really. Rose wouldn't be easy to replace, but Tess could find someone.

"I haven't told you the worst part," Rose said. "They offered me a twenty-five-hundred-dollar bonus if I could start tomorrow."

Tess's heart stopped. "Tomorrow?" No.

No. No. No. No. NO!

"I'm really sorry. I didn't want to say yes, but after Charlie was in the hospital, I've got nothing in savings and…"

Tess's heart was beating again, faster, making up for lost time. Rose had told them yes. She was leaving, with no notice. "I see."

"About the meeting with the potential client tomorrow…"

Oh, yeah, the meeting. She could postpone it, but it was the first of Madeleine's friends. And if the lake property didn't sell, she needed the business.

Tess gripped the edge of the wooden stair. Something solid. Something that wouldn't drop out from under her. She tried to think. "I'll drive in and take the meeting. I only need to do a couple of things before I leave." A couple dozen, but who was counting.

Rose let out a sob. "You're the best boss. I can't believe I'm leaving you."

"I can't believe it either."

"O—Okay," Rose said. "I'm going to hang up now, because I'm crying all over the counter, and I'm going to prep everything I possibly can for Monday."

"Thank you," Tess said. She wanted to snatch her words back, beg Rose not to leave, but she didn't. Because Rose's mind was made up.

There was a click and then silence.

Tess stared at the phone. How could Rose do this to her? After all she'd taught her? After she'd given her a raise? After they'd been friends?

At least, Tess had thought they were friends.

She'd been wrong. Nobody did this to a friend.

She'd also thought that tomorrow her life would be golden.

Wrong again.

ᖍ

Jack called three times before Mort returned from lunch. But when he finally got through, the gallery owner was thrilled to put feelers out about *Ring-Necked Ducks in Flight*. Jack was pretty sure the man had figured his possible commission by the time Jack finished his first sentence. And a bit rankled to learn that Mort had taken several photos of the painting five years ago when he stopped by the house after Kaitlyn's funeral. "Just in case," Mort had said. It sounded downright crass but did seem beneficial now.

Jack had barely hung up when his phone rang. Probably another question.

He answered and pulled a plastic tub of leftovers out of the fridge.

"Jack? Scott Albright, remember? From St. Louis?"

Jack paused, switched gears, and remembered the conservation agent he'd once met. "Scott, hi." Jack dumped the contents of the plastic tub—a mushy mess that might once have been slaw—into the trash, gave up on leftovers, and pulled out a can of soup.

"You know how you asked me to let you know if I ever saw anything unusual that you might want to paint? Well, I was out at the Marais Temps Clair Conservation Area the other day."

A flicker of interest shot through Jack. "What'd you see?" He poured the soup in a bowl and shoved it in the microwave.

"I probably shouldn't have called. You might not be interested. It's not a duck, and they're really hard to see."

"What was it?"

"A king rail. You know, that kind of secretive marsh bird about the size of a chicken? A guy I work with says there's a pair at the conservation area, but I've only seen one."

"Really? Those are rare in Missouri." A painting of a king rail would be a great addition to his body of work. Jack looked out the window, then checked the clock. The storm clouds had broken up and scattered. He could be in the St. Louis area by four. And maybe he wasn't a diehard birder, but he was up for a challenge. Rails weren't as showy as ducks or geese, and the work might not appeal to hunters. Still, he'd never painted the species and he was pretty sure there would be a market for the work.

"I tried to get a photo," Scott said. "But I wasn't fast enough. Probably wouldn't have been a good shot anyway. Even with my new phone, the camera's not made for wildlife photography."

Jack's new lens was attached to his camera, packed and ready to go on the coffee table in the living room. "I'll drive up this afternoon. If I get any good images, I'll share them."

"Have you been to Marais Temps?"

"I mostly stay up in the northwest part of the state," he said, trying to be polite. Frankly, he couldn't imagine many waterfowl hanging out that close to St. Louis, no matter what people had told him.

"It's a big place. You'll need a lot of luck. And you'll have to listen for the rail. Kind of a *kek-kek-kek* call. Hope you spot it."

"Thanks." Jack hung up. A minute later he was shoveling down his lunch and planning his route using an app on his phone.

He finished his soup and dumped his dishes in the sink.

Scott was right. Photographing a rail would take luck. And patience.

The chance that he'd see it was incredibly low. But if he did happen to, and if he got some good shots, it might be just the new project he needed.

ʚɞ

Tomorrow, except for the waiters and waitresses Tess hired by the job, Silver Platter would rest on her shoulders alone.

She leaned her hips against the counter and stared at the tile floor of Leticia's kitchen.

The van's needing repair, then dying. Rose's leaving without notice... Problems seemed to mount faster than Tess could deal with them. Probably why she was still barely making ends meet after four years of business. And what if pouring money from the sale of Leticia's house into Silver Platter was just throwing it away? What if she was kidding herself and Silver Platter would never be a success?

Her head swam and her breath grew shallow. Her blood felt as if it was shooting through her veins at double speed. She never should have gone into catering. It had been a knee-jerk decision four years ago, a way to avoid those awkward questions in a job interview like "why did you leave your position at the bank?" No, back then she should have gotten a normal job, one with a steady paycheck. Now the whole situation was a disaster, and it was all her fault. Probably, she should close Silver Platter and do something sensible like working in an office and getting an online degree in accounting. Mom had suggested that once. She could—

Hold on. Talk about a knee-jerk reaction.

Tess walked into the living room, sat on the couch, and took deep breaths. She had to stop. This was the same my-life-is-a-disaster thinking that had gotten her into even bigger trouble after she lost her job at the bank. And she had a pretty good idea that once she was thinking clearly, she'd see that accounting was not for her. Wasn't doing the books for Silver Platter her least favorite part of the job—even the months she made a profit?

No, now was not the time for rash decisions. Today she'd deal with losing Rose. She'd been fine working alone that first year.

She twisted her mouth to one side. Well, maybe three years ago she'd been even more stressed and overworked and lonely, but she'd survived. She'd survive again, especially if she had money from the sale of Leticia's house to help her business. She could do this—prioritize and take things one task at a time.

Tomorrow morning at eight, Rose had been supposed to meet with a potential new client. And Stacey was bringing the potential buyer—the person who could solve all of Tess's financial problems and keep the lake as Jack wanted it—tomorrow at eight thirty.

Which meant she had to do the world's fastest cleaning to get the house ready for showing, then hit the road.

Working as though she was being chased, she vacuumed baseboards, cleaned the windows to the deck, and gave the whole place a spritz with vanilla air freshener. But air freshener alone couldn't handle the upstairs bath, where she'd put Indy's litter box. She opened the window as wide as it would go and gave the room a double spritz of vanilla.

Once the cleaning was completed, Tess loaded Indy into her car and drove to Jack's to say goodbye. But he wasn't there, and he didn't answer when she called his cell.

She dug a pen and paper out of her purse and scribbled a note. "Hey, it's Tess. I had to run back to St. Louis. If it rains, could you get the key from under the red flowerpot and close the window in the upstairs bathroom? Stacey's showing the house tomorrow morning at 8:30, and I'd hate for the floor to be wet."

She stuck one corner of the note under the rubber doormat by his back door.

There. He'd be sure to see it.

For the first time since she'd talked to Rose, her pulse began to slow. She wasn't totally alone.

She had Jack.

# Chapter Twenty-two

The GPS was useless.

Jack turned into a long, narrow driveway and parked by the road. He jabbed at his phone, shut off the annoying voice of the navigation system, and pulled a state map from his glove box.

There. That was the road he needed to be on. The GPS had taken him right by the Marais Temps Clair Conservation Area—but on the wrong road, a road that had no access. He turned around and headed back the way he'd come.

He passed a house built on a mound of earth about three feet higher than the yard.

Smart. The land here was so flat it made Kansas seem hilly, one enormous floodplain in a narrow V of land between the Missouri River and the Mississippi, right before they merged.

Except for the roar of a jet's passing overhead, he'd never have guessed he was near St. Louis. Farms stretched out on either side of the road, and the warm spring air blowing in the open windows smelled like Sunset Lake.

A mile ahead he rounded a curve and pulled into a small parking lot for the conservation area. He grabbed his backpack, stuffed with his camera, binoculars, sketchpad, and a detailed map of the property that he'd printed at home off the Department of Natural Resources website.

He followed a path past one shallow pool of water, then another. At the fourth pool, a great blue heron balanced on one leg on the opposite shore. High above, an egret soared. His heart sped, and he returned to his SUV to get a folding chair.

He hiked along the path, consulted the map from time to time, and listened.

Two more blue herons flew past. Then another. Then three more. There must be a colony. Jack hiked another twenty feet, unfolded his chair, and set his sketchpad on it. He took a series of photos of the herons, growing more and more impressed with his new camera lens, then sat down.

He heard what he thought was an American bittern but couldn't spot it.

Half an hour passed. He shifted his weight in the folding chair and thought about dinner, wondered if he should try another spot.

*Kek-kek-kek.*

The call echoed over the water.

Jack sat up, his whole body on alert, and scanned the shore.

Nothing. At least nothing visible.

He pulled his phone from his pocket, opened his birding app, and played a recording of the call of a king rail to be sure. Yes. Exactly what he'd heard.

He focused the camera on the shore, then rotated his head a fraction of an inch at a time, barely blinking.

*Kek-kek-kek-kek-kek.*

Reeds swayed. And then a king rail moved out into the open and dipped its long bill into the water. Adrenaline zipped through Jack's veins and he visualized himself painting the bird's white throat, rusty-brown breast, and darker back. He fired off dozens of pictures, zooming in close with the new lens.

A flock of Canada geese flew past and honked raucously. As quickly as it had appeared, the king rail was gone.

Jack sat immobile, peering at the reeds.

The bird didn't return.

But he'd spotted it, gotten lots of photos, basically done the impossible and found the proverbial needle in a conservation area. Talk about good luck. He flipped through his photos, zooming in on some to see detail. The new lens was amazing. He pulled out his phone to call Tess and tell her about his day.

The phone battery was dead. Great. So much for being connected to the rest of the world. He probably should have told Tess—or someone—where he was going.

He shoved the phone back in his pocket and clicked through the images on his camera again.

No. No. No.

Yes. This one.

Ideas swirled in his mind. Before they slipped away, he needed to get them down. He settled back in his folding chair, picked up his sketchbook, and began planning a new project featuring a king rail.

CB

Stacey was not nervous.

She checked the mirror in her office bathroom, fluffed her hair, and added a bit more concealer under her eyes. Then she smoothed her coral cardigan. Not too bad. She could have run home to change, but that would have been trying too hard.

She'd been on plenty of dates before. With a few decent guys in California and, of course, with Earl Ray.

But not with a guy ten years younger.

What if they had nothing to talk about?

She found lip gloss in the bottom of her purse, put some on, and studied the effect. Too girlish. And too sticky. She wiped it off and redid her lipstick.

What if Earl Ray heard about her date?

This was Abundance. He'd hear. And Earl Ray did have a jealous streak.

She watched a smile spread across her face and quickly frowned. That seemed like she was using Brad. Really, she wasn't. This wasn't about getting Earl Ray back. She needed to accept that and make a life in Abundance without him. Brad seemed nice. And women did tend to outlive men, so a younger man might be a great idea. And talk about a cutie!

She gave her hair a final fluff and slid her purse on her shoulder. If she didn't hurry, she'd be late.

Across town, she pulled into a parking spot in the big gravel lot at Whole Hog. Three spots over, Brad climbed out of a red truck. A red Ford truck.

Nerves kicked to high alert in her stomach. Brad worked for a Ford dealership. And lots of people drove red Ford trucks. No reason to think about Earl Ray.

She got out and Brad waved.

His glasses were almost the same shape as Earl Ray's. She hadn't noticed that before.

Brad walked up beside her, and she smelled his aftershave.

She stopped.

He hadn't worn aftershave at the dealership, hadn't smelled like Earl Ray.

Hadn't sent her mind rocketing back through bonfires and hayrides and school dances with her husband.

Uh, ex-husband.

"Stacey?" Brad touched her arm.

She pulled back, ever so slightly. She couldn't do this, couldn't date someone else in Abundance, couldn't give up her dreams of Earl Ray.

"Are you all right?"

"Not really." Her voice shook. "You're a great guy, Brad, and I'm flattered that you asked me to dinner but…" Her chest felt like it was caving in.

"It's okay," he said in that tone a man uses when he doesn't want a woman to make a scene.

"I can't go out with you. I'm sorry. You're a good guy." She patted his arm and brushed the air near his cheek with a kiss.

His eyes searched her face for an explanation, and he angled his head to one side.

"I'm still in love with my ex-husband. I just figured out right this second that it's never going to change. I'm sorry I wasted your time." She spoke the words quickly, then turned away.

"Hey." Brad put a hand lightly on her shoulder.

She glanced back at him.

"Your ex is a lucky guy. If you ever get past this, call me." He gave her a look like he might give a customer whose credit got denied. "And I'll give my sister your card."

She blinked at the tears welling in her eyes. "Thank you."

Three people came out of the restaurant. They saw her and stopped talking.

Stacey sped toward her car.

Ten minutes later, she pulled away from the drive-thru at the mega-chain hamburger franchise and pawed through the bag on the console.

Fries. Not the glorious curly fries of Whole Hog—she couldn't go back there tonight—but fries all the same.

# Chapter Twenty-three

Talk about depressing.

Earl Ray tossed a box of pasta in his shopping cart. He hated eating alone, hated shopping alone, hated that he'd be going to his house alone. With Stacey back in town, everything he did felt alone.

If they were together, he'd pick out some rib-eye steaks, some of those frozen twice-baked potatoes with lots of butter and cheddar cheese, one of those bag salads, and that crumbled blue cheese she loved.

In that perfect world, the steak and cheese would sit just fine in his stomach.

In reality, he'd eat noodles, with a drop or two of olive oil to keep them from becoming a gooey glob, and even then his gut would act up. He'd even broken down and called his doctor for an appointment, faced the fact that he probably had stomach cancer. His life was just peachy.

Despite the fact that his shopping cart needed a front-end alignment, he managed to steer it over to Aisle 13 for toothpaste and more antacid. Then he needed a couple more things to refill his fridge, had to run by Jack's, and he could go home.

He rubbed a hand along his jaw. Those papers about the Brawley auction better be at Jack's. They hadn't been at his house yesterday morning, and they weren't in his luggage or his truck. He'd looked three times.

Earl Ray dropped a bottle of antacid in his cart and rounded the end of the aisle into frozen food.

The fluorescent light flickered overhead.

A redhead who worked over in city hall held the door to the frozen vegetables open and pursed her lips at the selection as cold air poured out.

He hurried past.

"Hi, Earl Ray." The redhead—Jenna or Jenae or some such name—strolled toward him, noisily chewing gum.

"Oh, hi. Just got back in town and needed a few things," he said. "Can't wait to get home." That pretty much said he didn't want to chat, right?

"Have you heard the latest?" She darted ahead of him and parked her cart diagonally in front of the frozen waffles, blocking his path. "I saw George Gilcroft at the drug store, and he told me Stacey's showing Leticia Palmer's house to some big developer from St. Louis. Wouldn't that be something, if we got some fancy boutique hotel here in Abundance?"

Earl Ray backed his cart up, ready to swerve around her. He had no intention of discussing a hotel at Sunset Lake. Or discussing Stacey.

"Oh, I'm sorry. I guess I shouldn't have mentioned Stacey, not after today," the redhead said and snapped her gum.

"Today?" Earl Ray stopped. Her words didn't have a drop of sympathy in them. Just a note that sent a tremor of dread through him.

"I guess you haven't heard." A look of malicious joy flashed in her eyes, then she rearranged her face into sympathy. "I hate to be the one to tell you, but your ex was kissing that car salesman Brad from the Ford dealership outside Whole Hog Barbecue."

Earl Ray couldn't move, couldn't breathe. A lump had formed halfway down his throat. No air in. No air out.

He knew Stacey had dated out in California. Nearly wrecked his truck the day he saw a picture of her and some guy on Facebook.

But she didn't need to be kissing some other man, especially not one right here in Abundance.

"I figured you'd want to know." The redhead oozed counterfeit compassion.

What he wanted was to shove his cart right through the freezer. But Stacey would hear about that. Probably in graphic detail.

He coughed, worked air past the lump in his throat, and choked out a hollow laugh. "No big deal. We've been divorced, what? Fifteen years." He pushed his cart away in a leisurely fashion and then tossed in a box of frozen breakfast sandwiches, something he never ate.

Once he made it into the next aisle, pet food, where no one was in sight, he barreled toward the self-checkout, correcting the course of the cart every few feet to make up for the wonky wheels. He could come back tomorrow for the rest of his groceries.

Food didn't matter tonight.

Any appetite he'd had was gone.

CB

Although it was after seven, Stacey didn't want to go home, didn't want to explain her puffy face and red eyes to Dad. She sat in her office with only the desk lamp burning, ignored the musty smell of the carpet, and crossed her arms tightly, trying to squeeze the ache out of her chest.

It didn't help. The fries she'd eaten didn't help. Even feeling useful at her job—running out to Leticia's to close the bathroom window after she got a frantic text from Tess—didn't help. Neither did the fact that, except for the window, Tess had done a great job getting the house ready to show.

Stacey shut her eyes and leaned on the desk. Once again she'd gone back to thinking she could handle everything on her own. Instead, she'd made a disaster of her life.

Back in California, when Delia took her to church, Stacey had heard a sermon series about turning every issue in life over to God and handling them as he led. Pretty much the antithesis of how she'd lived in high school and those first several years in California, when she'd thought she was in complete control of her life. These past few years, she'd tried to follow the advice in the sermon, but her progress had been shaky. She'd do all right for a day or two, then practically forget about God for three days, offering only rote prayers and skimming her Bible study in a hurry to get to her own solutions for her problems.

And since she'd come back to Abundance, she'd been so busy thinking about achieving her dreams, she'd forgotten about God. Once again she'd "fixed" things all on her own, without thinking about what God would have her do, without even praying about them. Had she taken the most ethical route and told Tess about her conflict of interest regarding Leticia's house? No, she'd followed the letter of the rules about conflict of interest that she'd learned in her real estate classes and ignored the feeling in her gut that told her she should discuss this with Tess.

Had she tried to make things up to people she'd hurt back in high school, like Louise Chambers? No, she'd simply viewed Louise as a tool to use to succeed in business. Definitely not a Christian mindset.

Had she apologized to Earl Ray for the way she left him, for abandoning their marriage? No, she'd tried to win his heart by flirting, never addressing the real problem. Even without praying, she had a feeling that wasn't how God would have her handle things.

And then, worst of all, she'd come up with her brilliant plan to find a new man. Look how well that had turned out.

Sometimes she wasn't any more mature as a Christian than she had been in high school. And back then, well, she'd been saved, but she hadn't been living it, hadn't been listening to God at all.

But he'd forgiven her. And he'd get her through this, if she'd just let him lead.

She shoved back her laptop, rested her elbows on the desk, bowed her head against her clasped hands, and began to pray.

*God, you know how much I want to get back together with Earl Ray. And I really believe I have to sell Leticia's house tomorrow for that to happen. Because if Bud doesn't buy the house, I think eventually Tess will sell to whoever will buy, and that will be a developer. And the sale will upset Jack and create an even bigger wedge between me and Earl Ray.*

A tear slipped down her cheek.

*At least that's how it seems to me. But you know more than I do, God. I'm sorry I thought I had the answers, sorry I didn't seek your guidance on Earl Ray or on anything else here in Abundance. I struggle so hard to trust you, but I'm going to try—really, really hard—to turn this over to you every morning. More often if needed.*

*Every time I seem to grab my problems back and start worrying. Every time I think I have to handle them on my own. Help me not to do it again.*

*Thank you, Lord, for loving me, in spite of all my failings.*

*Amen.*

Another tear ran down her cheek, and she raised her head. She felt better. If she was meant to be with Earl Ray, God would take care of it.

She would look over her research on the barbecue guy and the property one more time, then prepare for the showing just like any other, the way she'd learned in her class.

And she would trust.

03

Earl Ray climbed in his truck, set his groceries on the front passenger seat, and took a couple of slow breaths to steady himself.

They didn't help.

His Stacey. With some car salesman.

He gunned the engine and headed toward Jack's.

That moment when he'd met Stacey outside the diner, before his stomach acted up, he should have pulled her to him and kissed her senseless, made her forget she'd ever left him.

He took a glimpse in the rearview mirror.

There was gray hair in his goatee. His hairline had receded another quarter inch.

Old was bad enough.

But his skin was pale, and he had dark circles under his eyes that hadn't been there yesterday.

One glance and Stacey would know he was sick. All he could do was go home. But first he needed those papers.

He floored the gas and streaked through downtown at highway speed. On the county road toward Sunset Lake, the fence posts in the roadside fields passed in a blur.

He tore up Jack's driveway, gravel flying, and slammed on the brakes just in time to avoid hitting the 50-gallon drum of duck-poop tea on one side of the drive.

He shot a disgusted look at the swill and pounded on the back door. "Jack."

No answer.

Earl Ray sorted through his keys and let himself in.

Even compared to his house, the place was a sty—an empty soup can and drips of soup on the counter, dirty dishes in the sink, and a hint of something rotting in the trash.

But no sign as to where Jack might be.

Earl Ray sent him a text and started searching for his auction papers. After five minutes, he found them buried under the sports pages on the coffee table.

No reply from Jack.

He shrugged and went out the back door. A big drop of rain hit him in the head and thunder rumbled off to the west.

There, tucked under the edge of the mat, was a piece of paper.

He checked the sky, then picked up the paper and read it.

"Hey, it's Tess. I had to run back to St. Louis."

Earl Ray frowned.

The note continued. "If it rains, could you get the key from under the red flowerpot and close the window in the upstairs bathroom? Stacey's showing the house tomorrow morning at 8:30 and I'd hate for the floor to be wet."

Heat rose in Earl Ray's chest. The nerve of the woman. How could she possibly expect Jack to help her sell her house, expect him to welcome a hotel with open arms?

Because she was one more selfish woman, only thinking of herself.

Selfish. Like a woman who would leave a man, rip his heart in two, then move back to town to rub his nose in his loss.

A drop of rain hit his glasses, and he wadded the note in a tight ball and shoved it in his pocket. Whenever Jack got home, it would be too late to worry about windows. Besides, what Jack really needed to do was to stop that showing.

Earl Ray was more than willing to help.

A successful showing wouldn't simply mean a hotel at Sunset Lake. It would mean a big commission for Stacey. And once she was rolling in money, she'd be even more attractive to that car dealer. He knew how those guys thought.

Envisioning his wife—uh, ex-wife—eating a meal with some jerk and batting those gorgeous brown eyes at him was bad enough. Earl Ray couldn't even let himself imagine the rest of the date, the fact that at this very minute, they might be cuddled up, watching a movie. They might be saying goodnight on her doorstep and kissing—

His heart pounded and his hands curled into fists.

Head down, he strode toward his truck. Stopping that house showing would be good for all involved.

He'd text Jack again. There had to be a way.

His gaze slid past the 50-gallon plastic drum.

Doubled back.

And stayed.

CR

The light of day was fading at the conservation area.

A chorus of frogs filled the air. In a few minutes the last rays of the sun would slip away, and the sky would grow deeper and deeper blue.

Jack shouldered his backpack, folded his chair, and threaded his way down the path through the shadows.

By the time he got in his vehicle, it was dark. Probably after eight. No wonder he was hungry. Once he'd seen the king rail, he'd forgotten all about food. Forgotten everything but the new project.

Now dinner was priority one. He'd drive through some fast-food place and be home by midnight.

He turned the key in the ignition.

The SUV made an all-too-familiar *uh-errrrr*.

What now? He'd just had the battery replaced a month ago.

And his phone was dead. So much for his luck today.

He climbed out, slammed the door shut, and glared at his SUV. Great, just great. Now he'd have to walk someplace and ask to borrow a phone.

Two hours later, after a hike to a nearby house, a call to AAA, and a lengthy wait for a wrecker, he watched the tow truck pull out of the hotel parking lot. The guy had driven him through a burger place and dropped him at a hotel that he assured him was decent but cheap. And said he'd work on the SUV in the morning.

Jack shoved the last of his greasy burger in his mouth and crimped down the top of the bag to keep the remaining fries hot while he checked in. As soon as he got a room, he'd call Tess—

No. It had to be almost eleven. She was probably asleep.

He'd call in the morning. He reached in his pocket for his phone and remembered it was dead.

He spun to look back toward the parking lot, where the tow truck had been only a moment ago, and shook his head.

Probably just as well he was waiting until tomorrow to call. He didn't want to pay hotel long-distance rates.

And his phone charger was still in the SUV, on its way to the garage.

What a day.

# Chapter Twenty-four

At 8 a.m. on the dot, Earl Ray pulled into Jack's driveway.

Half an hour until Stacey would show Leticia's house. Thirty minutes to get ready.

He sent a hurried text to Jack.

Where are you? Call me now!

No response.

Should he wait until he heard back? Call off the plans?

No, that redhead had said Stacey would be showing the house to a developer. If Earl Ray wanted to help Jack, he needed to protect Sunset Lake.

He tucked the phone inside his jacket pocket and climbed out.

He picked up the 50-gallon barrel that held the mixture of duck poop and water. Luckily, it wasn't very full. Awkward, but not that heavy. He carried it to Jack's back deck and scooted it right up against the rail, with the spigot at the base pointed out toward the yard. Then he pulled on rubber gloves, took a gulp of fresh air, and removed the lid.

He bent to set the lid down and pain sliced through his gut. Without thinking, he inhaled deeply and drew in the stench.

Ewww. Talk about disgusting.

The things he did for family.

But he was not wimping out. Even if he was surrounded by the stink of duck poop and crippled with pain because he'd been stupid enough to eat one of those greasy breakfast sandwiches early this morning, he would manage. He used his key to let himself into Jack's garage, found a shovel, and used it to stir the swill in the barrel. Green scum from the surface mixed with sediment that swirled up from the bottom. Top-quality fertilizer to be sure.

And top-quality ammo.

He felt a grin tease the corners of his mouth.

A white pickup with an extended cab pulled into the drive. About time.

"Hey." Jim, one of his high school buddies from their garage band, climbed out, dressed in a faded red sweatshirt and jeans, looking as scruffy as ever.

"Jim, buddy." Earl Ray gave a quick wave, then walked down the deck stairs and over beside the base of the water barrel. He tried the spigot. A stream of the murky mixture ran out.

A warm breeze blew the smell of the foul brew back toward him, and his stomach twisted.

Was it his imagination, or were the pains in his gut getting worse?

Nah, it was probably the stench.

"What are you doing?" Jim's words held a note of disbelief as he came closer and peered at the package of balloons.

"Preparing my ammo."

Earl Ray positioned a balloon over the spigot and began to fill it.

"That stuff stinks." Jim backed away. "And nobody's going to get within range for you to throw those balloons."

"Distance doesn't matter. See that?" Earl Ray nodded to the Dynamic Duck Poop Launcher in his truck bed. The wooden catapult was small enough to haul easily and was pure engineering genius. A bit of retrofitting to the high school science project and it had been good to go.

"A catapult?"

"That, my friend, is the Dynamic Duck Poop Launcher." Earl Ray couldn't keep the pride out of his voice. He'd tried the device with a plain water balloon at his house and sent the balloon flying a hundred and fifty feet. "It won't reach across the lake, but if the buyer follows the arrow on the real estate sign over by the dam, which I happened to turn the wrong way, I'll be ready."

Jim shook his head. "You are one sick puppy. All this to screw up Stacey's first sale?"

Earl Ray pulled himself up taller. "It's to protect the lake for Jack."

"Right." Jim gave him a look that said he wasn't buying it and pointed at the balloons. "Like you'd be filling those if it didn't involve your ex-wife."

Earl Ray glared at him. "Just hurry up and rig those high-power amps you bragged about." He tied off another balloon and added it to his stash. "It's just us. All the rest of the guys had to work."

"Hold your horses. I'm moving a little slow. Pulled a double shift yesterday repairing storm damage." Jim ran a hand over his lower back.

"You may be the utility company's employee of the year, but right now, we've got a gig to play. The first reunion of the Rowdy Boys in ten years."

"You know we were lousy, don't you?" Jim opened the tailgate of his pickup.

"Lousy is what we need. Lousy—and loud."

"My wife will kill me if she learns I was in on this." Jim picked up two coils of orange extension cord.

Earl Ray snorted. Jim was a great guy, but he still had no guts. In high school, Earl Ray had concocted a fabulous plan to drive down Main Street while standing with his head out the sunroof of his mother's car, navigating with his feet duct-taped to the steering wheel. Main Street was straight as an arrow. The plan would have worked. But Jim, who from the passenger seat could easily have handled the accelerator—and if necessary, the brakes—had been afraid to try it.

And now Jim was afraid of his five-foot-two wife.

"She thinks I'm at the hardware store, getting paint for the living room," Jim said, and he rounded the corner to the back of Jack's house.

Earl Ray howled with laughter. Women only cramped a man's style. Losing Stacey had been a blessing in disguise. As quickly as possible, Earl Ray filled the balloons and put them in a wheelbarrow. Then he hauled out two wooden pallets, positioned them side by side on the wet grass, and covered them with plastic tarps so Jim could set up his drums. Extension cords snaked through the yard and connected to two huge amps sitting on another tarp.

With Jim's help, Earl Ray unloaded the DDPL from his truck, aimed it at Jack's driveway, with the wheelbarrow of ammo beside it.

He wiped his hands on his jeans and checked the time on his phone. Minutes were slipping by. He got his electric guitar from the cab of the truck.

"Ready?" Earl Ray plugged in his Epiphone guitar and played a quick C chord.

No sound.

Nerves tightened in his chest. He peered across the lake. There were no cars at Leticia's place, but it had to be close to eight thirty. "Jim," he shouted. "It's not working, and Stacey could be there any minute."

Jim shot a frustrated look at the speakers, hurried over, and checked the connections. "Okay, I think I got it."

Earl Ray tried again. Sound blared through the speakers, and excitement bubbled through his veins. He gave Jim a thumbs up. The plan was going to work.

A flash caught his eye. Sunlight, reflecting off a car headed for Leticia's house.

"It's show time," Earl Ray said. "Our favorite set from the old days."

Jim picked up his drumsticks, eyes gleaming. Finally, he'd gotten into the spirit of things. He counted off in a booming voice.

A pair of ducks squawked off the point and took to the air.

And then heavy-metal music poured over the lake.

Not quite in time.

Not all the notes correct.

But loud enough to send all the waterfowl into an uproar.

Loud enough to be heard across the lake.

And, quite possibly, loud enough to be heard a hundred miles away in Kansas City.

№

As soon as she turned onto Sunset Lake Lane, Stacey could hear music.

Bad music. She cracked the sunroof on her car.

The sound was vaguely like something from the eighties. If the lead vocalist been singing while giving birth. And his band had been playing while wearing oven mitts.

She scrambled out of her car in front of Leticia's house and scanned the area across the lake.

A bright red truck stood out like a beacon.

Her nerves tightened. This couldn't be happening, couldn't be part of God's plan.

Gravel crunched, and she turned to watch her client pull up behind her.

Bud Blake climbed out of his shiny black Cadillac.

An off-key chord screamed from across the lake.

Deep creases formed on each side of Bud's mouth.

Her throat constricted.

Bud stopped with his car door still open. The sun glinted off his bald head, and his round face flushed an unhealthy shade of red. "I thought you said this location was quiet."

"I—I'm sorry sir." How could Earl Ray be doing this? And how could Jack let him? It was ruining everything he and Tess wanted. She ducked in her car for her portfolio and popped back out.

Across the water, someone pounded on the drums.

Bud's jaw tightened and he gave Leticia's property a two-second glance. "This place is older than I wanted." He edged closer to his car.

Stacey's heart began thumping out its own drum solo. If Bud left, it was all over. "Sir, it's lovely inside." She could hear the desperation in her rushed words. "And you should see the view out the living room windows over that deck." She gestured toward the back of the house with an open hand. If she could only get him to shut his car door and walk toward the house.

"All I would notice from that deck would be awful music," Bud said with disgust. He got in his Caddy and lowered his window. "If you find another property, feel free to call me—once you make sure it really is quiet. I can get—"

An ear-splitting screech wailed out of the amplifiers across the lake.

Bud cleared his throat. "I can get noise in the city."

"But…" Stacey held out her arms, searching for something to say to stop him.

She was too late.

Bud backed up, turned, and sped toward Sunset Lake Lane.

Stacey watched him go, and the pulse in her temples grew faster and stronger. Then she jammed her hands on her hips and faced the lake.

She'd wanted one sale. One sale. Tess would have been happy. Jack would have been happy. And if Earl Ray had given her a second chance, the two of them could have been happy.

But he'd ruined it.

She blew out a sharp breath and got in her car. She cranked the steering wheel, threw up clods of mud from Leticia's yard, and drove to Jack's house as fast as she could take the curves. Waves of heat poured off her face and chest until she thought she might melt. She punched the button to open the sunroof wider and rounded the last bend.

Two trucks sat in Jack's driveway. A white one she didn't recognize, and a red one that had to be Earl Ray's.

The music stopped.

In the distance she heard a whoop and a faint cackle of laughter.

And then something hit the roof of her car.

She recoiled into her seat.

Had a small branch fallen from a tree? No, it was something purple and—

"Ew." Her shriek scaled two octaves.

Horrid, smelly liquid dripped through her sunroof and onto her head and into her lap.

She shoved the inner sunroof cover closed. A moment later she slammed on the brakes, parked beside the white truck, and got out of her car. She pulled what looked like a piece of purple balloon out of her hair and wiped at the slimy liquid on her best black jeans, smearing green and gray globs.

Across the yard, Jim, the drummer from Earl Ray's high school band, stopped, mid-chorus, with one drumstick aloft. His lips twitched.

Earl Ray stood in the muddy yard with his guitar hanging from the strap around his neck, watching her and laughing so hard that tears ran down his cheeks.

Adrenaline coursed through her body. Her breathing came heavy, as if she'd sprinted around the lake instead of driving.

How could he have done this to her? Wasn't there some corner of his heart that remembered what they'd had? That still cared about her? That didn't want to hurt her? She never wanted to hurt him.

Until now, of course.

Now she was going to kill him.

No one would blame her.

Not even Jack.

ɔʒ

"Are you out of your mind?" Stacey yelled from the driveway.

Earl Ray crossed his arms over his chest and smirked. No, he was not out of his mind. He was finally thinking clearly. He could tell her off and move on.

She lowered her head like a bull about to gore its victim and exposed a greenish-gray smear in her hair, a smear that matched the one on her pants.

His chest swelled. Those two smears were evidence of the incredible accuracy of the DDPL. Man, he was good enough to be a defense department contractor. He turned to point out the direct hit to Jim.

Jim was gone.

Coward.

No matter. Earl Ray did this for family. For Jack.

Stacey barreled toward him, surging forward even when her heels sunk in the wet grass. "Don't you know that was the one customer who wants to keep the lake the way it is?" Her voice was shriller than the worst feedback from Jim's amps, and the tendons that ran up the sides of her throat were stretched taut.

Pain clawed at Earl Ray's stomach, worse than ever before. He clenched his teeth together. He was not letting her see him look weak, not even for a second.

"You've ruined everything." She jabbed a finger at his chest with a force that jarred his whole body. "That man wanted Leticia's house as a private home. Exactly what your cousin wants. Or don't you care about Jack anymore?"

A twinge of doubt uncurled at the top of Earl Ray's spine. What if the redhead had gotten things wrong? What if Stacey had shown the house more than once and this wasn't the developer?

No. It couldn't be. "You're lying." He pulled himself up taller.

Stacey leaned in. "When did I ever lie to you?"

"Just once. When you told me you loved me."

Stacey paled and pulled back.

His gut twisted. How could he have said that? He knew the truth.

She had loved him.

Until he'd failed her.

He started to take back the words but didn't speak fast enough.

"You fool." Her voice dropped in pitch and grew harder. "When Tess ends up taking some commercial offer, it will be your fault." Stacey's eyes blazed—too self-righteous for her to be bluffing.

She was telling the truth.

Nausea slammed into him. What had he done?

"Got to tell Jack," he gasped. He pulled his phone from his pocket and, with an unsteady hand, sent a short text.

"Haven't you grown up at all? This is like some stunt you'd pull in high school. Playing horrible music, flinging stinky water balloons at me? I can't even imagine what you put in them."

"The music"—another spasm wrenched Earl Ray's mid-section—"was Jack's idea."

"Jack's idea?" Stacey looked lost.

"And the stuff in your hair—" Even to him, his voice sounded weak. "It's duck poop."

"Duck poop!" She hit a screeching note that reverberated in Earl Ray's ears, and she batted at her hair like it was infested with vermin.

Pain gripped his stomach, biting and twisting. His legs grew weak, and cold sweat covered him.

She kept talking, but he only heard bursts of static.

He clutched his stomach and fell to his knees.

Things seemed to fade.

"Earl Ray?" Stacey's frightened words cut through the haze. "Oh, my word, I'm calling 911."

"It'll...pass." He managed the words between spasms of agony. "No ambulance."

She dropped to her knees beside him and placed a hand on his shoulder. "Of course I'm calling an ambulance. You could be dying."

His heart thundered and he could feel sweat beaded on his forehead. He tasted something bitter. Dizzy, he collapsed onto the wet, muddy grass. But he gritted his teeth and managed to get out a few more words. "I think it's cancer."

# Chapter Twenty-five

Tess patted the clipboard and the plastic sheath of colored gel pens on the front passenger seat of the Honda. The eight-a.m. meeting had gone flawlessly. In spite of losing Rose, things were looking up.

It was the perfect job—deliver a buffet lunch for twenty-five, every other Wednesday. Easy, steady income with no wait staff to hire and no need to get up at three a.m. Ideal for Silver Platter. Before the meeting, she'd even placed an ad for a new assistant.

And now, as she headed west on I-70, past the St. Louis suburbs, she was dying to hear about the house showing. Using hands-free dialing, she called Stacey.

No answer. Showing a house couldn't take more than an hour, right? So if Stacey was still busy, maybe the client had a lot of questions because he was really interested in the house.

Tess's heart raced. If she wasn't driving, she'd have bounced up and down on the seat like she did when she was seven. Everything could be perfect.

If she could hire the right assistant, sign the client from this morning, and get more jobs like this one, maybe she could take Mondays and Tuesdays off. Jack's work was flexible. They could get together once a week, actually date. She could move past her failures and feel good about her accomplishments, maybe offset the lingering guilt from her night with Nick.

But Jack never had called back last night or answered her calls earlier this morning. Good thing she'd gotten ahold of Stacey to deal with the window.

So where was Jack? Granted, he didn't seem like the kind of person who faithfully charged his phone every night and kept it close at hand, but still... A niggle of worry crept up the back of her neck. Was he regretting their kiss? No. He'd seemed glad to see her when she'd told him about the showing. Maybe he was wrapped up in some new painting.

Her phone rang. It was Stacey.

"I've been trying to call," Tess said. "Did he want the house? Were you signing papers?"

"No." Stacey sounded odd. "I've been in the ER."

Tess hesitated. Not signing papers for the house. And the house was not what she should be asking about. "Are you okay?"

"I'm fine."

"You don't sound fine. Is it your dad?"

"No. It's—it's—" Stacey broke off. "Never mind. I need to tell you about the house and get back." She drew in an audible breath. "Jack's cousin sabotaged the showing."

"What?"

"He and his buddy played this obnoxious, super-loud music and the customer hated it," Stacey said quickly. "Bud wouldn't even go in the house."

Tess struggled to fit Stacey's words into slots in her brain. "Why—why would he do that?"

"The cousin, Earl Ray, he's my ex-husband."

"Ex-husband?" Tess blinked rapidly. Stacey had been related to Jack?

"Earl Ray said the music was Jack's idea."

Tess recoiled in her seat, as stunned as if the airbag had deployed. Her breath grew shallow, not quite reaching her lungs.

Muffled sounds came through the phone, then Stacey came back on the line, sounding scared. "Tess, I've got to go. There's a doctor coming out. He might know about Earl Ray." Without waiting for a reply, she hung up.

Tess pulled off the highway and parked at a rest stop. She sat, numb, and tried to take in Stacey's words.

Stacey had been married to Jack's cousin.

The showing was a bust.

And Jack had wanted her to fail.

☙

Twenty minutes after Jack woke up, he walked out of his hotel room—showered, dressed in last night's clothes, with his teeth brushed with the hotel's complimentary toothbrush and a sample of some fancy new kind of toothpaste. He was leaving two hours later than he'd planned, but that was his own fault. Last night he'd managed to set the hotel alarm clock to p.m. instead of a.m.

At least he'd lucked out with the mechanic. A scheduled job hadn't come in, and he'd taken care of the SUV first thing. He'd left a message at the desk that it should be done soon.

Pickings were slim at the complimentary breakfast buffet, most of the good stuff already back in the kitchen. Jack grabbed a granola bar, a banana, and a cup of coffee and hurried out to wait for a cab to the garage.

The mechanic had replaced the starter, and soon Jack was headed west on I-70 with the sun high overhead and the SUV running better than ever. The problem, according the mechanic, had never been the vehicle at all. It had been the guy Jack took it to for repairs in Columbia.

Jack gobbled down the chocolate-peanut-butter granola bar, swallowed the last of his lukewarm coffee, and plugged in his phone. He couldn't wait to tell Tess about the king rail.

A minute later, his phone came to life. It let out a string of notifications—beeps and dings and chimes—of texts and calls and emails. One eye on the road, he glanced down. The screen showed the last text, from Earl Ray.

On my way to the ER.

The ER? Earl Ray had seemed a little off lately but not that bad.

Jack pulled up the previous text. Also from Earl Ray.

House showing not good. Sorry.

How would Earl Ray know about the house showing? Had he heard at the diner or—?

A semi's horn blared near Jack.

His heart leapt to his throat, and he yanked the SUV back into his own lane. He'd almost hit a motorcycle.

The motorcyclist sped ahead, clearly willing to get a ticket if it would save his life, and the semi roared past Jack.

No more reading while driving, but he had to find out what happened. He used voice dial to call Earl Ray's parents, Aunt Patsy and Uncle T.J.

No answer at their house. They might be at the ER too, but he didn't have their cell numbers in his phone. He tried Abby's shop and got the machine. Should he call the hospital? No, they wouldn't tell him anything.

He called his parents.

Neither of them answered their cell.

If he had to bet, he'd say their phones were in their golf bags on the fairway, and his parents had gone hunting for Mom's last ball. The woman had an unerring ability to send new balls far into the rough.

"Call me," he said on her voice mail. "I need Patsy's cell number. Earl Ray's in the ER." He bumped the cruise control up a couple of notches. If the only way Jack could find out about Earl Ray was to get to Abundance, he wasn't wasting any time.

And Tess must be devastated about the showing. Exactly what he feared.

He called her, but she didn't pick up.

What if she was already uncomfortable, thinking she might have to sell to a commercial developer if she wanted to save her business?

He tapped the steering wheel with one finger and ran numbers in his head. If he could get a decent price for *Ring-Necked Ducks in Flight*, even three-fourths of what his last piece sold for, he might be able to make it work. He wouldn't be taking Tess out to any fancy dinners, but if she was happy with Steak 'n Shake, if he stopped all savings and put his money into property, he could do it. He just needed an offer.

He dialed Mort.

"Jack, I was about to call you and—"

Jack cut in. "Any news?"

"I've got two brothers that are clients, always trying to outdo one another. And they both saw that photo I took of *Ring-Necked Ducks in Flight* and have been bugging me for years about it. How does double your last sale sound?"

Jack pumped a fist in the air. "It sounds amazing. Sell it." He could buy Leticia's property himself. Sunset Lake could stay as it had when Kaitlyn was alive. And his relationship with Tess would have a chance.

He thanked Mort repeatedly, stretched in his seat, and tried Tess's number again.

Still no answer.

He had a long way to drive, but as soon as he checked on Earl Ray, he could tell her in person.

He'd solved all their problems.

# *Chapter Twenty-six*

Tess turned off Sunset Lake Lane and onto Leticia's gravel drive.

It was noon, two hours after she'd talked with Stacey, but she still felt numb. How had her life become such a disaster?

She pulled up to the house on autopilot and braked suddenly.

Indy's carrier slid forward and bumped into the back of the front passenger seat. The kitten let out a yowl.

Tess gave Indy an apologetic look, then stared across the lake at Jack's.

How had she ever thought he could love her? Especially after she'd foolishly bared her soul?

She'd believed he cared.

And believed he'd be happy if the property was sold to a private homeowner. But really, he didn't want any change at all. Leticia had been the perfect neighbor. One old woman, who probably never came out of her house beyond her deck, had been ideal. Because he wanted complete control over Sunset Lake. And if he could sabotage every potential sale, no one would ever move into Leticia's house.

Probably exactly what he wanted.

Memories slammed into Tess's brain, memories of Jack Hamlin's manipulations.

He took her on that walk to show her the ducklings—to manipulate her. She'd seen it and then foolishly believed him when he smoothed his way out of it.

He'd given her that drawing of a duckling—to manipulate her.

And he'd brought those gorgeous irises and been so charming—all to manipulate her. Probably just to make her think he cared. So he could know when the house would be shown.

She'd been crazy to ask him to help her last night. Shutting that window was the last thing he wanted to do. The worse her property looked at the showing, the better. Probably, when she'd tried calling for help, he'd been scheming with his cousin. She had absolutely horrible judgment when it came to men.

All along, Jack had lied to her.

Why? Because she didn't matter. She wasn't worth loving. She squeezed her eyes shut, pressed her fingertips into her forehead, and let out a shaky breath.

Her phone rang and she pulled it out of her purse.

It was Jack. Again. He'd called four times since she talked to Stacey. Probably to tell her more lies, to set her up for more misery.

She dropped the phone back in her purse. After what he'd done, she was never speaking to him again.

She climbed out of the car, dragged out Indy's carrier, and hauled it into the house. Once inside, she released the kitten. Then she pulled the paperwork for the low offer from the neat pile of papers on the end of the breakfast bar.

She skimmed through it, her heart beating faster and faster, until she found the answer she needed.

There it was. The offer had not expired.

Stacey had said it contained all the right clauses and legalese. It was good, except for the price.

But how much could she trust Stacey's opinion about the price? Sure, she had seemed motivated to help sell the house at first. But Stacey was connected to Jack, and she'd never said a word. She was at the hospital with his cousin right now.

Had she been acting in Tess's best interest?

No. Tess pulled out her phone. Adrenaline poured into her veins. She would have to handle this alone. Her future was with Silver Platter. In St. Louis. She needed to make sure she had that future. All she had to do was sign this document.

If she didn't, if she wasted any more time on Jack Hamlin and Sunset Lake, she might lose Silver Platter.

She'd be a failure at everything.

Absolutely everything. Again.

A shudder ran through her.

She found the number for the commercial developer online and dialed.

A couple of phone transfers later, she reached the person who had made the offer, Jeremy Seasky.

Something crinkled in the background, as if he'd reached into a bag of chips. "Miss Palmer, we were sorry things didn't work out."

She grew shaky. He spoke as if it was over, as if the offer she held wasn't good anymore. She tried to think what to say next. "I wanted to make a counteroffer." She tried to keep her voice calm enough to hide her desperation.

"But I"—his words dribbled out, slow and questioning—"I told your agent we weren't interested in a counteroffer."

"Hmm." Heat rushed into Tess's cheeks. She hadn't thought this through. Didn't know enough about how real estate worked.

"Is there a problem with your agent?" Jeremy still sounded baffled, but his words now also held a note of curiosity.

"Stacey can't help me. She's at the hospital with a…a loved one who's having surgery."

"This is very unusual, but I would still like to acquire that property for my uncle. And my budget has become a bit more flexible in the interim." The man spoke slowly, as if he was weighing his options. "What were you thinking, for a counteroffer?"

Tess gripped the edge of the breakfast bar. What should she say? She couldn't go too high or he might laugh and hang up. She swallowed and named a price forty thousand above Seasky's initial offer.

For a long moment, he said nothing.

Her heart raced and she squeezed the edge of the counter harder.

"All right," he said. "We can do that."

She froze, not quite willing to believe her ears.

"With your agent unavailable, it would be difficult for you to initiate the paperwork. I could send a new offer, at the increased price, to you. I can copy your agent on all our correspondence."

"You'll send a new offer? At the higher price?"

"I'll email it to you within the next half hour. You print it out, sign it, scan it, and email it back."

She drew in a choppy breath and slowly released her grip on the counter. "That would be perfect. Thank you."

She'd done it—found a way to sell Leticia's house.

She'd find a copy shop with a printer and email access, send the signed offer back, and leave in the morning.

She was finished with Sunset Lake. Finished with foolish dreams. And finished with Jack Hamlin.

CB

When Jack was stopped for gas, he'd gotten a call from his mom. Earl Ray was still in the hospital. They should know more in a few hours.

Jack called Tess again and again, but she never picked up.

So he drove to the lake. Had her phone died as well? Unlikely. She was too on the ball, too worried about her business.

Was she so upset about the bad showing that she didn't want to talk? Had she, too, realized that they'd be right back where they started, with his desire to keep the lake in its natural state squared off against her need for cash for her business?

He turned off Sunset Lake Lane onto Leticia's long driveway. The afternoon sun reflected off the water and into his eyes from the side, around the edge of his sunglasses.

Once he told her how he'd sold a painting and could now buy Leticia's house himself, all her worries would be over. He'd tell her the news, then take her in his arms and kiss her again and again. Maybe Aunt Patsy was right. Maybe God really did want good things for him.

And as soon as he'd set Tess's mind at ease, the two of them could go by the hospital and make sure Earl Ray was all right. By then, they might know what was wrong with him.

Jack parked, dashed across the driveway and up the porch stairs, and pounded on the door.

He heard a rustling and moved back, waiting to see Tess pull the door wide, waiting to draw her into his arms.

The door didn't open.

He leaned his ear closer to the door. He knew he'd heard sounds. And not kitten-sized sounds. Human footsteps.

Unable to stand it any longer, he tried the knob.

It turned.

He swung the door wide and burst inside. "Tess? I've got great—"

She sat on the couch, the only furniture left in the living room, and spun her head to face him. Her skin looked splotchy and her eyes puffy, as if she'd been crying.

He ran toward her. "What's wrong?"

She sprung up and pointed at the door. "Get out. I don't ever want to see you again. Not ever!" She drew the last word out in a roar of anguish.

He moved closer. "I know the showing didn't go well—"

"Didn't go well?" Her back stiffened and she stared at him, eyes burning. "The only reason it 'didn't go well' was because of you."

"What are you talking about?"

"Stacey told me all about your plan. Getting your cousin to play that loud music so the buyer wouldn't even go in the house."

Jack's throat tightened, and he raised a hand to his mouth. No. Earl Ray wouldn't.

He might. But how could he make music loud enough to be a disturbance across the lake?

"It doesn't matter," Jack said. He'd prepared for the worst. "I sold *Ring-Necked Ducks in Flight*."

"So? I couldn't care less about your painting." Tess's lips drew into a thin line, and she crossed her arms over her chest.

"I'm sorry about whatever Earl Ray did. But I was afraid the guy from Kansas City might not like the house. I sold the painting so I can buy the house."

Her eyes narrowed and she angled her head to one side. Confusion flashed over her face, then what looked like horror.

She didn't understand. He charged on, determined to make her see that everything was fine. "Trust me. This will solve all our problems. I'll buy the house and—"

"You can't," she said, almost too faint to hear. Her face paled, and her hands hung limp at her sides. "It's already sold."

He stared at her. She wasn't making sense. "I thought the barbecue guy didn't like it."

"I didn't sell it to him." She inched back. "I sold it to a commercial developer."

Jack's blood stopped moving. Every cell in his body went rigid. "You what?"

"I thought you sabotaged the showing on purpose. That's what Earl Ray said. That it…was your idea." She spoke with odd pauses like the delays in a bad cell connection. "Because…you never wanted the house to sell…at all."

Emptiness filled him, as if an elevator had dropped and his stomach stayed six flights up. How could she even think such a thing? "But what about—what about us?" He spread his hands, palms up, beseeching her to explain, to say he'd misunderstood.

"I didn't think there was an 'us.'" Her voice grew thin and her shoulders curved forward. "Not after you didn't take my calls, not after the showing. I thought it was all a lie."

His blood began to flow faster and faster and faster, pounding through his veins and ringing in his ears. "I had nothing—NOTHING—to do with that music!" he shouted, leaning in toward her. "I was at a conservation area over by St. Louis yesterday, thinking that we had a future. And because my phone was dead, because the starter on my SUV failed, because mechanics don't work at night, you sold the house to a developer?" He gasped for breath. "I can't believe I thought for a single minute that I could trust you." He spun around, strode down the hall, and slammed the door behind him.

The drive to the other side of the lake was a blur. Somehow three minutes later he was in his living room, sitting on his couch, with adrenaline still pulsing through him so fast that his hands shook. He stared at *Ring-Necked Ducks in Flight.*

By Monday, he had to ship it.

He turned to look at the lake, where his memories with Kaitlyn would be violated. He could almost see the shape of a huge hotel gripping the far side of the lake.

How had he been foolish enough to believe Tess cared? To believe God cared? To believe he might be happy?

His memories would be destroyed.

All because of Tess Palmer.

He would never trust a woman again.

Never.

Ever.

Ever.

# Chapter Twenty-seven

The duck poop wouldn't come off.

Not off her jeans and not out of her hair.

In the hospital bathroom outside the operating room, Stacey tried to remove the muck with water and a paper towel, but it only smeared on her jeans and added an unattractive streak to her hair, ruining the natural-looking color she'd worked so hard to achieve.

And it smelled.

It didn't matter. Neither did the mud stains on her jeans from when she knelt beside Earl Ray. She was not leaving the hospital until she learned if he was all right.

Right now, he was in the OR. She'd seen one of the paramedics in the hall, and he'd told her.

She threw the paper towel in the trashcan and walked toward the hall.

"Patsy, I'm sure he'll be fine. Becky's right, you need to eat." The voice, almost like Earl Ray's, floated out of the waiting room.

Stacey froze, then scurried back to the alcove by the bathroom, her heart pounding. She had no desire to see Patsy Hamlin.

Earl Ray's dad, T.J., she could handle. She'd seen him at the discount store right after she moved back to town, and he'd been pleasant, almost as though she and Earl Ray were still married. And Stacey liked Becky, Earl Ray's sister. But Patsy? Since Stacey got back in town, she'd gone out of her way to avoid Patsy. The woman never had approved of her, not after that day in high school when Earl Ray told his folks she was pregnant.

"The receptionist says it will be a while," T.J. said. "She'll text Becky when we can see him. Let's go down to the cafeteria and get some food."

Someone said something Stacey couldn't hear. Possibly Patsy.

"Mom, Earl Ray will come through this fine. He's tough. Think of all the times he's been in the ER after breaking a bone doing some dumb stunt."

Stacey leaned her head farther toward the hall and the conversation. That had to be Becky talking.

"If you sit here in the waiting room, it won't make the doctor come out any faster," T.J. said.

Perfectly logical. That didn't necessarily mean Patsy would listen.

But after a moment, several sets of footsteps came closer to Stacey.

She ducked into the bathroom. A minute later she peeked around the corner.

The three Hamlins disappeared down the hall toward where the elevator dinged. From the back, Becky looked about the same, but Patsy's hair was now that pale blonde some women used to hide a lot of gray.

Stacey hurried into the waiting room.

A new receptionist sat behind the glass and Stacey's heart leapt. The last one had been an old biddy, but this woman looked like she might be sweet.

Stacey hid the duck poop on the side of her jeans with her hand and headed toward the window, chest tight.

The receptionist opened the window.

"Hi. I'm wondering about Earl Ray Hamlin."

"Are you related?" Far from sweet, the new receptionist sounded snippy.

"I was married to him."

The receptionist's eyes narrowed. "Was?"

Stacey gave a slow nod.

"We're not allowed to give out any information unless you are next of kin or have Power of Attorney," she said in a bored tone. "Do you have a POA?"

"No," Stacey said. What man would give his ex-wife power of attorney?

"That information is protected by—"

"I know," Stacey said with a groan. "HIPAA."

The receptionist slid the glass closed with a clunk.

"I could go over your head," Stacey shouted at the window.

The woman's eyes turned to slits, as if giving an unspoken warning that she had security on speed dial.

Stacey's shoulders sank. In addition to the segment of town that already hated her, she'd just made a new friend. Maybe she should slip the woman a business card.

In the meantime, Stacey would wait until Earl Ray's family was called back, then bite the bullet and talk to T.J. or Becky or even...Patsy. Whatever it took to learn how Earl Ray was.

Stacey trudged to a vinyl chair and shivered in the Arctic breeze of the air-conditioning. Which no one needed in April, thank you very much. The hospital probably wanted to make more people sick, drum up business. Same tactic with their free coffee, if that's what it really was. She'd tried it, decided it might be poison. Of course, it might taste that bad because of the pervasive smell of duck poop.

She sat, hunched back into the torn, vinyl upholstery to try to keep warm, and picked at her nail polish.

So what if she could smell the duck poop on her jeans and in her hair, even over the sick, antiseptic smell of the hospital? She wasn't leaving.

Not without seeing Earl Ray.

And apologizing for how she left.

And telling him how much she loved him.

He'd looked so pale in the ambulance. So mortal. As if he might not make it.

Emotion pricked at her throat and she swallowed it back. If Earl Ray had cancer, if he was dying, she'd take care of him. It was the least she could do after the way she left fifteen years ago.

Minutes crept by. Earl Ray's family took their time in the cafeteria. Concerned family members and friends of other patients wandered in and out, the lucky ones called to the double doors for conversations with doctors or nurses that ended in smiles. Except the receptionist behind the glass, every other face in the room showed fear. Stacey twisted her hands together, picking at the polish on her nails, then pulled out her phone and dialed.

Finally, he picked up.

"Dad? I'm at the hospital." Tears pooled in her eyes. "I was talking to Earl Ray, and he collapsed. And it's been hours since they took him into the OR and there's no news."

"Do you want me to come over there?" Dad's words flowed through the phone and wrapped around her, as comforting as a fleece blanket.

"No. Not yet at least. But will you pray?"

"Of course. I've been praying for Earl Ray every day since before you all got married."

"Thank you." The tears escaped and dribbled down her cheeks. "Dad, Earl Ray said..." She hated to even mention the disease that had killed Mom, but she was so scared. "He said it might be cancer."

For a moment, Dad didn't speak. When he came back on the line, his voice was husky but encouraging, as if he knew she needed his strength. "Stacey Lynn, doctors can do a lot these days. You just stand by him and pray. Call me as soon as you see him."

"I will, Daddy." A sob escaped. "I will." She hung up, bowed her head, and began to pray herself, pleading with God, explaining that her earlier prayer—that he bring her and Earl Ray back together—didn't matter. All she asked was that he let Earl Ray live.

At a sudden noise, she glanced up.

A man in scrubs barged through the double doors and scanned the waiting area. He rapped on the glass window.

It opened.

"I thought you told me you texted the Hamlins," he said to the receptionist. "Where are they?"

"Sorry, doctor. I must have written down the number wrong." The receptionist twiddled a pen nervously.

"If they come back, tell them I'll stop by the ICU waiting room in half an hour." The doctor ran a hand through his thinning hair. "And next time, try to get the number right for a change." He strode back toward the double doors.

Stacey's heart jumped as if she'd been shocked with those electric paddles on TV.

If Earl Ray was in the ICU, he wasn't dead.

She leapt up, wiped her tears, and dashed toward the elevator, thanking God again and again, with every step she took. A glimpse of Earl Ray's face. That's all she needed. That and a chance to hold his hand.

A few minutes later, she'd talked her way into the ICU.

She stopped outside his door and ran a hand over her hair. Hopeless. How could she look good with duck poop in her hair? But she had to see him. She peeked in.

There he was in the bed, asleep.

She walked closer.

His eyes opened and he blinked, as if bringing her into focus. "Stacey, love," he said in a raspy voice. "You came to see me."

Her throat closed. Her face grew hot and her eyes filled again with tears.

He'd called her 'love.'

Why, oh why, had she spent fifteen years running from the truth? This was the man she should have been with all along, the only man for her.

And now—though she didn't deserve it—he called her 'love.' That had to mean there was a chance she could win him back.

But what about the cancer?

What if he was dying?

&#x2767;

Stacey's eyes were red and puffy, as if she'd been crying a long time. Her jeans were muddy. Her hair had an odd streak of color and hung flat on one side. And the stench of duck poop wafted toward Earl Ray.

Without question, she was the most beautiful woman he'd ever seen.

And she was here with him in the hospital, hadn't even gone home to change.

Things were fuzzy, but he forced himself to concentrate, and he sent up a silent prayer that somehow, some way, he could show her he was worthy of her love.

Stacey moved closer and laid a hand on his arm. "Oh, Earl Ray…" Her fingers were cold, but her touch made his chest grow warm.

He tried to sit up, moved a fraction of an inch, and crashed into pain. Clutched at his gut and felt bandages.

Her face grew tense. "Is it…is it cancer?"

"No—it was my gallbladder." He'd made her worry. "They say I'll be fine, but I had some kind of rare complication. It's a good thing I got to the hospital when I did. If you hadn't been there, hadn't called the ambulance…"

Her shoulders sagged, and tears ran down her cheeks. "You'll live?"

"You bet."

"Thank the Lord." She brushed her fingers along his jaw. "I need to tell you something that's been bothering me a long time. I'm so sorry. I shouldn't have left you. I…I couldn't handle the guilt."

"Guilt?" He wiped a tear from her cheek. "You mean because I got you pregnant?"

She shook her head. "Not that." Her voice grew high and shaky. "Something worse."

"What?" He touched her arm. "You've got to tell me."

She turned away for a moment, then faced him. "I was so scared about becoming a mom when I was only seventeen, and every month that it got closer, I got more nervous. You were excited, but"—she drew in a deep breath—"sometimes I didn't want the baby. For a long time, I thought"—she bowed her head and held a hand over her abdomen—"that was why she died."

Earl Ray felt as if his heart had been put in a vise. His poor Stacey. His poor, dear Stacey. He laid his hand over hers. "You know that wasn't true."

"I do now." She paused. "My boss, Delia, back in California told me about a baby she'd lost, a baby she desperately wanted. I finally saw that my miscarriage had nothing to do with my state of mind. But I didn't understand that back then, not completely."

"Stace, I should have been with you that night here at the hospital."

"You were scared."

"Too scared to be there when you needed me." He spat out the words. He'd been such a coward. "I know that's why you stopped loving me."

She jolted back. "I never stopped loving you," she said emphatically. "Never ever. Why do you think I came back to Abundance?"

His heart raced. She loved him? Stacey loved him? "Aw, hon, I never stopped loving you either." He grabbed both her hands and held them.

Her face glowed. "Oh, Earl Ray."

He stared into her eyes, her beautiful eyes. He needed to tell her what she meant to him, tell her he would help with her father and her business, tell her he would do anything to have her back. "Stacey, I—"

Before he could find the words, she leaned down. Her precious face drew closer, and she brought her soft lips to his with a kiss.

A kiss that was everything he remembered. And more.

Happiness spread through him. His Stacey. His wife. His love forever.

He drew her nearer, back where she belonged, close to his heart. Never, never would he let her go again.

She sank to the edge of the hospital bed and gently wrapped both arms around him.

Was it just the drugs that they'd used to knock him out? No. It was real. Life spread before him, full of blessings. Stacey loved him. And he didn't have cancer.

He wasn't going to die.

But, here in her arms, he was already in heaven.

# Chapter Twenty-eight

Jack hated hospitals.

The smell of antiseptic. The ugly tile floors. The people.

He wanted to be home. Alone.

But he needed to check on Earl Ray. Aunt Patsy had said he was fine, but Jack wanted to see for himself, find out if there was anything his cousin needed.

Even though his gut was hollowed out by Tess's betrayal, even though he wanted to hide away and lick his wounds, Jack had driven to the hospital.

He punched the button for the third floor. Patsy had said Earl Ray was awake. Maybe the anesthesia had worn off enough that he could explain what had gone on with Tess. Clearly, she'd exaggerated. Earl Ray's best amp couldn't make enough noise to drive away the guy who came to see Leticia's house. Jack needed the real story.

And needed someone who would agree that women were evil. If he was awake, Earl Ray was the answer.

Jack wasn't immediate family, but a nurse he'd gone to school with let him into the unit.

A woman's throaty laugh floated out of Earl Ray's room.

He stopped. It sounded almost like Stacey. Slowly, he looked into the room.

It *was* Stacey. She hovered beside Earl Ray's hospital bed, and her bright red lipstick was the exact same shade as the smear on Earl Ray's hospital gown.

"Once I get out of here, I'll fix that leak in your office," Earl Ray said. "Then I'm going to take you out on the town and prove to you that you are the most precious woman in the world."

"Absolutely not," Stacey said. "I'm going to fix you a bowl of homemade soup to help you heal. And make you rest. Didn't you listen to the nurse?"

"Too busy looking at you, hon," Earl Ray said in a tone that turned Jack's stomach.

His face grew hot. His own cousin. With Stacey, the woman who'd sold Tess's house, who'd helped destroy Sunset Lake.

Jack grunted and spun away.

"Jack, I'm in here." Earl Ray called, with enough volume that Jack couldn't ignore him. Not in the ICU. Not in Abundance, where everyone knew him and three people at the nurses' station looked at him.

He took two steps into the room. "I'm glad you're all right," he said curtly to Earl Ray. He looked past Stacey.

"Yeah, they took out my gallbladder. They said I'll be fine." He turned back to Stacey. "Stacey called the squad,

306

probably saved my life. By the time I was in trouble, Jim was gone."

"Jim?" Jack came closer to the bed.

"You know, from the Rowdy Boys? He works for the utility company now, wired up these massive amps."

Heat rushed to Jack's chest. Tess hadn't been exaggerating. "You did drive away the potential buyer," he growled. "I can't believe you."

Earl Ray folded the edge of the hospital blanket between his fingers and studied it. "I thought it was a developer wanting to build a hotel." He gave Jack a quick glance.

Jack averted his eyes.

"On the plus side, the DDPL was remarkably accurate," Earl Ray said under his breath.

Jack glanced back at him. The DDP—? Oh. Had Earl Ray been crazy enough to do that too?

Stacey glared at Earl Ray.

Jack grimaced. Yep, his cousin was that crazy. And he was pretty sure that was duck poop in Stacey's hair.

"I hit her sunroof." Earl Ray looked at his ex with puppy-dog eyes and an ingratiating grin. "But you forgave me, right?"

Stacey's eyes hardened, as if Earl Ray ought to shut up. "Only because I thought you were dying." She walked around the bed toward Jack, her eyes serious. "I'll get right back on the job tomorrow. Maybe I can find a new buyer who would keep the property residential."

Jack stared at her. "You don't know?"

Her forehead wrinkled.

"Tess sold the land to a commercial developer." Even saying it out loud brought a bitter taste to Jack's mouth. "With the noise Earl Ray made, and you telling her it was my idea to sabotage the showing, she was furious."

"But I wasn't even contacted." Stacey pulled her phone from her pocket and touched the screen rapidly. "Oh, you're right." Her voice rose in pitch and her words tumbled out. "When she couldn't get ahold of me, she called the developer herself. The buyer's agent handled the whole deal. He sent an email." She held up the phone. "Said he was 'helping' me because I had a family emergency."

Earl Ray shrank down into his pillow.

Jack backed toward the door. There was nothing left to say.

"Jack, I'm sorry," Earl Ray said. "I thought I was doing what you wanted, protecting the lake. I never meant to mess things up."

"Mess things up? I find a woman who's authentic, who I want a relationship with, and you destroy it."

"You?" Earl Ray said, incredulous. "Wanted a relationship?"

Jack said nothing.

"So what are you doing here, man? You gotta do something big, something bold, to prove to her how you feel. Women like that, don't they, hon?" Earl Ray gave Stacey a lovesick look.

The air in Jack's lungs grew thick and sluggish.

Do something bold?

He'd just sold a painting, a heart-shaped chunk of his memories, so he could buy Tess's property and the two of them could have a future together. And, thanks to Earl Ray, it hadn't helped a bit. How much bolder could he be? How much could a man sacrifice for love?

Chest heaving, Jack strode from the room.

Yelling at his cousin, banging him over the head repeatedly with a cafeteria tray, strangling him with an IV tube—all were probably frowned on by the hospital.

And none of them would ease Jack's pain.

CB

"Bye, Stacey. Thank you." Tess hung up the phone.

Stacey had been—well, she'd been shocked at what Tess had done, that was clear, even though she'd tried to hide it. And she'd been nice. But she hadn't offered any real hope.

Tess wandered through the first floor of Leticia's house, mentally saying goodbye. Once she left Sunset Lake tomorrow morning, she wasn't coming back. Ever.

Tomorrow she'd check out the van in Kansas City, then drive the five hours back across the state to St. Louis. And she'd hire a mover to bring her the dining room set and the couch.

For now, she needed to finish her list of questions to ask about the silver van in Kansas City, the one positive thing she could focus on.

But it was hard to care. About the van or a list or even about a catering job planned for next week.

All that really mattered was Jack.

And the fact that she had destroyed their future.

Once again she had slipped into catastrophe mode, believing all hope was lost. Once again she'd acted rashly.

And once again she'd created an even bigger disaster and hurt someone else in the process.

Just like she had four years ago.

And just like four years ago, it couldn't be fixed.

All she could do was go back to St. Louis, back to Silver Platter. Only now she saw her life there differently. A month ago, she'd known she was overworked and lonely. She'd thought it was temporary, thought everything would solve itself if her business could succeed.

Now she knew the truth. The money from Leticia's house would help her business, but it wouldn't make her happy. Because Jack had changed her. He'd made her want more. He'd made her see that the success she'd been working so hard to achieve could never make her life complete. If her life was a glass measuring cup, then making her business a success might refill the part that had been splashed out four years ago. But what she hadn't seen, as if she hadn't looked through the side of the clear glass cup, was that even before that awful day and awful night, the cup had only been half full. Her boyfriend at the bank hadn't filled her heart, not like Jack did.

If all she had in her life was her work, she'd still be half empty. She'd talk to clients, vendors, waiters, and waitresses she hired for events. She'd smile and laugh and act as though everything was fine, but it would all be fake. All hiding how much her heart hurt. And all knowing that at the end of the day she'd go home to her apartment—alone.

No friends.

No Rose.

And worst of all—no Jack.

She walked into the living room, found Indy lounging in a sunbeam on the carpet, and picked her up.

The kitten nestled in close and purred.

Someone knocked on the door.

Tess's heart sped, and she gently placed Indy back in the sunbeam and bolted toward the hall. Even if Jack was still mad, if he'd come back—

Abby and Becky waved at her through the narrow window beside the front door.

Not Jack.

Tess cracked open the door.

"It can't be that bad." Abby rushed in, carrying Emma and a giant diaper bag. She dropped the bag and pulled Tess into a one-armed hug.

Tess's throat grew tight. Even Abby and Becky would hate her. "It is. You haven't heard yet, or you wouldn't be here."

"We have heard." Becky said. "That's why we're here, to make sure you're okay." She walked into the living room and sat on the couch like an old friend, determined to give help whether it was wanted or not.

Tess and Abby followed her in. Abby propped up Emma on the floor and sat on the carpet beside her, then looked pointedly at Tess. "Are you okay?"

"No. I never should have sold the house without talking to Jack or Stacey." She joined Becky on the couch and blinked rapidly, trying to keep her tears at bay.

Becky patted her shoulder, and Abby pulled two tissues from a pocket of the diaper bag and held them up toward her.

Tess blew her nose. The honk echoed in her ears.

"Can't Stacey fix this? Get you out of the contract?" Becky said.

"She says it's a signed legal document," Tess shoved the tissue in her pocket. "If I refuse to sell, I can be sued. And she said the buyer mentioned that his company had its own lawyers. She thinks I have a chance, but how can I win against someone who can afford endless legal action?"

"Oh." Becky looked at Abby.

"It's no use. I've ruined everything," Tess said. "Jack will never love me. Just like God will never love me."

"What are you talking about? God loves you no matter how many mistakes you make," Becky said.

Tess kept her mouth shut. She didn't want to be rude, but she knew the truth. She'd felt God's love before that night with Nick. And it had never felt the same since.

"You need to talk to Jack," Abby said. "Straighten things out."

A raw ache built in Tess's chest. Straightening things out was impossible. "How could he ever forgive me?" She pulled a throw pillow against her chest.

"If it was your fault, you apologize," Abby said.

From the kitchen, Tess's phone rang.

Her heart raced, and she blew her nose again and ran to the phone. Maybe it was—

No, not Jack.

It was a number she didn't recognize. A Missouri area code, though.

"Hello?"

"This is Rodney Friedman, from The Blue Caboose. Can I speak with Tess Palmer?"

She blinked and tried to regain her composure. "This is Tess."

"Miss Palmer, glad to reach you." Friedman's voice was scratchy, as if he spent a lot of money on cigarettes. "One of my mom's friends, Madeleine McCullen, was just here talking about your catering work, your desserts and gourmet ice creams."

Tess snagged paper and a pen from the breakfast bar. Maybe Friedman ran an art gallery that needed desserts for an opening. "What type of event are you planning?"

"Let me explain. The Blue Caboose is a restaurant in Columbia. We're expanding and I need to hire someone dedicated to desserts."

"Oh." She set the paper down on the dining room table.

"Madeleine said she heard you inherited property near here. I was hoping you might be interested in a job. I'm calling on a Friday night, if that gives you any idea of how desperate I am. Or how much Madeleine sang your praises."

Suddenly Tess understood. She could have made desserts, could have had a life with Jack. But it was too late. Her heart wedged into her throat. "I'm sorry. I no longer own the property. I'm going back to my business in St. Louis."

Friedman let out an expletive and a cough. "Back to square one. Madeleine really had me sold."

"It's probably for the best," Tess said, almost to herself. "I've never worked in a restaurant. Before catering, I did special events."

"Clearly, you can cook. And those ice creams would be a big hit. So, if you change your mind in the next couple of days, call me."

Tess murmured her thanks.

"I'm not kidding. I've worked in catering. I can imagine what it's like as a small operation. I've got two words for you." He paused dramatically. "Days. Off. Think about it." He told her his number, waited while she numbly repeated it back and wrote it down, and hung up.

She returned to the living room, barely seeing where she was walking, and collapsed onto the couch. "It's worse," she wailed.

Abby's brows drew together. "But it sounded—I didn't mean to eavesdrop—but it sounded like the guy offered you a job."

"He did. In a restaurant in Columbia. The Blue Caboose."

"I've eaten there." Becky gave an encouraging nod. "It's delicious."

Tess's eyes felt hot, her heart, ripped open. "I could have lived here. I never thought of working in a restaurant." Never considered herself qualified. But even though she'd never been to culinary school, she had spent hours and hours creating desserts. "But I could do it. Most desserts I could make ahead of time, so it wouldn't be like a chef who has to make eight different dinners at once. If only this guy had called earlier."

"It's a sign." Becky leaned forward and her words rang with conviction. "God has a plan for you. You need to talk to Jack."

"No." Tess sunk back into the couch. God didn't make plans for people like her. And things with Jack were over. "The land is sold. They'll build some huge hotel, and all Jack's memories of the lake will be ruined. Every day he'll see a reminder of what I did to him. How I didn't trust him."

Abby got up off the floor and sat on the other side of her. "God loves you, Tess. And I'm pretty sure Jack does too. You can fix this and have a wonderful future here in Abundance."

Tess shook her head.

"Really, you have to try," Becky pleaded.

Tess rose from the couch. Her disaster of a life wasn't their problem. She needed to deal with it on her own. "I...I kind of want to be alone. And I need to call about this van in Kansas City. How about I stop by the shop on my way out of town in the morning to say goodbye?"

The two women exchanged glances. Neither got up.

"Are you sure?" Abby pulled Emma onto her lap.

"We could stay, order some pizza," Becky said, her words racing out. "And I could go get chocolate pie from the diner. I know Grace always has chocolate on Fridays."

"No." Tess took a couple of steps toward the hall and glanced back at them.

Becky's mouth tightened. "All right, I guess."

315

"If that's what you want." Abby still didn't sound convinced.

Tess nodded.

They looked at each other again, then rose and hugged her. Abby scooped up Emma, and the two women walked out slowly, both glancing back.

Tess shut the door behind them and squeezed her eyes shut. She was not going to cry. She needed to think about her future back in St. Louis.

She had a business to run, a business that needed a van.

She pulled up the car dealer's website on her laptop.

The silver van wasn't listed anymore.

Unease skittered through her chest, and she dialed the dealership.

Two minutes later she hung up.

There'd been a mix-up. They'd sold the silver van to someone else.

Everything was a failure.

Every. Single. Thing.

# Chapter Twenty-nine

A chilly gust of wind tossed up choppy waves on Sunset Lake near Jack's house. Gray clouds hung low as evening approached. Across the water, a tiny beam of sunlight slipped through the gloom and reflected off Tess's car.

A lone Canada goose circled, gave a haunting cry, and landed in the middle of the lake. Near Kaitlyn's Point, a large flock of Canada geese swam together, but the single goose didn't join them.

Jack stood on his deck with his arms crossed and watched the goose. Off by itself, as though it had lost its mate. All alone.

Like him.

Only the female goose had probably cared.

Unlike Tess. How could she have done this to him? Sold Leticia's house right out from under him? He'd thought…well, he'd thought a lot of things, like the fact that he and Tess had a future. He'd been wrong.

He grasped the deck rail with both hands and let out a long breath. After a moment, he went inside and opened the freezer, then the fridge. Out of pizza. And milk.

He poured a bowl of dry Frosted Mini-Wheats and a glass of water to wash it down with.

If he viewed things logically and tried really, really hard to put away his anger, he could almost see how Tess had taken things the wrong way. The stunt pulled by Earl Ray. The fact that she couldn't reach him by phone. He could even see, with what had happened in her past, that trust was hard for her.

He could relate.

Trust didn't come easily after Chloe.

Yep, if Tess was totally focused on the negatives, she would have felt rejected. Majorly rejected.

And at least she hadn't lied like his wife had. Hadn't tried to manipulate him. She'd overreacted. Big-time, nuclear-launch-style, but in essence simply over-reacted.

And talk about fallout.

But she'd been good for him. He'd been—he could admit it—a hermit. He'd avoided people as much as possible, had focused on his past, his grief, and his anger. Tess had turned things upside down and made him happy. Deep down, honestly happy. For that brief time they'd had together, he'd even wanted to think about a future with her.

And now?

Now she would go back to St. Louis. Some hideous hotel would be built. Obnoxious teenagers and drunk men going through mid-life crises would overrun the lake. The waterfowl would fly away.

Jack would be left alone, with no Kaitlyn.

No Tess.

No reason to stay.

He dropped a Mini-Wheat back in the bowl and pushed it away. What was he doing, eating dry cereal with water, living in misery? He ought to just move, not to some rustic retreat built by a Frank Lloyd Wright fan, but somewhere closer to Tess.

He grabbed his phone and pulled up a map from the Missouri Department of Natural Resources. There. The Marais Temps Clair Conservation Area. Where he'd been yesterday. Where his creativity flowed. And only an hour from St. Louis was another conservation area, the B.K. Leach. It was even larger and designated an Important Bird Area by Audubon Missouri.

He could move closer to St. Louis, and he and Tess could get to know each other better.

What? Move?

His stomach tensed and his heart thudded as if he'd wandered near the edge of a cliff.

He ran the idea through his brain one more time.

Forgive her? Follow after her? Was that foolish? Was it weak? And wouldn't he be setting himself up for rejection? He had to be crazy.

But he could not get the idea out of his mind.

He went back out on the deck and stared across the water at Leticia's house.

The breeze quieted. The air warmed. And the clouds parted, revealing the sunset bit by bit. One super-saturated color after another spread through the sky and reflected off the water, creating a work of art no human hands could form.

His heart rate slowed, and the tension in his body eased.

He caught his thumbs in the front pockets of his jeans, rocked back on his heels, and tried to take in the incredible colors—a rich tangerine, a deep indigo, a pink as soft as cotton candy. Colors and shading he could work days to achieve and still fall short. Here, they just happened.

He rocked forward, and his feet landed with a solid jolt that reverberated up his body and into his brain. How had he lived here at Sunset Lake, seen thousands of sunsets melt into the water, and not thought about it? The beauty wasn't accidental. To his eye as an artist, it was a creative work designed for a specific audience. For mankind. Who knows? Maybe this one sunset, with the colors so intense when seen from this very spot, was made just so he could see it.

And see that God didn't change. He was good all the time.

For years Jack had thought that if God had let Kaitlyn die, he couldn't possibly care about Jack or any of the rest of the world.

But now, the things Aunt Patsy kept telling him began to make sense.

God did care. The evidence of his love was all around.

Jack had been too deep in his grief to understand.

To see that God brought gifts into his life, like sunsets.

Like Tess.

Out on the water, the lone Canada goose turned its head toward the sunset, then glided toward the other geese. And on the shore, Jack took one last look at the horizon, then went inside and put on his jacket.

He still didn't know why Kaitlyn had to die. Maybe he wasn't supposed to. But deep inside him, something had changed. It was time to be grateful for God's gifts.

Time to make one last attempt to keep Tess in his life.

CB

Tess lugged her suitcase onto Leticia's front porch.

With no van to see in Kansas City tomorrow, she had no reason to stay at Sunset Lake. She could be in St. Louis late tonight and just send Becky and Abby a card.

Now that she'd thought about it, she realized that with the house sold, she could buy a brand-new van and have it customized on credit. It wasn't the same as long-term debt. She could repay it with money from the house in a couple of weeks.

She ought to be happy, excited about what she could do with Silver Platter, thinking up new ways to get clients and new ice cream flavors to make.

But she couldn't care less about ice cream. Or new clients. Or Silver Platter.

She gazed across the lake at Jack's house, then forced herself to look away, at the sunset, a spectacular show where minutes ago there had been only clouds.

The sun hung halfway below the horizon, and orange and red layered the sky. A deep purple hugged the land and swirled upward as if pulled by eddies.

She sighed. It was a sunset meant for strolling by the lake and watching the ducklings and holding Jack's hand.

If only she'd stopped herself and not reacted so rashly—even waited just long enough to get that offer from The Blue Caboose. Things might have turned out differently.

She gave the lake one more look, went back inside to the dining room, and picked up the final box she needed to load. A few mementos, papers, and on top, Leticia's Bible. Tess certainly didn't plan to read it, but she couldn't get rid of it. It had meant too much to her great-aunt.

From out of nowhere, Indy darted into the hall, her fluffy tail brushing Tess's bare leg right above her socks.

Tess faltered, unable to see over the box. She took one step back, heard a yowl, and lurched forward. A second later, she slammed against the carpet, and the box flew ahead of her.

With a low moan, she pulled herself up to her knees.

Indy perched on the breakfast bar and tilted her head as though she found Tess's clumsiness bewildering. She let out a *mrrrooowwrrr*.

"Some of us aren't as graceful as you are." Tess made sure the kitten was okay and eased her into her carrier.

She rubbed her elbow and began to put the papers back in the box. She could sort them out later. Now she just wanted to leave.

She reached for the Bible, which lay open, one page partly ripped out after the fall. She nudged it back into position. Halfway down the page, bright yellow highlighter shone. Unable to stop herself, she read the marked verses, Psalm 103:9-12.

*He will not always chide: neither will he keep his anger forever. He hath not dealt with us after our sins; nor rewarded us according to our iniquities. For as the heaven is high above the earth, so great is his mercy toward them that fear him. As far as the east is from the west, so far hath he removed our transgressions from us.*

She skimmed over it once more, then put the Bible back in the box, carried the box outside, and set it on the wide rail of the front porch.

Wait. Transgressions were sins, right?

She opened the Bible to the loose page and read the marked verses again.

Her sin, put as far away as the east was from the west. God's mercy as high as the heaven is above the earth. What was it Becky said? *"God loves you, no matter how many mistakes you make."* That was pretty much what this verse meant. And it had to be an important one. Leticia hadn't just highlighted it, she'd underlined it in ballpoint pen as well.

Tess ran a finger over the words. An odd, unsettled feeling stirred inside her chest. God did love her, in spite of her mistakes. Seeing it in black and white was hard to ignore.

How had she gotten things so wrong? And how come she felt so far away from God?

And then in a split second, she understood. Tears welled up in her eyes as it sank in.

She'd pulled away.

Ashamed of that night with Nick, she'd stopped praying, stopped reading the Bible, stopped going to church.

God had been there all along, loving her, willing to forgive her. But she hadn't forgiven herself and had been too ashamed to seek him.

Yes, she had been hurt all those years ago first by the bank, then by her boyfriend, by the guy in the bar, and by her own actions. She'd lost her confidence and bearings and her belief in her self-worth. But most of her misery had been of her own making—not just in what she'd done, but because she'd let one day more than four years ago rule her life ever since.

Because she had let her sin and perfectionism separate her from God.

She didn't need to be perfect. She needed God's forgiveness. Her legs grew weak and she sank to the top step, still holding the Bible open. Her tears dripped on the loosened page.

She wiped them away with her sleeve and read the verses one more time. Then she closed the Bible, squeezed it against her chest with her arms crossed over it, and bowed her head.

A few minutes later an engine roared to life across the lake, and an SUV moved from behind a patch of trees.

Tess's breath grew choppy. Was there a chance, even a shred of hope that he might forgive her? Might want her back?

As if in answer to the question in her heart, the SUV drove past the dam, toward Leticia's driveway.

Tess stood, clutching the Bible, her chest bubbling with hope, adrenaline pouring into her veins. She placed the Bible back in the box.

And then the enormity of what Jack had done for her in selling his beloved painting, the one he'd created with his daughter beside him, slammed into her.

What could she say to him? She'd sold the lake, what he saw as a memorial to his daughter, right out from under him. She'd failed entirely in their relationship. She had no right to even dream that he'd forgive her.

But she had to ask.

She leapt down the stairs and sprinted past the sidewalk and out Leticia's driveway, running as fast as she could.

Jack drove closer and then—right before he reached her—parked and got out of the car.

She stopped for a second, gasping for air, then raced toward him. "Jack, I'm so sorry I sold Leticia's house." Her voice caught. "I never should have done anything when I was so upset."

"Tess." Tension melted around his eyes. He moved closer and took her hands in his. "I'm the one who's sorry. I did talk with Earl Ray about playing loud music. A long time ago, before I really knew you. But I was kidding. I never, ever thought he would actually do it."

"I should have talked to you." She blinked back tears. "But I was so mad and depressed, and I wasn't thinking logically." Her hands shook, and he squeezed them tighter.

"How could you talk to me? I forgot to charge my phone, and I went to St. Louis without even telling you."

"But because of what I did, your memories of Kaitlyn will be destroyed."

"My memories of Kaitlyn are right here." He brought her hands to his heart, and his eyes filled with emotion. "With my love for you."

For a second, she couldn't breathe, couldn't get air past the giant lump in her throat. "You love me?"

"I do," he said solemnly, as if he had no question, no doubt, even though she had made another huge mistake.

"Oh, Jack, I love you, too," she whispered. She gazed up at him, heart pounding.

He slid his arms around her and pulled her closer.

She raised her head, aching for him to kiss her.

Slowly—oh, so slowly—he did.

And warmth and love filled her chest until she felt it might burst, until her knees grew weak.

At last he stepped back and looked down at her tenderly.

Moments passed. Lifetimes of hope and possibility and promise.

Peace and rightness and connection with the other half of her heart.

God loved her and offered forgiveness.

And Jack loved her, in spite of her mistakes.

She didn't have to be perfect.

# Chapter Thirty

She loved him.

She. Loved. Him.

Jack's heart hammered inside his chest, and he gazed into her eyes, letting the reality of her love sink into his heart.

A chilly breeze flowed off the lake.

She shivered, and a lock of hair escaped her pins and feathered across her face.

He ran his fingers across her cheek, tucked the hair behind her ear, and angled his head toward Leticia's house. "Can we go inside? Talk for a minute? I have an idea I want to run by you."

"Okay."

On the porch she reached for a box with a Bible on top.

"Were you leaving?"

She raised the box. "I only needed to load this and Indy."

He took the box from her. If he'd been ten minutes later, she'd have been gone. Along with his dreams.

Inside, the house seemed emptier than before, without even bowls for Indy on the kitchen floor.

"Come in," she said. "The dining room furniture and couch are still here." In the living room, she released Indy from the carrier and gestured Jack toward the couch.

He put down the box, sat, and pulled her to sit beside him. "So, I found two areas near St. Louis that are amazing waterfowl habitats." He waited a second, then plunged ahead. "We need to get to know each other better, but if things work out, one day I could move near the city. I could see you and I could still paint and—"

She inhaled sharply and her eyes narrowed. "Move to St. Louis?"

His chest tightened. What if he'd spoken too soon? If she didn't want—

"You'd move? For me?" She sounded shocked.

"Not if you don't want me to. But with your business in St. Louis and me three hours away. I want..." No more living in fear. He just needed to say it. "I want us to have a chance. I'm willing to move to make sure we get it."

"Oh, Jack," she whispered. Her blue-gray eyes softened and shone. Twin spots of color glowed on the perfect skin of her cheeks. She moved closer, until the sweet scent of honeysuckle surrounded him and wrapped him in the warmth of summer. "I can't tell you what that means to me." She stretched her arms around his neck.

Happiness and hope swirled through his heart, warming icy corners he'd forgotten even existed. He pulled her closer and kissed her.

After a moment she moved her hand to his shoulder, stopping him. "But..." Her tone had changed and her eyes held an odd expression. "I don't want you to give up the connection to Kaitlyn. Earlier today, I had a job offer in Columbia. I want us to live here. I want to try to fix this."

Jack sat back against the couch cushions. Fix this? How could they fix this? The house was sold. And he didn't want Tess to make sacrifices for him and then resent him. He wanted her to feel like a success, not a quitter. "Even if we could, if you give up your business, I'm afraid you'll regret it."

"Sunset Lake is important to you. Kaitlyn is important." Her eyes filled with caring.

"Not the way I thought. At least not the lake. Kaitlyn is. But she's not the lake, and you've worked so hard for your business."

Tess shifted her position on the couch, and her face scrunched up as if she was concentrating. "You know, I thought being a success with Silver Platter was what I wanted more than anything. But when the house sold and I knew I could invest in my business, even when I got a great new catering client, it felt empty." She raised her shoulders and made a who-knew face. "I don't know what you were planning to offer for the house, but maybe if you offered Seasky Enterprises a little more than they paid, so they'd make a profit on the deal, they'd sell it to you." Her voice grew hopeful. "Then I could rent it from you and take that job in Columbia."

Jack's muscles tensed. He was grateful—incredibly grateful—for what she was offering, but real estate didn't work that way. "I'd be happy to buy this place. But I can't see why they'd want to sell it back."

Her face fell. "The guy I talked with did say his uncle really wanted the land—"

"We ought to accept the situation." Jack said the words as gently as he could. His idea was the only way. She'd see.

"We can still ask," Tess said. She nodded her head like her own enthusiasm made the idea more logical.

It didn't.

෴

The only thing worse than the choking sensation of wearing a tie was the dread building in Jack's chest.

He parked in a visitor's spot outside a huge St. Louis office building and tugged once more at his collar. It had been a week since Tess had her idea. A week when he'd tried in vain to convince her to accept that Leticia's property was gone.

He glanced at Tess, absorbed in her phone, then at the tower before them. Somewhere up there Seasky Enterprises, the new owner of Leticia's land, covered an entire floor. A business that successful didn't give up newly acquired property simply because someone said please.

Or what if they would give it up, but at a price he couldn't afford?

Tess had convinced herself that buying back the land was practically a sure thing.

He turned off the A/C, cracked a window, and shut off the engine. The first day of May and already as hot as July. "We're here," he said, and he pointed at the office building.

"Just a second. I'm reading the last of those new articles I found about Edward Seasky." She squinted at her phone, touched the screen, and gasped.

"What?" He leaned closer.

Tess held the phone toward him. "Look. This is a profile of Seasky from a St. Louis business magazine, and it's got a picture of him in his living room. He's got a painting over his couch that looks almost like one of yours."

Jack took the phone and peered at the tiny image. A tingle of electricity ran through him. "It is one of mine. *Mallards in Autumn.*" He scrolled across the photo. "Judging by the size of it over that couch, it might be the original. I don't think they made prints that large."

Tess let out a breathy laugh and her mouth spread into a broad, overly confident smile. "This guy is going to sell you the property. I can feel it."

"We don't know that. I don't want you to be disappointed."

"I won't be," she said as she got out of the car. "This is going to work."

They walked toward the building, passing a huge fountain.

Ten minutes later, on the seventeenth floor, Jack and Tess followed a thin, older woman down a long hall. The walls were paneled with wood that looked like cherry. The plush brown carpet felt two inches thick. Even the air smelled better, as if Seasky Enterprises paid to have it purified and enriched.

Jack shot a look at Tess. She wore the same black heels as she had at the funeral and a conservative dark suit, a suit that fit right in at Seasky Enterprises. Today, though, unlike at the funeral, her hair fell over her shoulders. The contrast between her uptight suit and her flowing hair, her gentle blue-gray eyes, and her velvety cheeks made her even more attractive, more kissable.

He took hold of her fingers and squeezed.

Then forced his mind back to the business at hand.

The receptionist knocked, opened the door, and gestured them in.

Inside the office, two men rose to their feet. The man behind the huge desk was probably in his sixties, dressed in a custom-made suit, and had short salt-and-pepper hair. His eyes gleamed with confidence. The pen on his desk probably cost more than Jack's suit.

"Edward Seasky," the man said, walking from behind the desk.

"Jack Hamlin." He took a step forward and they shook hands.

There wasn't a bit of art in the room. The walls were decorated with awards. And Edward Seasky didn't seem like an art lover. He seemed like a man who, if offered the opportunity to own a masterpiece by Monet or Matisse, would actually prefer mutual funds.

Edward introduced himself to Tess.

"And this is my nephew, Jeremy, whom I believe you've spoken with, Miss Palmer." Edward made a broad gesture toward the young man hovering at his elbow.

Jeremy was shorter than his uncle, and seemed more cocky than confident. He came closer, almost strutting, and greeted Tess, then reached a hand toward Jack. "Jeremy Seasky, V.P. for Real Estate for Seasky Enterprises."

Jack shook his hand. "Jack Hamlin."

"You know, the wildlife artist." Tess directed her words toward the older man.

"Hamlin?" Edward focused on Tess, then Jack. *"Mallards in Autumn?"* he said with excitement in his voice.

Jack nodded quickly.

"Come, let's sit." Edward led the way to a couch and two chairs near the windows. "We own that original. My wife has practically had the whole town over to see it. I never would have made the connection if you"—he gestured to Tess— "hadn't said 'wildlife.'"

Jack sat on a buttery leather couch. "Thank you. Always good to hear of a fan." But Edward wasn't the fan, his wife was. Jack shouldn't expect any favors. Disappointment squeezed at his heart.

Still, Tess would want him to try. And maybe the guy had found some obstacle to developing the property after he bought it. Glossing over Earl Ray's music and Tess's impulsive sale, Jack began to explain how the property had been sold.

333

Edward held up a hand. "Jeremy and I have discussed how things were handled. What were your thoughts?"

Jack's lungs felt as if they couldn't fully expand. Time for the offer. "I'm here to ask if you'd consider selling the property back to us."

Not a single muscle moved in Edward's face.

Jack swallowed. This was such a bad idea. Edward was going to say "Sure, at double what I paid." Jack cleared his throat. "What price would you consider fair?"

Edward sat silent for a moment, eyes narrowed. Then he named a price. A low price. Considerably less than what Tess said he'd paid.

Jack's heart stuttered. He must have heard wrong. He looked at Tess.

Her eyes were round and her face quivered as if she might explode.

Jeremy might have stopped breathing.

"And one painting. On the same scale as *Mallards in Autumn*. Within the next year," Edward said. "Something that no one has even seen yet."

Jack stared at Edward. He must have misunderstood.

Tess elbowed him and gave him a face that said he should hurry up and say yes.

"Done." Jack numbly stuck out his hand to shake Edward's.

Tess's plan had worked.

"But, but—" Jeremy stretched an arm toward his uncle as if to pull him back from a precipice.

Edward gave him a stony stare. "We'll talk more later, Jeremy, about good business practices."

Jeremy's arm fell, and he wilted into his chair.

Tess glanced at Jeremy, then spoke to Edward. "It's not all his fault. I did rush him. And my agent wasn't available."

"Even so..." He shook his head at Jeremy, then looked at Jack. "You won't back out on me, will you?"

Jack chuckled. "Sir, I'll have to work out the details with my gallery, but painting a commissioned work for you would be a pleasure."

"Getting back in my wife's good graces after I forgot her birthday will be the real pleasure." Edward rose. "And I want to set things right for all parties here. There are a million lakes in this country. I'll buy another one."

"Thank you, sir." Jack did his best to stay calm and glanced at Tess.

She looked ready to turn cartwheels across the floor.

Somehow, they maintained their decorum as they passed the secretary and zipped down in the elevator. Jack didn't say a word. He couldn't. If he opened his mouth, he'd yell so loudly he'd disturb the whole building. So he beamed at Tess, and Tess—who must have felt the same way—beamed back.

But once outside the building, he let out a shout.

A man inside the door jerked to attention and looked at him.

"We did it," Tess said. Laughter bubbled from her, and her face shone.

"*You* did it."

Behind her, the fountain sprayed ten, then fifteen feet into the air. The water fell into a basin and overflowed into a lower, larger pool.

Overflowed, like Jack's heart. He slid one arm around her waist. "You are amazing. If you hadn't found that detail, hadn't mentioned what type of painting I do..."

"Your art is what made it all possible." She tilted her head up toward him, and the sun lit her hair like golden fire. The way she looked at him, as though he was Michelangelo instead of a guy who simply painted ducks, made his heart soar.

Raw emotion filled his chest and the back of his throat. He couldn't believe he'd been blessed with this woman. A woman who loved him, who respected his memories of Kaitlyn, and who found a way for them to forge their future together at Sunset Lake. "What made it possible," he said, "was the two of us. Together."

"And God," she said gently.

"Yes. And God." Definitely God. Because deep in his heart he believed that the Lord had brought them together, that Tess was a gift brought into his life.

She reached up, took his head gently between her hands, and brought her lips to his. She kissed him sweetly and gazed up at him, eyes tender.

Jack slid his other arm around her waist and held her, their bodies barely touching, but their hearts entwined.

Droplets of water splashed in the fountain behind her, a million diamonds sparkling in the sunlight.

It was too soon to propose, he knew.

But he'd found the woman he could trust, the woman who truly loved him, the woman he would spend the rest of his life with at Sunset Lake.

# Epilogue

*Sixteen months later*

Tess Hamlin leaned over the breakfast bar in her kitchen and went through the list on her clipboard once again. Up since five, she'd rushed home, recounted the bowls and spoons, and re-taped the plastic tablecloth so it wouldn't blow off the big table on the back deck.

This event was going to be a success.

And the home she shared with Jack, the house that used to be Leticia's, was the perfect spot for the ice cream social to end the week of Vacation Bible School.

After Tess had moved to Leticia's, even before she and Jack got married, the two of them had started attending Abundance Community Church, sharing a pew with Stacey and Earl Ray almost every Sunday. And Becky, who not only taught school but was the church choir director, had encouraged all four of them to help out with VBS—Tess working with the snack ladies each night, Stacey and Earl Ray helping with games, and Jack being in charge of arts and crafts. The party tonight was the grand finale for the week, a celebration for the staff, the kids, and their parents.

Inside, she'd cleaned everything until it gleamed. Outside, Sunset Lake lived up to its name. Across the water, the sun sank into the treetops, partly obscured by puffy pink and lavender clouds, each edged in brilliant orange.

Wood ducks and mallards and a pair of Canada geese swam across a rippled reflection of the colors, as if they enjoyed the warm August air. Honeysuckle wound up the railings of the deck and filled the air with its sweet scent.

Tess flipped her braid over her shoulder and peered across at Jack's old house, which Earl Ray and Stacey had bought after they got remarried. Any minute, they ought to be bringing over the ice cream tubs Tess had stashed in their freezer, Coconut Lemon Bliss and Chocolate Praline Crunch. Not her most exotic flavors, but sure to be popular with the kids.

A glint of light caught her eyes as the sun reflected off an SUV headed down Sunset Lake Lane. Finally, Jack getting back from the church.

Indy rubbed against Tess's leg, then wandered into the living room and settled herself on the back of the couch.

Jack came inside, gave Tess a quick kiss, and sank onto a stool at the breakfast bar, facing her. "I survived." His purple VBS staff T-shirt and khaki shorts were covered with splotches of paint, and he let out a put-upon sigh.

"I knew you would." Tess giggled.

"I can't believe I let Becky talk me into running arts and crafts."

"You did have two youth helpers."

"I don't care. Those groups that came to my station—easily eighty kids at a time. And me, remember? Practically a hermit."

Tess considered him with mock pity. She knew for a fact that each group was twelve kids. And, much as he complained, he was grinning from ear to ear. Abundance Community Church had been good for both of them—in so many ways.

Over the past year, her faith had grown stronger, her outlook changed. A couple of times recently she'd even had a pleasant conversation with her mom. Not that everything was wonderful, but Mom's comments—even those comparing Tess to her golden-boy brother—hurt less after Tess had more perspective. Knowing God loved her, knowing Jack loved her, and focusing on her blessings helped her deal with Mom's criticisms. And helped her avoid going into catastrophe mode when she made mistakes. Most days she could see that she was a work in progress, being shaped every day by her faith.

She gazed at Jack. She still couldn't believe how full her life was—working at The Blue Caboose four days a week, being surrounded by believers at church, and being married to this amazing man.

Soon, though, the VBS children would arrive with their parents. She needed to get things ready. "If you've recovered from arts and crafts, can you bring up the three tubs of ice cream from the basement freezer?"

"Is one of them Peanut Butter Banana Split?"

"Of course." As if she'd make five flavors of ice cream and skip his favorite.

"Be right back." He headed down the stairs.

The next minute, Stacey and Earl Ray burst in the door from the deck, both laughing, their VBS staff T-shirts still damp from water night at the games station.

"The kids should be here in fifteen minutes," Stacey said.

"That's great, but where's the ice cream?" Tess said.

"On the deck," Earl Ray pointed.

"He insisted on carrying both of them." Stacey's voice held a note of amusement.

"Well, I would think so." Stacey's dad, George, strolled in behind them, carrying a baby boy who looked exactly like Earl Ray, minus the glasses. "You only delivered this little fellow six weeks ago."

Tess's heart flooded with love at the sight of Stacey and Earl Ray's baby, dressed today in a tiny Kansas City Royals uniform. Absolutely adorable. And who knew an eight-pound person could bring utter joy to a couple and to a grandpa?

"Do you want me to take him, Dad?" Stacey took a step toward him.

"No way." George settled onto the couch, the baby snug in one elbow. "This little guy is my medicine."

Tess caught Stacey's eye. It was true. Modern medicine may have helped George avoid heart surgery, but his true healing came in two parts—when he had walked Stacey down the aisle a second time and whenever he held his grandson.

"Stacey," Earl Ray said, "why don't you sit down by your dad and rest a bit?"

She waved a dismissive hand. "I'm fine."

"Humor me," Earl Ray said. "I'll get the ice cream for Tess. Even bring you a full bowl of your favorite." He turned to Tess. "I can't get her to slow down at home either, and her real estate business is booming. At least I got her to hire an assistant."

"I knew my girl would be a success," George said, his words rich with pride.

Stacey beamed, hugged Earl Ray, and sat beside her father, making an exaggerated show of slipping off her flip flops and putting her feet up on a cushion on the coffee table.

Earl Ray cast an approving eye over her and went out to the deck.

A minute later Becky stuck her head in the front door. "Anybody home?"

"Becky, come in." Tess went to meet her and gave her a big hug.

"I'd say you've got ten minutes until the kids and their parents arrive." She turned toward the living room. "Oh, the baby's here?" Her brown eyes lit. "May I?" Becky stretched her arms toward George.

"For a little while, I guess." He adjusted the tiny Royals uniform, tugged up the little socks, and handed her the baby.

"Hard to believe such a sweetie could be related to Earl Ray." Becky snuggled the baby close, and her dark hair fell down over him. "The good Hamlin genes must have missed Earl Ray but ended up in me and the baby."

341

"I heard that," Earl Ray said, halfway in the French doors from the deck with the ice cream. He gave Becky a dirty look.

Becky ignored him.

Tess laughed.

"Knock, knock," Abby called from the front door. "Look out! I pulled Emma out of the nursery early."

Emma, almost two, raced in, light-up shoes flashing.

Jack came back upstairs, set three tubs of ice cream on the breakfast bar, and scooped the little girl into his arms. "Hey, there, princess."

Emma giggled.

"Jack," Abby said, "I brought what you asked." She angled her head toward the front door.

"Thanks." Jack set Emma down and moved toward the hall.

Tess touched his arm. "What is it?"

"Just a little surprise." But he sounded delighted with his secret. He and Abby hurried out.

A minute later they returned. Jack carried a huge sheet cake, plenty for all the kids. On top, in bright green script, were the words, "Happy Birthday, Tess." He set the cake on the dining room table.

Tess waved her hands in front of her, reaching uselessly for words. "But it's not—I mean, my birthday isn't until—"

Jack stepped beside her and wrapped an arm around her waist. "Next week. I know. This way you didn't suspect a thing."

Her face grew hot and tears welled up in her eyes. She looked around the room, stopping to gaze at each face, each person who had become so dear to her, until at last she reached Jack and realized what he'd given her with the cake. A special event—not just for VBS, but also for her—where she was surrounded by people who loved her. Her heart felt so full it could burst, too full to keep her own secret a minute longer.

She checked the clock. Yes, there was time.

"I have a surprise too," she said to Jack.

"Oh?" His eyes narrowed.

"Next year I may need to take a VBS position that requires a little less time beforehand."

He angled his head to one side, and his face clouded. "But you've done such a great job, and I thought you loved it."

"I do," Tess tried to keep her expression neutral. Two could play I've-Got-a-Secret. "But we're moving VBS to June next year, remember? Next June I think I'll be really busy."

"With?" Jack drew out the word, clearly wanting an answer.

She slipped in the kitchen and pulled a wrapped package from the cabinet where she kept the baking supplies. Her heart faltered. What if it upset him? Should she have told him when they were alone?

Too late. He'd already walked up beside her and seen the package. She held it toward him.

"But it's your birthday, not mine." He ripped off the paper and pulled a double picture frame from a box. His brow wrinkled.

Tess took a deep breath. "One side for Kaitlyn," she said quietly. "The other for our baby."

Jack's eyes widened. A smile spread across his face, stretching until the corners of his eyes crinkled. "A baby, Tess? Our baby?" His voice was low, each word filled with joy.

Her throat tightened, as if her heart had expanded and filled it, and she could only nod.

Jack's eyes shone with a hint of tears. He pulled her toward him, wrapped her in his arms, and kissed her.

Around her, her friends and family cheered, the special people she'd found near the little town of Abundance, Missouri.

She was so blessed.

Jack Hamlin would always love Kaitlyn, but he also had plenty of room in his heart for her.

And for their child.

Truly, Tess had found meaning for her life—in casting fear aside and trusting in the abundance of God's love, the love she found at Sunset Lake.

**All of Sally's books are available in paperback and e-book from Amazon. For a complete list, or to sign up for her author newsletter and get a free novella, please visit her website at www.sallybayless.com.**

# A NOTE FROM THE AUTHOR

Dear Reader,

Thank you so much for reading *Love at Sunset Lake*. I hope you enjoyed it!

My Missouri friends often ask the location of Abundance. It, along with Prattsville and Miller's Junction, are in an imaginary county in north-central Missouri, somewhere between Moberly and Chillicothe.

And I want to assure you that, despite Earl Ray's paranoia, in the real world, information about blood donation is kept confidential.

People also ask me about wood ducks laying eggs in a tree. That is definitely real! If you haven't seen a video of baby wood ducks leaving the nest, I highly encourage you to search for one on the Internet. The ducklings jump out of the nest when they are only *one day old!*

Whenever I see aspects of our world like those ducklings or breath-taking sunsets, I just can't believe they're accidents. Every time I spend time in nature, even a simple walk in my neighborhood, my spirits are lifted and my faith renewed. I pray that you, too, can see all around you the evidence of God's love.

If you enjoyed this story, I'd be really grateful if you would write a review on Amazon or Goodreads. Those reviews are the best advertising around, and you wouldn't believe how fun it is to get feedback!

I love to hear from readers! If you'd like to say hello, please visit my website, www.sallybayless.com, where you can email me or find me on social media.

If you'd like a free copy of another sweet Christian romance set in the little town of Abundance, please sign up for my author newsletter at www.sallybayless.com. You'll get a link to download the holiday novella *Christmas in Abundance* for free in ebook or PDF!

Keep reading for an excerpt from *Love and Harmony*.

May God bless you,

Sally Bayless

# ACKNOWLEDGMENTS

A huge thanks to the many, many people who helped me write this book.

First, I could not have pulled all the details together without help from a number of experts. Huge thanks to Realtors Meg Van Patten of Crye-Leike Real Estate Services in Murfreesboro, Tennessee, and Michelle Blackwell, who worked for years with Moody Real Estate in Salem, Missouri. With their extensive knowledge of the right way to do things in real estate, they helped me shape the character of Stacey, who—as a brand-new agent—sometimes did things wrong.

Thanks also to experts Robert A. Holm, Jr., D.O. FACEP, and M.V. Freeman, a fellow author and an R.N., for their help with medical issues. To Peggy Bowsher Aoki and Wendy Merb-Brown, who answered my questions about all things related to catering. To Lori Gray, a fellow author and a paralegal, who helped me find answers about legal matters. To Jennie Klein, Associate Professor of Art History, Ohio University, who answered questions related to art. To Erin Bowald, who helped make Jack's canoe adventures realistic. And to numerous people from the Missouri Department of Conservation and Department of Natural Resources who helped me better understand wildlife and wetlands. I cannot tell you how grateful I am for all of your help— both for answering my questions and for volunteering information in areas where I didn't even know to ask. If, in spite of all this help, errors slipped in, they are my own mistakes.

I am also incredibly grateful for my wonderful critique partners, authors Susan Anne Mason and Tammy Doherty. Your friendship, support, and insight into fiction are amazing. I cannot imagine writing without you.

Thank you to my fabulous beta readers—Carrie Saunders, Diana West, Jan LeBar, Kristina Gerig, Leisa Ostermann, and Stephanie Smith. Each of you made this story stronger and more enjoyable to read.

Sally Bradley, my developmental editor, is a gem. She not only offers brilliant suggestions but also with each book kindly teaches me to be a better writer. What a gift you are to me!

Thanks as well to Christina Tarabochia for a wonderful copy edit and all her encouragement. What a blessing!

Jenny Zemanek of Seedlings Design Studio created the cover. Thank you, Jenny, for making it beautiful and being such a joy to work with.

Huge thanks to my family—Dave, Michael, and Laurel—for your love and support. Now that this book is done, I promise there will be no more talk of duck poop at dinner. You can return to your regularly scheduled insanity.

Finally, a huge thank-you to Jesus for all you teach me through my writing, for a life full of blessings, and—above all else—for my salvation.

# ABOUT THE AUTHOR

After many years away, Sally Bayless lives in her hometown in the Missouri Ozarks. She's married and has two grown children. When not working on her next book, she enjoys reading, watching BBC television with her husband, doing Bible studies, swimming, and shopping for cute shoes.

Please turn the page to read the beginning of

*Love and Harmony*
*The Abundance Series*
*Book 2*

# Chapter One

With every new calendar year and every new school semester came a chance to begin again, to become the person you were meant to be. Or the person you once had been but somehow lost.

Yep. Seth Williams nodded. Today, January 7, was the first day of a new semester at a new high school, and it was time for Tony, his half-brother, to get back on track.

And Seth was starting over as well. His new job as interim principal at Tony's school meant big challenges, but they were challenges he was willing to face if it meant Tony might get his life straightened out. Stepping in mid-year—after the previous principal, his secretary, and the athletic director had been fired for misappropriating funds—would require flexibility, which was not Seth's strongest suit.

He rose from his desk, straightened his tie, and walked out of his office, right into a stampede. Only worse. In a stampede, all the cattle headed the same way. Here, kids plowed four directions at once, and the beige concrete-block walls reverberated with loud conversations and the clang of lockers.

"Is that the new principal?" a red-headed girl said.

"He looks like we should salute, doesn't he?" replied a girl who had to be her twin. Both wore too much makeup and showed too much skin for a northern Missouri school day in winter—or, really, a school day in any season.

He ignored the twins—for now. But they were in for a rude awakening during the third-period assembly, when he would introduce himself to the student body and set forth some straight-forward rules, starting with a dress code.

Call him old-fashioned, but Seth had made it clear to the school board that if he ran the high school, things would change. He wouldn't promote the "Christian values" one board member had suggested, but he would expect the students to show respect for themselves and for others.

He passed the twins and almost collided with a chunky boy carrying a tuba case.

The boy detoured around him.

Seth pulled his phone from his pocket and checked the time. Five minutes until the bell and still no text from Tony.

After much begging, Tony had been allowed to drive to school in the ancient pickup truck Seth had bought him as a gift for his sixteenth birthday, a symbol that Seth really believed Tony was going to make a fresh start. But if Tony didn't text to say he'd arrived, tomorrow he could come in an hour early with Seth or ride the bus.

Seth shoved the phone back in his pocket.

Twenty feet ahead, the hallway made a T. From down to the right, a whoop echoed, followed by a gleeful cry—"Fight!"

A second later, a chant began, the students sounding as bloodthirsty as the Romans at the Coliseum. "Fight. Fight. Fight."

He set his jaw, hurried around the corner, and looked over the students' heads. A beefy blond kid was holding a dark-haired boy on the floor and landing solid punches.

Students ringed the pair, but teachers from the nearby classrooms were nowhere to be seen.

Seth pulled a police whistle from the pocket of his khakis and blew on it long and hard. "Break it up!" he shouted. "Now." He pushed his way through a trio of girls in leggings and T-shirts.

The blond boy paused, fist raised, and looked at Seth with wide eyes.

The dark-haired kid took the opportunity to slam a punch into his opponent's nose.

Seth gritted his teeth. The past week had been so quiet as he settled into his office and prepared for the semester. He'd only rarely seen a student pass through the halls for basketball practice.

That honeymoon was over.

He grabbed each of the boys by the arm and yanked them to their feet.

The blond slumped, head down.

The dark-haired boy spun toward Seth with his jaw clenched and his fists tight. Then the kid looked up.

Way up.

At six-four, close to two hundred pounds, and still mostly muscle from his days in the Navy, Seth could break up most fights with one glance.

The boy was tall but thin, no match for Seth. The kid lowered his fists. His square jaw, though, didn't relax.

A jaw that looked exactly like that of Seth's boss, Superintendent Roscoe Grange.

"Boys, I'm your new principal, Mr. Williams," Seth said. "And you are?"

"Johnny Driscoll," the blond mumbled.

"J.W. Grange," the dark-haired one said with a note of defiance.

Just as Seth had feared. Suspending the superintendent's grandson on the first day of class was not the best way to start a new job.

A group of girls whispered, and one pointed down the hall.

Roscoe Grange was walking straight toward them. Familiar square jaw, buzz-cut gray hair, unreadable steel-blue eyes.

Seth's stomach tightened. He couldn't guess how the man would react, so Seth had to go with his gut. Which said that this group of high school students shared several traits with a pack of wild dogs. There might be consequences later from Roscoe, but Seth had to show he was in charge. "My office after school for detention," he said to the boys. "One hour, every day this week."

Johnny nodded.

"But I can't miss basketball practice." J.W. glanced toward his grandfather. His voice rang with an assurance that he was above the rules.

"I'm seeing your coach in half an hour," Seth said. "I'll explain that you'll be late. Be grateful it's my first day. Once we go over the new student handbook during the assembly, fighting will get you an automatic two-week suspension. Understood?"

"Understood," Johnny said.

J.W. shot a look at Roscoe, his eyes hopeful.

Seth glanced at Roscoe as well. He really didn't want to have to find out if his old job teaching Advanced Placement Physics was still available in Tennessee.

Roscoe's bushy gray eyebrows pulled together. He glared at J.W. and shook his head, once right, once left.

J.W.'s face fell. "Understood," he said to Seth.

Roscoe walked over to Seth and said under his breath, "You're doing fine."

Seth's stomach relaxed. "Thank you, sir." He turned to the two boys. "You two stay here. The rest of you, get to class."

"I left those papers we talked about on your desk," Roscoe said. Without another word, he left.

Seth took the boys to his office, determined that their fight was caused more by hot heads than by a significant issue, and sent them to class.

One crisis resolved.

And he hadn't been fired. He still had a shot at making this interim position a permanent job.

He checked his phone again. Still no word from his brother.

But Tony hadn't been one of the boys fighting. That was a plus. And if he had a problem driving, Seth would have heard. Maybe the kid was nervous, being at a new school, and forgot to text.

Seth could wander down the hall and take a peek in his brother's homeroom.

No, that wouldn't go over well. Too controlling.

He forced himself to take a deep breath and let it out deliberately. He needed to relax. Everything was fine.

CB

A loud metallic crunch, followed by a *clinkle*, echoed across the parking lot.

Becky Hamlin stopped at the doors of the Abundance Community Church and squinted back over her shoulder, into the winter-white sun, at her car.

Just past the side yard of the church, in the lot it shared with Abundance High School, a full-size pickup was stuck to the front bumper of her cute little blue Toyota. After a few seconds, the truck backed slightly and stopped. The vehicle, once green, sported some white replacement body parts and had seen better days. The crash, however, appeared to have barely scratched it.

And the tall, blond boy climbing out appeared unharmed.

"Are you all right?" She retraced her steps along the icy sidewalk until she reached the parking lot.

"Yeah, I'm fine, but"—his voice grew thin and nervous—"I'm sorry about your car."

Becky hurried over. So much for being on time to her meeting. She'd even gotten up half an hour early to go through the new drive-thru donut place to get Pastor Corey's favorite, a sour cream cake donut. And of course, a donut for herself, which she'd accidentally already eaten.

"I can't believe I did this," the boy said. "I was late and—"

"Let's see how bad it is before we get too upset." She bent down and checked her front-passenger-side headlight.

Completely shattered.

Pretty much how the boy looked.

She stood, brushed some flecks of powdered sugar off her red coat, and looked down at a baggie caught on a crack in the pavement.

A baggie that held what looked like a tiny bit of pot. Inexperienced drivers weren't the only downside of the church sharing a parking lot with the high school. Pastor Corey had shown an educational video so the whole church staff could understand the drug problem.

At least the pot didn't seem to belong to the kid who'd just hit her car.

She turned to the boy. "I'm Becky Hamlin."

"Tony Williams." He glanced at her Toyota and zipped up his gray jacket.

"These things happen," she said. "We just need to exchange insurance information. Do you have any paper?"

He leaned into the truck and returned with a brand-new notebook, a pen, and an insurance card. A minute later, he handed her a sheet of paper that he'd carefully ripped along the perforations. "I wrote it all down, like they taught us in driver's ed."

"Thank you." Tony sure was polite. And, though she didn't think she'd met him before, there was something familiar about his eyes. She used his notebook and pen to write down her information.

The first-period bell rang at Abundance High, loud and clear in the parking lot. The private school forty miles south in Columbia, where she taught music, might not return from winter break until tomorrow, but the Abundance public schools were back in session.

"You'd better get to class now," she said. "I'll call your folks later."

"It's my brother. He should be here any minute. I texted him. He's coming over from the high school."

Becky scanned what the boy had written down. Tony and...*Seth Williams?* She looked at the boy more closely. No wonder his blue eyes seemed so familiar. "All right. I'll wait." Despite the circumstances, a tingle of excitement zipped through her heart. She'd read in the paper that Seth had taken a job in Abundance, but she hadn't seen him since all those years ago at church camp. And now...

Clearly today had been the perfect day to wear her new red coat. The color set off her dark hair and brown eyes and matched the red boots she'd found on clearance.

"I read about your brother in the paper." Becky pulled her hair out from where it was caught inside her scarf. "New principal, huh?"

"Yeah." He leaned against the truck, and his face tightened as if his stomach hurt. "That's my brother, My-Way-or-the-Highway Williams."

"Oh." *My-Way-or-the-Highway?* That was not the Seth she'd known. "And you just moved to town?"

"Yeah."

Poor Tony. Today must be his first day at a new school.

"The kids here are going to love me." Tony's words were thick with sarcasm. "Everybody wants to be friends with the principal's brother."

She gave him a sympathetic smile and peeked at her phone. Her meeting with Corey should have started about the time that bell rang. He had the local ecumenical leaders' breakfast at nine, but had said if she came in at eight thirty, they could talk for fifteen minutes. She slid off her right glove, decided it was too cold to take off the other one, and awkwardly tapped out a text with one finger. Not her usual *Sorry, running a bit late* because she'd gotten too caught up talking with someone, but *Someone hit my car. Be there soon. Can't wait to tell you my idea.*

An idea she thought was brilliant. The perfect way to make up for how she'd let the town down. And it would help her get her dream job—teaching in the Abundance public schools.

"There." Tony pointed.

A tall man in a navy ski jacket strode across the parking lot from the high school.

The Seth she'd known had been skinny and barely taller than her own 5'3". This man had shoulders like a football player and had to be over six foot, but she'd have recognized those blue eyes anywhere.

"Tony." Seth's voice was deeper but still familiar. "How bad is it?"

Tony winced and gestured to her car. "I gave her the insurance information and your cell number. And got hers."

Seth took the paper Tony offered, glanced at the two vehicles, and turned toward her.

She stood up straighter, glad the red boots had heels, and tried to suck in the five pounds she'd gained since the new donut shop opened.

"Seth Williams." He shook her hand, then looked down toward the plastic baggie in the pothole. He jerked his head toward his brother.

He'd barely looked at her.

Of course he'd be more concerned about his brother if he thought the boy might be involved with drugs. But Tony didn't smell like pot.

"I'm sorry," Seth said, now facing her. "I'll call our insurance company as soon as I get out of my first meeting. I thought he was doing okay driving, but…I take full responsibility, ma'am."

Ma'am? Becky's heart shriveled into a raisin. Seth didn't even recognize her and called her *ma'am?* Granted, she was thirty-two, but had she changed that much since she was sixteen and he'd given her her first kiss?

"I hate to rush off," he said. "But I've got a meeting, and I don't want to be late." His lips narrowed, as if being a little late now and then was a crime. "Let me know if I can do anything."

"I will," she said.

Seth reached down toward the baggie just as a gust of wind caught it and swirled it away, high out of reach. He watched it a second, then took a step sideways, half-turning toward the school. "C'mon, Tony. You better run by attendance and get a tardy slip."

Tony looked once more at her car, gave her an apologetic shrug, and followed him.

A second later, Pastor Corey drove up next to her. He pointed at his wrist, where someone might wear a watch, and drove out of the parking lot.

Becky pulled her phone out of her purse. Eight forty-five. Corey was on his way to the ecumenical breakfast, and she'd missed their meeting. Completely.

All to find out that the man who she'd been so excited to see didn't even recognize her. Because he was too busy to even look at her.

Talk about rude.

**All of Sally's books are available in paperback and e-book from Amazon. For a complete list, or to sign up for her author newsletter and get a free novella, please visit her website at www.sallybayless.com.**

Made in the USA
Coppell, TX
25 August 2021